NONE STANDS TO SHIELDBREAKER

The demon Akbar had once more returned and now was rushing again upon the Prince, sweeping from the doorway the last shreds of protective magic.

The Sword of Force came literally leaping up out of its velvet casing to meet Stephen's grasping fingers. Shieldbreaker continued its upward movement, pulling the young Prince's right arm violently with it.

Shieldbreaker, hammering thunderstrokes, lashed out against the demonic intruder. Stephen's right arm was pulled helplessly forward even as his body staggered back. Pain stabbed at his shoulder, where the movement of the Sword twisted it.

The demon, an image of horror, emitted no bellow of outrage this time, but rather a choked cry, a grating and unbreathing sound that was to haunt the young Prince in nightmares.

Tor books by Fred Saberhagen

THE BERSERKER SERIES

The Berserker Wars
Berserker Base (with Poul Anderson, Ed Bryant, Stephen Donaldson, Larry Niven, Connie Willis, and Roger Zelazny)
Berserker: Blue Death
The Berserker Throne
Berserker's Planet
Berserker Kill

THE DRACULA SERIES

The Dracula Tapes
The Holmes-Dracula Files
An Old Friend of the Family
Thorn
Dominion
A Matter of Taste
A Question of Time
Séance for a Vampire

THE SWORDS SERIES

The First Book of Swords
The Second Book of Swords
The Third Book of Swords
The First Book of Lost Swords: Woundhealer's Story
The Second Book of Lost Swords: Sightblinder's Story
The Third Book of Lost Swords: Stonecutter's Story
The Forth Book of Lost Swords: Farslayer's Story
The Fifth Book of Lost Swords: Coinspinner's Story
The Sixth Book of Lost Swords: Mindsword's Story
The Seventh Book of Lost Swords: Wayfinder's Story
The Last Book of Swords: Shieldbreaker's Story

OTHER BOOKS

A Century of Progress
Coils (with Roger Zelazny)
Earth Descended
The Mask of the Sun
The Veils of Azlaroc
The Water of Thought

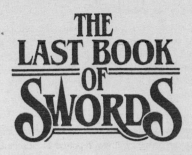

THE LAST BOOK OF SWORDS

SHIELDBREAKER'S STORY

FRED SABERHAGEN

TOR
fantasy ®

A TOM DOHERTY ASSOCIATES BOOK
NEW YORK

This is a work of fiction. All the characters and events portrayed in this book are fictitious, and any resemblance to real people or events is purely coincidental.

THE LAST BOOK OF SWORDS: SHIELDBREAKER'S STORY

Copyright © 1994 by Fred Saberhagen

A Tor Book
Published by Tom Doherty Associates, Inc.
175 Fifth Avenue
New York, NY 10010

Tor® is a registered trademark of Tom Doherty Associates, Inc.

ISBN: 0-812-50577-8

First edition: February 1994
First mass market edition: June 1995

Printed in the United States of America

0 9 8 7 6 5 4 3 2 1

THE
LAST BOOK
OF
SWORDS

ONE

HUNCHED in his saddle on the flying demon's back, buffeted by winds of air and magic, Vilkata the Dark King confronted catastrophe with a snarl of defiance. In his left hand Vilkata gripped the magical reins of his monstrous steed, and in his wounded right fist he clutched the black hilt of the naked, god-forged Mindsword, its flashing steel blade stained lightly with his own blood.

The cuts on his right wrist and hand had been inflicted perhaps three minutes ago. After that the Mindsword had been sheathed again, its powers muffled; but when the Dark King had finally succeeded in getting control of the Sword, only a few moments ago, his first act had been to fling the scabbard clear, unleashing all Skulltwister's magic.

Too late.

Even armed and mounted as he was now, the ancient wizard, survivor of a thousand dreadful perils, could not doubt that this time, at last, the doom of utter destruction had overtaken him.

With facial muscles clenched hard around the long-empty sockets of his eyes, the Dark King uttered a tremendous scream, venting all the agony of his soul in a bellowing curse, a malediction as profound as it was impotent, directed at all his enemies, known and unknown, and at the universe itself for spawning them.

The Dark King's enemies were many, and what was happening now gave proof, if any proof were needed, that some of them were very strong

Around Vilkata, from the quasi-material throats of the two dozen or so flying, shape-changing demons who formed his hideous escort, there rose despairing howls of such pitch and volume as to suggest that the end of the world had come.

He, Vilkata, together with his mount and his entire escort—these now including in their number the mighty demon Akbar, at one time the Dark King's mortal foe—the whole swarm of them, despite the Mindsword's presence, regardless of anything that any and all of them could do, were being swept away, helpless as leaves in a tornado.

Only moments ago, a mere few heartbeats in the past, the wizard Vilkata had been, as he thought, on the brink of triumph. He had been locked in airborne combat above the torchlit palace of his archfoe, Prince Mark of Tasavalta. And then, in the twinkling of an eye, not only had the Tasavaltan palace passed quite out of the Dark King's sight and reach, but so had the whole night-shrouded city of Sarykam, as well as all of the human enemies and temporary allies by whom Vilkata had been surrounded. It seemed that he had been cut off from the whole world.

And the Dark King knew the cause. It was impossible to avoid the bitter truth, even if he could not understand it. He had heard the incantation of his doom, foolish-sounding but irresistible, shouted by Prince Mark.

An instant after those words had fallen upon the air, the shouts, the clash of metal, the glare of torches, all were gone. Vilkata and his demons had been wrapped up, bundled together as if by hands of divine power, and thrown away. Now blackness and near-emptiness surrounded him and the two dozen hideous, half-material creatures whose loyalty the Mindsword had compelled. They were now encapsulated within an almost featureless void that was pervaded by a sense of movement, caught in helpless hurtling flight at some indeterminable but awesome speed.

They were in rapid motion, certainly. But toward what destination? Speed and destination were both completely out of their control. Gravity, as modified by the flying demons' magic, seemed to come and go in yawning leaps. All sense of direction had been lost; even "up" and "down" no longer seemed to have consistent meaning.

Vilkata understood that his own greatest weakness, as was so often the case among humans, was the mirror image of his strength. The fact was that the Dark King's own skills in magic had long ago led him to depend almost absolutely upon demons. The man was physically blind, by his own hand and choice, and had been so for most of his long life. Only by magically borrowing the vision of a demon was he able to see at all, but ordinarily the vision thus provided was keener than that of any merely human eyes. Not now. Currently his perception of his surroundings was only sufficient to suggest that the tornado of material and non-material energies evoked by Mark was carrying him and his inhuman escort into a strange realm indeed.

The exact nature of this realm, or condition, was obscured by the same forces that enveloped Vilkata and bore him through it. But at least his immediate fate was not to be annihilation, as he had feared at the outset. Perhaps, he told himself, there even remained a glimmer of hope for ultimate recovery.

Meanwhile, defeat, even if it should prove only temporary, was made all the more bitter by the fact that only moments earlier he, the Dark King, had been, as he thought, so close to final victory. So close to winning, to gathering in the gods' great Swords all for himself! But that chance had now been obliterated. He, who had long played the great game for ultimate authority, was in the grip of forces that held him helpless as an infant. Now, despite the awesome power of the one Sword he still possessed, despite the strength of the demonic mount between his knees and the other terrible monsters flying near at his command—despite all this, disaster.

Still, moment after moment flew by, and he remained alive. The ultimate blow had not yet fallen.

At least he had no fear that the demons droning and murmuring around him now were going to turn against him. No, Vilkata's sense of magic assured him that, even here in this peculiar domain of darkness and of hurtling movement, the Mindsword still retained its power to compel obedience, loyalty, and worship.

Only moments before Mark's curse of banishment took effect, Akbar and Vilkata had been opposed to each other in deadly combat. But then, suddenly, the demon had been deprived of Shieldbreaker, the Sword which had for some time protected him, and almost at the same time the Mindsword had come into Vilkata's hands. Akbar, along with every other thinking being within its radius of operation, had fallen immediately under the domination of the Sword.

Now silence held. And duration, in this strange and shadowy and almost timeless realm, had become difficult to quantify. Now, more than ever, the man could tell that he was dependent upon his demonic escort for his continued survival, his very existence. Compelled by the power of the Mindsword to an uncharacteristic loyalty, they were magically supplying him with air to breathe, as well as eyes to see with. It was as if the sealed-off space which enclosed Vilkata and his creatures during their helpless flight had quickly come to lack any atmosphere of its own.

Yes, the calculation of time was certainly a problem in this state . . . . More and more the wizard became convinced that time here—wherever "here" might be—was evolving very strangely. Had this enforced passage endured for a day, an hour, a month, a year? Vilkata had lost all confidence in his ability to tell.

Whatever might have been the correct objective reckoning of time, an epoch at length arrived when one of the demons, murmuring deferentially as it hovered near its worshipped master, informed him that it had fabricated for his priceless Sword a new sheath (the original was irretrievably lost), of some leathery material obtained from the gods knew where. In this sheath he could put his priceless Sword to rest while he tried to heal his injured hand. That was all right; the Dark King knew from experience that the Mindsword need not be held unsheathed continuously to maintain its compulsion, once that influence had been established.

Sword sheathed, he was able at last, with a sigh of relief, to let go the reins of the huge magical creature he was still riding. Let go, for the time being, and try to get some rest. In truth he was very weary. At a murmured command from him the saddle he had been sitting in reshaped itself to suit his comfort, becoming something like a bed or hammock. The demon-beast he had been riding reshaped itself as well, a trick they could do practically at will; then it vanished for the time being from his ken. Still it continued to re-orient itself as necessary, providing for its worshipped master some semblance of consistency regarding "up" and "down."

For many, many years the Dark King had had no eyes to close; but now he did the trick of magic that allowed him to disconnect his borrowed vision. With sight now gone, he could still hear and feel his faithful demons around him.

Ever since disaster struck he had drawn some measure of comfort from the fact that he certainly was not going unaccompanied into the peculiar night which had so totally engulfed him. His erstwhile enemy, the mighty Akbar, was drifting near him now, and the Dark King with only a minimum of effort, performing an act magically analogous to slitting his eyelids open, was able to see, through Akbar's inhuman perception, his own physical body: albino white of skin and hair, tall and strong and ageless. And currently somewhat damaged.

The demon Akbar, doubtless taking note of this activity, commented sadly and unnecessarily that its master had been wounded. Vilkata's right arm and hand had by now ceased to bleed, but were still somewhat painful, gashed from an earlier accidental contact with the Mindsword, the Blade of Glory. This particular weapon was known, among other things, for the ugliness, the resistance to treatment, of the physical wounds it could inflict.

"See what you can do in the way of healing me," the magician ordered brusquely. He held up his right hand, on which all of the blood was not yet dry.

"Yes, Master."

The damned monsters could probably do some good if they tried, Vilkata thought. Though in the ordinary course of events the healing of any living thing, especially a human, would certainly be among the least likely actions to be expected of any demon.

Once before, years ago, the Dark King had enjoyed an extended possession of the Mindsword. When in that epoch he had carried the weapon into battle, his demonic vision had shown it to him as a pillar of billowing flame long as a spear, with his own face glowing amid the perfect whiteness of the flame. And so the weapon appeared to him now.

Hand resting uneasily on the hilt of his newly resheathed Sword, he totally blanked out his vision once again and endeavored to rest. But anger and resentment prevented anything like complete relaxation.

And exactly what was it that had mobilized this impersonal and overwhelming force against Vilkata? Almost nothing, or so, in his present state of brooding helpless rage, it seemed to him.

No more than a few words of incantation cried out by his archenemy, Prince Mark.

Such was the mysterious power against demons, and against those who depended upon demons, enjoyed by Mark, the Emperor's son.

♣   ♣   ♣

When the Dark King decided that he had rested enough, and reclaimed his demonic vision, there was really almost nothing to be seen. This bizarre state of darkness and movement which had been imposed upon Vilkata and his escort by some enigmatic, overwhelming power, this rushing passage into an incomprehensible distance, protracted itself for what he began to find, subjectively, to be a very long time indeed. It seemed to him that he endured an immeasurable epoch, divorced from any objective standard of duration.

Little more in the way of deliberate, articulate communication passed between the man and the members of his demonic escort while the journey lasted. Vilkata had begun to fear that this condition might prove to be eternal, when at last hints of change broke the monotony. A murmuring developed among the demons. Something like a normal flow of time seemed to resume, and presently demons and man alike were able to sense that the darkness and the sense of rushing movement were also coming to an end.

And now, Vilkata realized with mingled relief and apprehension, the compelled journey had at last concluded. The sense of encapsulation persisted for the moment; but seeming weightlessness had been supplanted by gentle gravity. Once more "up" and "down" had become perfectly consistent— though the magician retained the odd impression that his body was now considerably lighter than it had been.

Now finally the sense of encapsulation was fading. Man and demons were free to move about. For the first time since the Prince had cursed him, Vilkata could feel a solid surface under his booted feet, a surface that felt like sandy soil.

Issuing crisp orders, making sure his compulsively loyal escort were deployed as a bodyguard ranked closely about his own person, Vilkata magically grafted the vision of first one of his enslaved creatures and then another to his own mind, in hopes that at least one of their viewpoints would be able to provide him with useful information.

Having thus done his best to transcend the handicap of his own empty eye sockets, the Dark King looked about him warily.

He was standing on a dusty, heavily cratered, windless, airless plain—he could breathe, he sensed, only because his demons were loyally providing him with air. The Sun glared, with abnormal brilliance, out of a black sky. The temperature of his surroundings was extremely high, well past the point of human endurance, had he not been magically protected.

Vilkata's first impression of this environment was that it was a hellish place indeed to which the Emperor's son had exiled him. This land, this airless space, were virtually as dead as the encapsulation he had endured on the long journey. This place was breathless and silent, in fact altogether lifeless, to a degree that the Dark King had never before encountered or even imagined.

Now, beyond the foreground of dusty, almost level plain, he could perceive hills of assorted sizes, rounded and smoothly eroded but harshly cratered. The farthest of these elevations marked out a sharp horizon under the clear but dark sky, which was strewn with unlikely numbers of hard, unwinking stars. Already, as the last traces of encapsulation disappeared, there were many stars to be seen, and more were steadily becoming visible.

In the middle distance of Vilkata's field of view were clustered a dozen or so strange buildings. These were unmistakably relics of the Old World, structures fabricated of unknown crystalline and metallic materials, the basic dome shape elaborated in incomprehensible variations. Certainly no human skills available in Vilkata's world could have created anything like them. Some were no bigger than peasants' huts, others the size of manor houses.

The inventions of the Old World were not completely foreign to the Dark King, whose education had not been restricted to matters of statecraft and magic. Like every serious scholar, he had read how the arrogant humans of that long-gone era, armed with their mysterious *technology,* had admitted no limits to their ambition—and yet had been overtaken by destruction all the same.

Issuing orders to his demons in a steady voice, Vilkata sent a couple of them ahead to scout among the buildings. In less than a minute the pair were back, saying they could detect no danger. Irritated by what he considered their casual attitude, he told them to go and look again, to make absolutely sure.

But despite his irritation the Dark King had been reassured, and in his impatience he did not wait for his scouts' second report. Hand ready on the Sword hilt at his side, he started to walk toward the apparently deserted settlement. As soon as he began to walk, new strangeness almost overcame him; his strides on this ground were awkward and bouncing, almost a slow bounding, as if his body had indeed somehow been deprived of most of its weight.

Before he had covered half the distance to the nearest of the strange, domed, half-crystalline structures, his pair of scouts, who could move with the speed of quasi-material beings, were at his side again. Still the two demons had discovered no clear and present danger. But they were obviously excited and worried by things they had just observed, babbling to their Master about Old World *technology* beyond anything that they had ever seen before. Below the visible settlement there stretched extensive underground passages and rooms, many of them still in a good state of preservation; and in some of these there appeared to be wonders indeed.

The Dark King brushed aside talk of Old World things; he

simply was not interested. "And people? Is this place inhabited?"

"Not as far as we can tell, Master. There has been no one, I think, for a very long time indeed."

Vilkata grumbled some more at the excited creatures and kept on walking. It was not that he had any wish to explore this alien land, where so much strangeness, so much—*technology*—was going to make it difficult to concentrate on the familiar and important things of magic. But the Dark King wanted to learn where he was as quickly as possible because he was eager to reassure himself regarding his chances of returning to more familiar regions without inordinate delay. Only when he had done that would it be possible to get on with his own business. And he had plenty of vital business demanding his attention: first, of course, glorious revenge, and, when the lust for revenge was stated, a return to the methodical accumulation of power.

Walking toward the Old World buildings with steps which were still mystically light and springy (even though not magically assisted), over a crunchy soil, the Dark King put the question of location to another of his demonic servants. Instinctively he chose for this purpose the demon who might be expected to be most knowledgeable and capable, the Mindsword's most eminent recent convert, Akbar himself.

"Where in the world are we, Akbar? Tell me, you cloud of slime, are we still on the same continent as Tasavalta and Sarykam?"

Akbar now assumed in Vilkata's perception the shape of a sturdy, reliable manservant who walked beside him, crude boots crunching in the soil. In apologetic tones the manservant informed the Master that the journey they had just concluded had evidently been indirect as well as protracted. They had been helplessly following for approximately two earthly years a long, wandering course through airless space. Akbar, in his usual smooth, oily fashion, did his best to take credit for making the experience as relatively comfortable as it had been for the human wizard.

But Vilkata, staring incredulously at his informant, was shocked. Outraged! Two years, wasted in confinement, as surely as if he had been clapped into a dungeon!

The Dark King snarled at his faithful demon, sending the manservant image cowering back in fear and disappointment. A demon could ordinarily take any shape it chose, within broad limits, and Akbar's likeness was now abruptly transformed into that of a young woman. Her body, voluptuous and nearly nude, minced along on delicate bare feet beside Vilkata, moving hesitantly and awkwardly, as if she were on the verge of darting away to take shelter behind one of the boulders occasionally dotting the landscape. The look on the young woman's nearly perfect face confirmed the impression of her utter helplessness and fear. In fact, her countenance reminded Vilkata strongly of a young servant girl whose name he had forgotten—it was years since he had amused himself for an evening by torturing her to death, but he still retained fond memories of the experience.

At the moment, the adoption of this particular image by the demon struck the Dark King as disgustingly stupid. Akbar could be that way at times—as though he thought his Master wanted or needed distraction, when his true need was to concentrate intensely on his problems!

Akbar, as Vilkata thought to himself, had always been one of the most cowardly and self-effacing of demons, though by no means one of the least powerful. The race were hardly noted for their bravery; but always this one had preferred to avoid even the slightest risk of death or punishment, whenever possible using other creatures—human, animal, or demonic—to attain his ends.

But right now the wizard had more important problems demanding his attention than trying to fathom the depths of a demon's character—if one could attribute such a quality as character to any member of the race. His physical environment was the first thing he had to understand. Where exactly was he, and in what kind of place? Here the pervasive ascendancy of forces other than magic made him uneasy.

He paused in his springy walk toward the enigmatic buildings. His demonic escort stopped as well, and waited, droning and half visible, in the space around his head. He was close enough now to the Old World structures to see that many of them were ruined. Whatever information might be discoverable among them could wait. Just now, with the utter alienness of his surroundings impressing itself upon him with ever-increasing force, he wanted a simple answer to a simple question: Which way was home, and how far?

Distractedly, Vilkata ran trembling fingers through his white beard, which—as he just noticed for the first time—had indeed grown long during the involuntary voyage just completed. Staring around him at the strange hills, he once more demanded the clear answer he had not yet been given.

"And where have our coerced wanderings brought us? What is this place?"

The cringing image of the young woman, becoming suddenly even more attractive, looked up brightly and edged closer. Her eyes turned bright and hopeful as she replied: "Sire, we are now standing on the Moon, upon that portion of her surface perpetually most distant from the Earth."

TWO

THE demon who had pronounced the shattering words, together with all his colleagues, peered in anxious silence at his Master, concerned to see what effect this news might have upon him.

Vilkata, stunned by the announcement, said nothing for a few moments. It was impossible to hear such an unprecedented claim without doubting it. Yet the unearthly strangeness of the environment, impressing itself upon him more intensely with every moment, immediately undermined his doubts. And the Dark King reminded himself again that the Mindsword compelled perfect loyalty; whatever his demons' natural inclination, they would not, could not, lie to him. Not unless they deemed that their Master's best interests would be served by such deception—and that condition hardly seemed likely to apply in the present situation.

Was it conceivable that a demon could be mistaken in such a matter? No, not likely either.

Seeking to establish beyond all doubt the truth of his situation, and wanting the best advice he could obtain on what to do about it, the Dark King summoned the whole number of his faithful demonic horde close about him. There were about two dozen of them in all, at the moment assuming a variety of human and almost-human shapes. Though Vilkata recognized them all individually, he had never taken a count of their exact number.

One reason for this summoning was that he did not want any of the demons straying for any dangerous length of time beyond the physical distance at which the Mindsword's influence would, in time, begin to fade.

When he was sure he had the full attention of each member of his escort, he demanded proof of the incredible statement one of their number had just made. Characteristically, he phrased the request in the form of an accusation.

"We are on the *Moon?* Do you really expect me to believe *that?*"

Judging by the expressions on the faces of his slaves and guardians, such belief was indeed what they, in their current state of enforced loyalty, had expected. The angry tone of their Master's question disturbed them.

"What proof can you offer?" the Dark King demanded.

If he had expected Akbar and the others to be perplexed by this demand, he was mistaken. To prove to their choleric Master as clearly as possible that they spoke the truth, they lifted him gently and carried him at arrow-speed over the rolling hills of the peculiar landscape, directly away from the clustered Old World domes. When his bearers put him down a minute later, the Dark King found himself gazing by means of his borrowed vision at an almost recognizable Earth, just risen straight ahead of him above the sharply defined and not-too-distant horizon.

The great orb, vastly larger than the Moon as seen from Earth, and nearly full, was now hanging motionless among the crowded stars, for all the world like some blue-white Moon, monstrously swollen.

There was half a minute of silence before the Dark King, in a changed voice, murmured: "That is . . . what I think it is?"

"Indeed, Master."

As he stared at his native planet, Vilkata's magically augmented vision was able to descry, beneath the white film of distant clouds, the shape of continents and oceans. The sight was finally convincing.

Suddenly his homeworld, so eminently recognizable, also looked so *close,* almost within reach. Vilkata wanted to reach up and pluck blue Earth from black sky, crush all the juices from the planet in his grip.

Impulsively he demanded: "How long will it take us to get

back there? Surely not a matter of years again? Such delay would be unendurable!"

Akbar, speaking with a fanatic's vehemence, and quickly supported by a chorus of his lesser colleagues, assured his Master that they would find a way to make the homeward leg of their journey infinitely faster.

"Never years, Master!"

"Never!"

Vilkata glared at them all. "Months, then? That would be almost as bad. Assure me that the return trip to our own world will not be prolonged over months."

Akbar now turned supremely smooth and reassuring. "Days only, Master, I am sure. Never more than days."

"How are we to travel? I have the feeling that this place is still connected to the Old World, that it does not support magic as well as it might. *Technology . . .*"

"Yet magic here works well enough for your purposes, Master, for here *we* are. As for getting home, I can see already that there are several ways. We will soon determine the swiftest and most secure," the demon promised.

"How?" Vilkata's voice, demanding particulars, grew louder, threatening. He waved the glowing torch-vision of his Sword. Even before the lengthy voyage just concluded, he had flown uncounted times on demons' backs, and was very familiar with the process. The idea of deliberately setting out to travel from the Moon to the Earth by such means was unsettling, whatever magical protection might be provided.

"We will discover the best way," Akbar assured him vaguely. The demon, evidently sensing that his Master considered the maidenly form inappropriate just now, had taken that of a stout male warrior. "I suggest we begin, great Master, with a thorough investigation of those buildings we had sighted."

"Be it so."

Again Vilkata was lifted gently by his guardians, and in

moments they were all back at the abandoned Old World settlement—if that was the right word for this collection of enigmatic and apparently deserted structures. As they flew above the pockmarked surface, the Earth once more slipped back below the strangely foreshortened lunar horizon.

With the complete dissipation of the encapsulating force, whatever it had been, which had confined the man and demons together through their outward voyage, the demons' vision had dramatically improved, as had that of the wizard who shared their perceptions. Now a truly unreasonable number of stars were crowding the dark sky. Standing out in the display were a pair of the brighter planets, the latter familiar to Vilkata from his long-ago studies in astrology. And always there was the mercilessly glaring Sun, which so far had shown little inclination to move from the place low in the sky where the Dark King had first seen it.

Flying, he was able to observe more clusters of human construction in the distance. Whatever the true nature of this place, whatever its true location (he still clung fiercely to an atom of doubt about being on the Moon—he did not *want* to be there!), it was certainly marked, in scattered locations, with other clustered, abandoned settlements, the ruins of strange buildings and devices.

Vilkata had learned the fact in his studies long ago—had learned but until now had never totally believed—that the arrogant humans of the Old World had indeed, even without the benefit of any magic at all, colonized the Moon.

One of the first things he had observed upon his arrival here was that the landscape was heavily cratered, pocked and blasted with marks as of violent impacts or explosions. These concavities came in all sizes, from kilometers in diameter—all distances here were hard for a stranger to estimate by sight, and Vilkata thought that ordinary human vision would have done no better than his—down to only centimeters. Some of these scars, whatever their provenance, overlay older craters and were as fresh looking as if they had been formed only yesterday. In depth and width and conformation these craters seemed to testify to titanic explosions, waves of heat which had slagged and melted native rock and buildings alike.

Directing his demonic guardians to put him down again in the middle of the first cluster of Old World constructions they had observed, the Dark King could see that many or most of the house-sized domes were more than half destroyed, looking empty and airless as the surrounding landscape.

Hand on his Sword hilt, moving again with enforced slow springy strides, Vilkata at last stepped warily in through one of the fractured walls, entering one of the broken, glassy shells. The tiled floor, looking quite ordinary, was by far the most familiar thing in sight. Now at last he was able to see enough details to convince himself completely that these buildings were the work of the legendary folk of the Old World, constructed with the aid of all their mysterious technology. Indoors and outdoors the place was littered thickly with the leavings of that antique race of humanity, the piled debris of their colossal failure. Even as the tracks of their booted human feet remained here and there visible in the crunchy soil around the buildings, evidently preserved neither by technology nor magic, but only by the unearthly nature of this environment.

The Old World culture of technology, Vilkata knew, had died some fifty thousand Earthly years ago.

In response to mumbled orders from the increasingly tired and bewildered wizard, his escort soon located for him, in one of the better-preserved ruins, a real bed, solid furniture upon a solid floor. They filled his vision with bright, cheerful light, supplied his new quarters with air, and found for him, miraculously preserved by more Old World technology, wine to drink and real food to eat. A volume of comfortable living space the size of a small house was magically sealed off.

Once a secure and comfortable physical environment had been provided for their Master, half a dozen demons, borrowing the shapes of young and beautiful humans of both sexes, came crowding together on his bed to tempt him with their bodies. He considered this display thoughtfully for a few moments, then snarled at its creators. Waving the naked, flaring Mindsword at them, he bade them get out of his sight, ordered them on pain of destruction to concentrate their efforts upon vigilantly standing guard.

When, about eight hours later, Vilkata awakened from the first real sleep he had enjoyed since his banishment—his first in two years, if Akbar was right about the time—with the hilt of the sheathed Mindsword still gripped in his long-since healed right hand, he felt considerably better. The Dark King was once more in command of himself, and ready to resume control over his own destiny.

A good thing, too, that he felt rested. Because within a few minutes of his awakening his demons came to inform him of certain unsettling discoveries they had made while he slept— there were ominous hints from beneath the lunar surface of a whole domain of ongoing mysterious activity seemingly not native to the Moon. The centerpiece of this phenomenon seemed to be a certain very ancient but still active individual presence, no more than a hundred kilometers away.

At the moment when his demons brought this news, the Dark King was standing before a mirror of magic which presented him with a demonic vision of his own eyeless countenance. He paused in the act of magically depilating his two-year beard.

"What sort of activity and presence?" he demanded. "What are you talking about?"

The demon-image of a voluptuous woman—this time one

of Akbar's lesser colleagues was acting as spokesman—observed him warily. "Great Lord, it is certainly connected with the Old World, and yet it is not entirely of that."

" 'It'? What? What kind of information is that? Either tell me something definite and meaningful, or— or—"

Again it was Akbar's turn to speak. He loomed in insubstantial form, a talking cloud. "Great Lord, it is very hard to say exactly *what* it is that we have discovered. There is much *technology,* as one might expect in any Old World settlement, and besides that there is much that is alive."

"Alive? Where? What is alive?"

"As to where, Sire, some kind of life exists here under the surface, in places not readily accessible to our examination. We cannot be more specific at the moment because there are barriers, magical and otherwise, to our close approach. We might assault those barriers successfully. Whether we might gain or discover anything that would be worth the cost . . ."

The Dark King thought. "Human life? You told me earlier that there was none."

Akbar's cloud shape contracted, suggesting a humble bow. "To our infinite shame, Tremendous Master, we may have been mistaken. What kind of life it is is hard to say without obtaining a closer look."

"Dangerous to us? To me?"

"I think not, Sire. Rather such life as exists here seems—quiescent. Of course, what might happen if we probe harder in our investigations . . ." Akbar gave the image of a shrug.

"You are babbling," Vilkata accused his faithful slave. Then he took thought before he added: "I do not intend much exploring here. I suppose you have already carried out some local investigation, or you would not have detected this supposed life."

"A rather thorough probing of our surroundings within a kilometer or two seemed only prudent, Master."

The Dark King had to admit as much. "What else have you

found? But never mind, it's plain I must look the situation over for myself. You can tell me of your discoveries while I walk."

An hour after he had awakened, the man, holding the Mindsword drawn, was standing in a tunnel several meters below the lunar surface, at the very rim of the territory his demons had already thoroughly explored.

Within a few hundred meters of the room where he had rested ran at least half a dozen underground tunnels, all lighted at convenient intervals with undying globes or panels of Old World radiance. One of these passages, bending deeper underground than others, seemed to lead on to the heart of the domain of mystery, the locus of the individual presence which, according to his demons, might or might not be alive.

Vilkata, now probing alertly with his own magical sensibilities, soon perceived certain attributes of the thing his advisers had been struggling to describe. Great but ambiguous power in repose. *Some* kind of life. And, as seemed inevitable in Old World matters, *technology*.

The Dark King had to agree with his servants. The evidence so far, he thought, the fine emanations picked up by his demons and himself, indicated that somewhere in the deeper passages there dwelt an intellect, an awareness of some kind, neither human nor demonic—and certainly not bestial.

"We think it is asleep, great Master," a minor demon offered timidly.

" '*It*'? What do you mean?" But the Dark King did not really expect an answer to the question.

In his own estimation he was being patient. He yearned—for no particular reason—to beat and punish his slaves, but sensed that in this case such treatment would only interfere with their genuine efforts to be helpful.

Acting on impulse, he advanced again.

Within a hundred paces he came to a halt, standing before a sign carved high on a wall.

This was an array of large, clearly marked symbols in a type of Old World script that neither he nor his inhuman companions, all of whom possessed several languages, could begin to read. The notice—he estimated no more than a score of words—was cut into the wall with Old World precision, just above the place where the passage Vilkata was following changed direction and turned sharply downward.

"What do the symbols mean?" To Vilkata's thinking they had an urgent, imperious look about them.

"Master, we regret that none of us, in our abysmal ignorance, possess the capability of reading them. Certainly they are an Old World script."

"I can see that, fool!"

Considering his situation, the Dark King, somewhat to his own surprise, now felt a certain perverse temptation to continue along the descending passage, to explore this world much more thoroughly. But it was only a faint craving and easy to resist. Instead of yielding he ordered a retreat.

On the way back to his comfortable quarters, trudging with springy steps through one branch of tunnel after another, he forbade his slaves to go digging any further after such potentially dangerous mysteries; what he really wanted was to get back to Earth, and his servants should all concentrate their efforts to that end.

As for the presence slumbering beneath the lunar surface, Vilkata approved the arrangement Akbar had already made— three demons posted as sentries round the suspicious area, lest the nature or attitude of what was there should undergo a sudden change.

Whatever the true nature of the mysterious underground lunar entity, the Dark King thought it well to be wary of it. It could not be *greater* than Sword-power, he supposed—he believed that no force could be—but if it was inanimate he could not expect it to be subject to the Mindsword's control.

Meanwhile his demons had turned their energies to the problem of getting their Master safely home. Since the Old World folk had obviously come here in substantial numbers without benefit of magic—the lack of any serious power of enchantment was really what defined the Old World—it followed that they must have used *technology* for the purpose, and some of their machines of transportation, like those of other types, might still exist.

The researches of Akbar and his colleagues in the field of transportation had not made much headway before they were interrupted by yet another discovery. This, too, was of something underground, but at a distance of a hundred kilometers or more from the first. Here again was life, of a kind much more familiar to Vilkata and his demons, and which seemed to have nothing directly to do with that earlier mystery.

Cautiously responding to loud inhuman cries, demands for rescue audible on both psychic and physical wavelengths, the Dark King's demons notified their Master before taking any other action. Vilkata had himself transported to the site, and ordered further exploration. His demons cracked rock and cleared it away, and he himself dissolved binding spells of enormous power.

The passage through solid lunar rock, along which the Dark King and his faithful slaves so tenaciously fought and forced their way, ended in a great hollow shell of a chamber, like the interior of a glassy ball ten meters in diameter, physically and magically sealed away from the outside world. Filling this chamber and reverberating through the nearby rock, almost deafening the human explorer, was the nerve-shattering droning, tormented screaming of the nearly immortal beings who were confined within.

Demons, of course. A swarm, a score of them at least, a horde whose existence the Dark King had never suspected until now, had been here mercilessly imprisoned.

Nearing the place by means of a freshly blasted tunnel, Vilkata approached with the Mindsword drawn this fearsome chamber inside a convoluted, crystallized and enchanted mass of lunar rock. Breaking his way into the howling kennel, then entering it boldly, the Dark King shouted to silence the evil creatures who were bound within, and with the same shout proclaimed to them that they were now his slaves.

Unfamiliar though these captive demons were to him as individuals, Vilkata immediately found communication with them easy enough. They spoke, in addition to several archaic human tongues, the basic, common demonic language in which he was well versed. In moments he had learned their names, which, like their identities, were utterly unfamiliar to him.

The largest of these newly-discovered beings, named Arridu, at once assumed the role of spokesman. Arridu, who gave the impression of being much stronger than even Akbar, went so far as to describe himself as equal in power to Orcus of ancient legend, and Vilkata, awed despite himself, was not sure that the fiend before him was exaggerating.

Then the human wizard, assisted by Akbar, set about finding the proper modes of magic with which to free Arridu and his colleagues from their present bondage. The mere forcing of a tunnel into their prison was not going to suffice.

To say the locks and keys and barriers of enchantment were stubborn was to understate the case. But the Dark King was able to work on them without being himself confined, and he was one of the premier magicians of the world. Some hours of concentrated labor were required, but in the end his success was assured.

Vilkata was greatly impressed by this imprisoning, and not at all sure that he could have managed anything of the kind himself. Who, he demanded to know, had entrapped them thus?

The Dark King was at first amazed when Arridu and the demons with him insisted that they did not know their conqueror. But then Vilkata realized that the partial destruction of these demons' memories must have been part of their punishment, perhaps necessary to keep them so long confined.

Arridu, when pressed, related some disconnected scenes, about all he could remember, from the early years of his existence—or at least his version of events, which, under the Mindsword's compulsion, might be assumed to be close to what he actually believed, if not really the truth. But the fragmented memories were of little help. All that could be said with certainty was that some thousands of years ago, how many thousands the speaker could no longer tell, he and a handful of his most evil colleagues had been sealed by overwhelming magic—or by some other energy having the effect of magic—into this sublunarian vault, or crypt.

Questioned by Vilkata regarding the strange underground domain of non-demonic life and technology which lay approximately a hundred kilometers from the site of their confinement, the newly-freed demons were unable to give him much, if any, information.

Next Vilkata demanded of them: "Tell me, all of you, where are your lives?" Almost without exception among demons, it was the rule for the life, the vulnerability, to be concealed in some ordinary physical object, generally innocuous in itself, often at a considerable distance from the creature's manifest presence.

Akbar and his colleagues would have eagerly surrendered to the Dark King their life-objects as well as their names—but, in fact, the formerly imprisoned demons did not know where their own lives were.

The Dark King at length had to admit the truth of this

surprising development—he supposed it only natural that if the creatures' gaolers had known where their lives were hidden, they would have killed them.

But even without the extra advantage which would have been offered by possession of the life-objects, these demons were now the Dark King's slaves. Vilkata's eyes gleamed with ambition, with dreams of revenge and conquest, when he assessed the strength of the force over which the Mindsword had now given him absolute authority.

Arridu and his colleagues would have been disappointed that their deliverer should be a mere human, and that this mere human seemed quite capable of managing them—they would have been so disappointed, even dismayed, had not the Mindsword shown them their deliverer as the incomparable being that he was. From the moment the Dark King, with Skulltwister drawn, approached their place of confinement, their age-long despair had given way to elation, to transcendent joy. It was the one perfect being in the Universe who had come to make them his servants and worshippers!

Akbar chose a moment when all of the Dark King's new servants were elsewhere to approach his Master with a warning. Compelled by the Sword into genuine concern for Vilkata's welfare, Akbar warned the man that loosing a demon of Arridu's power and malignancy upon the world, no matter under what conditions of magical compulsion, could not but be fraught with peril.

"Tut. My Sword controls him, does it not? Even as it compels you, and the others."

"But I like it not, Master. I like it not."

And Akbar, who until now had rightfully considered himself the pre-eminent demon in the Dark King's service, sulked a little in jealousy. But under the Mindsword's influence even Akbar was compelled to rejoice at any development that really augmented Vilkata's power.

* * *

Within minutes after the lunar demons had been released, the imperfect memory of one of the long-term residents contributed to an important find:

Here was a large underground chamber filled with Old World devices intended to be used for interplanetary transportation.

Leading Vilkata along an underground passage the man had not walked before, Arridu and his contemporaries soon revealed to their Master the collection of spacecraft they had discovered.

A vast underground chamber contained a great number and variety of units, obviously Old World machines, the smallest as large as a small house. Investigation disclosed more than one underground hangar, occupied by ranks of bubble-type devices, with all the appropriate launching and support and control equipment.

Vilkata at first resisted the idea that these devices could have been meant to fly—there were not even rudimentary wings, such as birds, reptiles, and griffins sported, and even demons wore, at least in his demonic vision, when they soared into the air. These works of technology appeared almost magical in their outward simplicity: rounded, almost spherical things of glass and metal, interiors furnished with seats and couches of various styles, showing that the things were indeed intended for human occupation. The richness and variety of interior furnishings indicated strongly that they were definitely not meant as mere cells for confinement.

Over the course of the next few hours or days—the man tended to lose track of days because, compounding the unearthly nature of this world, there was only a very gradual shifting of the position of the Sun against the pattern of stars in the black sky—some demons cautiously experimented with these spacecraft.

Others ransacked certain Old World stores surviving in the deep caves. There the faithful, jealous creatures discovered supplies of air, and of preserved food and drink, more than sufficient to last their master comfortably through the return journey. This time, he warned them, he meant to retain his full awareness and alertness.

In moments when Vilkata allowed himself to be distracted from his mission of getting home, he again curiously questioned the old lunar demons, seeking to learn what they could tell him of the events leading to their imprisonment.

But all their most important memories were permanently gone. At certain moments some of the creatures spoke with chilling familiarity of the Old World, as though perhaps it was something they had seen for themselves, and of Ardneh and Orcus, of whom they must have heard much; but as for the mysterious regions, the other life possibly existing on the Moon, they could only warn their beloved new Master to stay clear. These warnings only reinforced his own inclinations.

Having learned what little his new recruits could tell him that seemed of any practical value, Vilkata, giving his most savage imitation of politeness, invited new demonic recruits and old servants alike to join him in his conquest of the Earth, which had been delayed, but not, he was now sure, prevented.

His formal invitation was, of course, accepted enthusiastically. Not that his hearers had any choice, being as tightly bound as ever to loyalty under the Mindsword's influence.

Knowing as much about demons as he did, the Dark King felt certain that, even apart from their enforced loyalty, his escorts were as spontaneously glad as he was to be returning to the Earth, to a place where they would once more be creatures of great size and importance.

*   *   *

Within an hour after the command had been given, his protectors—mighty Arridu now claiming priority among them—announced that they were ready to bear him, and his protective bubble of atmosphere, on the flight. Either magically or depending almost totally upon the powers of the Old World craft.

The Dark King's return flight was already under way—the hurtling glass-and-metal sphere escorted by quasi-material demons, some inside the craft and some outside, the huge blue roundness of the Earth dominating the black sky ahead—before one of the escorting creatures inquired: "And whereabouts on Earth, Master, are we to land?"

"What better place than the very spot from which we left? Conduct me back to the palace at Sarykam! I have unfinished business with that proud Prince who hateth demons. And business with his people too."

The Old World spacecraft was satisfactorily comfortable, much more so than the limbo-like conditions of the outward voyage. Shortly after leaving the Moon, Vilkata began to consider seriously at what hour he wanted to arrive at Mark's palace. In the middle of the night? Or just before dawn? That was always a favorite hour for a surprise attack. But it was more important, he soon decided, to time his arrival at Sarykam for a day and an hour when he could be sure that Mark himself was elsewhere—he was not pleased by the prospect of being immediately whirled away into another two years' exile.

Therefore, all his brave speech and muttered vows to the contrary notwithstanding, the Dark King did not really want to fly directly to the palace. No, it would be vastly preferable to land somewhere nearby—in the ocean, possibly, or along the rocky Tasavaltan shore—somewhere where he could hide his Old World flying device until he could discover how things might have changed in Sarykam in two years, and just where Prince Mark was now.

"We will discover a good place, sire."

Ought he to send a demon ahead to scout? That was a decision requiring careful consideration. If he did so, he would have to take the chance that the thing might well be tempted to turn against him when it had been away from his Sword for some hours at a distance of hundreds or thousands of kilometers.

Still, he had controlled demons before he had the Sword, and expected he could do so even if deprived of Skulltwister's advantages.

Vilkata decided to send at least one scout ahead, and perhaps several more after the first; to begin with, he wanted to select one of the demons whose lives he already carried with him. He had in mind a creature who on occasion had served him as his eyes, whose life-object, a small mirror, rode securely in the Dark King's pocket, and whose loyalty the man felt confident he could compel even without depending on the Mindsword's power.

What better choice than Akbar himself?

THREE

N EAR the middle of one of the shortest nights of early
summer, a single bright light, an Old World lamp of
cool and eerie brilliance, burned in one of the deepest and
most heavily guarded rooms of the central armory below the
palace at Sarykam. A brace of fascinated moths were circling
the round lamp of strange, smooth glass and metal in its
mounting on an oak beam over a workbench. The lamp
showed no flame and required no external source of power,
but cast superb illumination, balm for tired eyes, upon the
bench, the surrounding walls of whitewashed stone, and the
faces of the two people present.

One of these was Prince Mark's fourteen-year-old son, Stephen, who had been hard at work for half a day and half a
night upon a certain private project; the other was an elderly
man called Bazas, one of the senior armorers, who had volunteered to stand by and give advice. The young Prince was
making it a point of honor to do all the actual labor on this
particular job with his own hands.

The task Stephen had set for himself was that of crafting
some piece of armor (whether a breastplate or a shield was still
to be determined) from dragons' scales. And the project was
private, more accurately semi-secret, because the product was
intended as a gift for Stephen's father, on the occasion of
Prince Mark's fortieth birthday.

Prince Mark was currently absent from the palace, not expected back for two or three days, when he would return in
time for the semi-official birthday celebration. At the moment
Mark was some sixty kilometers from Sarykam, having spent
the last several days in a lightly populated region of his compact realm. Mark and Princess Kristin had gone there, with a
small military escort, to help some citizens who had recently

suffered from a local plague of dragons. The scales Stephen was working with were a byproduct of the relief expedition.

From the five Swords available in the Tasavaltan armory at the time of his departure, Stephen's father had chosen to carry with him only two—the harmless Woundhealer and the ruthlessly efficient Dragonslicer. The latter Sword had been returned to the armory, under guard, as soon as the need for it in the countryside had passed.

For more than a year now the land of Tasavalta had been at peace, save for the occasional natural violence of dragon-incursion, or of earthquake—thank Ardneh, there had been only minor temblors lately.

Inside the palace, peace reigned with special felicity. These days the royal couple, Stephen's parents, were doting on each other, spending by choice a great deal of time in each other's company; although they were temporarily separated now and then by the need to accomplish important business in two places at the same time, they were firmly reconciled, following an earlier period of near estrangement.

For more than a year Kristin, thanks to Woundhealer, had been completely recovered from the physical injuries she had incurred at the time of the Dark King's assault upon their palace.

Approximately two years had now passed since the vicious attack by Vilkata. That onslaught, the cause of so much pain and suffering for everyone in Tasavalta, was only a bitter memory.

But tonight, Prince Stephen's thoughts were concentrated on the matter of a birthday gift. To make a shield of practical size, two dozen or more of the hand-sized scales would have to be fastened to a wooden frame, arranged in overlapping rows. Putting together a suitable frame ought to pose no problem; but working a dragon's scales was something else. Try to cut or simply bore a hole in one, at least in any scale which was big enough to use for armor, and you were likely to wear out your tool or weapon of mere mundane steel, no matter how well forged and honed, before you had made much of an impression on the material.

Stephen had argued, and the expert armorer had grudgingly admitted, that dragonscale shield or armor, provided it proved feasible to make at all, ought to offer some real, practical advantages over any metal breastplate or shield—gram for gram of weight, such a defense would probably be a lot tougher and more protective than any human smiths could make of steel.

The special material for this project, the actual scales of a genuine landwalker, had of course been harvested in the field in the course of the recent emergency, by a skilled fighter who had been loaned the Sword of Heroes for the task. The detached scales had been brought back to the armory with the Sword, and were now being shaped with the same god-forged implement which had slain the monster and had cut the scales loose from its otherwise almost impervious hide—the only feasible way to do the job.

The setup on the bench in the armory workshop, with a Sword, one of the world's enduring wonders, clamped in place like some mere ordinary tool, was remarkable to say the least, and in the earlier, daylight hours of the job other workers had occasionally stopped to stare at the work in progress. Stephen had sworn each new witness to secrecy until Prince Mark's birthday came and the gift could be presented.

Stephen's hands, well coordinated though not yet extremely skillful, were already big, and hardened from frequent work with tools and practice weapons; his arms and shoulders were still on a smaller scale, not nearly as thick and strong as they would be in a few years.

At the moment the boy's hands were gripping a single dark scale, approximately the shape of a giant freshwater clamshell, slightly convex on its upper, darker surface, and with something of a clamshell's rugose texture.

Clamped immovably into place (earlier attempts to use it as a drill bit had been abandoned), the magical weapon began making its customary shrilling sound as soon as Stephen began to work the scale against the more-than-razor keenness of the Sword's bright tip. Using point and edge in alternation, the youth was with comparative ease shaving, carving, and boring holes in the material which would have quickly dulled or broken any ordinary tools.

Stephen, impatient to get the job finished before his royal father could be expected home, pushed harder, and suddenly the scale, tormented by the shrilling Sword which carved at it, broke neatly down the middle. The youth narrowly avoided cutting his own fingers.

It was not the first time during the past few hours that such a problem had arisen. The tough, hard scales seemed soft and malleable as cork when Stephen put them to the test with Dragonslicer; but the material was stubbornly reluctant to yield in the precise way the young craftsman wanted. The floor near the bench was littered with the debris of these mishaps.

The Sword's noise ceased abruptly when it lost contact with the scale. Into the sudden silence Stephen swore, using soldiers' oaths with a veteran's casual instinct, his adolescent voice breaking awkwardly in the middle of the utterance. He had heard a great deal of soldiers' talk during the last year or so, when the armory had suddenly become one of his favorite places. The armorer meanwhile looked on dourly, this time restricting himself to a single laconic comment; in truth old Bazas had never thought much of the plan of making a shield, or anything else, from dragonscale. In his view, if the idea had any real merit, some expert would have done it long ago.

As far as the old armorer had ever heard, only one being had ever used dragonscale armor: the god Vulcan, the limping smith who'd forged all of the Swords. Mere humans—so

Bazas was ready to tell the world, royalty or not—mere humans ought to be content with the kinds of armor humans had always worn.

Now Stephen bit his lip. In his cooler moments he was well aware that he needed to demonstrate patience and control his chronically difficult temper if he was going to make a real success of this job.

For one thing, his stock of available scales—his original intention had been to use only those in a narrow range of size and color—was far from unlimited.

Wiping his hands on his simple workman's shirt, he went to work again, longish hair falling over a face that was swiftly losing its childish looks; his hair was growing dark, soon to be even darker than his father's had been until a year or so ago, when Mark's hair and beard had started to show some gray.

Long hours ago, during the sunbright afternoon, the youth had been sweating from his work, but now the deep armory was almost chill. Tasavalta was a coastal land, whose climate, though subject to abrupt and sometimes unpleasant variations, lingered for the most part in a state approximating perpetual spring.

Now for a time the work went more smoothly. But the young prince soon paused again, with a technical question for his old adviser, one for which old Bazas, as usual, had a ready answer. Other voices, those of bored sentries exchanging passwords outside the thick walls, drifted in faintly through a high grilled window. It had been necessary for Stephen to inform Karel, the realm's chief wizard, and also General Rostov, the military commander, that he was opening the heavily guarded Sword-vault to get out Dragonslicer. But he had not needed any special permission to work with the dragonscales. At least he had not asked specifically, though he had told his mother what he was going to do, before she left Sarykam with her husband.

Now, having shaped one more dragonscale to his own satisfaction, the boy added it to the small pile of finished work and picked out a fresh scale from a small box nearby. Then once more he set to work under the critical eye of the grizzled armorer.

Mulling over the subject of gifts in his own mind as he worked, wondering whether he ought to try to discuss it reasonably with Bazas, Stephen's thought turned briefly to his two-years-older brother, Adrian, who was now absent from home while performing—or undergoing—the last stages of a years-long tutelage in advanced magic. This was a subject for which Adrian, unlike Stephen, had a tremendous natural aptitude. It now occurred to the younger brother, trying to carve scales, to wonder what, if anything, Adrian might be getting their father for his birthday. Mark himself, though a child of the Emperor, was no magician, apart from one great and apparently inherited talent—his amazing ability to hurl demons into distant exile.

Now for a time Stephen forgot about his brother and the subject of gifts in general. On the workbench things for a change were going well. Presently another of the exotic scales had now been cut and bored into the desired shape. Stephen held it up, inspecting the small, neat holes in the hand-sized slab, openings through which tough thongs could be laced, binding it to a light wooden frame. The surface of the shield (or, alternatively, the breastplate) when it was completed would be comprised of rows of overlapping scales, like shingles on a roof, each protecting the otherwise vulnerable lashings of the scale below.

With satisfaction the young Prince laid the latest scale on

his small pile of finished work. Five or six more of the same size, he told himself, ought to be enough.

Soon Stephen paused again, briefly, to ask Bazas another question having to do with certain details of the shield-maker's craft. Months ago when he began to frequent the armory the young Prince had discovered that it was necessary to speak loudly to the old man, who had been left somewhat deaf by his years of labor at the anvil. Except for Stephen's loud voice the vaulted room beneath the palace was very quiet at this hour, now that the Sword on the bench had once more ceased the shrilling sound it made in action.

In the near silence, the lad noted in the back of his mind that there did seem to be, after all, at least one other worker present there at midnight. The faint thudding sound of someone industriously, almost continuously, hammering came drifting in from one of the armory's relatively remote chambers.

The young Prince made some passing comment on this sound, mentioning the evident presence of another worker to his companion. Old Bazas, who had not yet been able to hear the noise, only grunted noncommittally. He was a proud man, who at any time during the past several years could have had his hearing restored by Woundhealer for the asking—but had not wanted to admit he needed help.

Stephen went back to work—he had become grimly determined to finish cutting, in this session, all the scales he was going to need. And the old armorer, gnarled hands behind his back, resumed the pose of an alert overseer.

But before another minute had passed, another difficulty arose with the scale currently being carved. Maybe, thought Stephen to himself, the shape of this one just wasn't quite right to begin with. . . .

Thud thud thud thud . . .

The sounds from the other room were growing louder,

becoming a real distraction. Not just because they were loud; during the afternoon just past, the armory had been a much noisier place than it was now. No, the young Prince thought, the disturbing thing was that something fundamental must be going wrong with whatever project was under way in the other room. He hearkened to another random, senseless-sounding barrage of impact-sounds from that direction.

Abruptly Stephen looked up, frowning, and turned his head, listening intently; that didn't sound like rational constructive hammering at all, but rather like some angry workman taking out his spite upon his bench. No, not like that either, but more like some deranged drummer, who had been locked inside a big chest and was trying to get out.

No, not even that.

Really what it sounded like was—was—

Stephen's eyes, widening, met the suddenly frightened gaze of the old man who stood across the bench from him. Even Bazas could hear the racket now, and in this he had been quicker-witted than his young Prince.

Realization had come to man and boy at the same time, and they both uttered almost the same words, almost in unison: "It is the Sword of Force!"

Shieldbreaker only gave such warning when actually in use, or when combat impended. So Prince Mark had taught his sons; and Mark had impressed upon the two young Princes also that in his experience the Sword was never wrong when it sounded the alert. This current uproar from the chamber where the Sword of Force was kept must mean that a serious assault was about to fall upon the palace at any moment.

Stephen, having been taught the lore of Swords almost from his cradle, realized that whatever kind of armed attack might be impending, they had only a few minutes, or perhaps only a few seconds, in which to act before it struck.

The troublesome dragonscale fell unheeded from the hand of the young Prince. Everything but the alarm forgotten, Stephen turned away from the workbench, his first impulse being to run up the nearest stair into the palace, shouting out a warning . . . but before he had taken more than two steps, he realized that there was no figure of real authority near at hand, none close enough to relieve him of the burden of decision and action which had been so suddenly thrust upon him.

He had no time to seek out Great-Uncle Karel, or General Rostov, or even the officer of the day; besides, the latter was not privy to the secret code of magic necessary to get the Swords out of their vault and bring them into action. Neither were any of the regular armorers, not even trusty old Bazas. The only person able to act immediately and effectively was the young Prince himself.

With swift agility Stephen turned in the opposite direction. Two driving strides and he was running at full speed toward the chamber in which the Swords were kept.

Just in the last few moments Shieldbreaker's noise had swelled to a hammering bedlam of terrible urgency. The young Prince experienced a choking sensation as he thought that there might be just time for someone as near to the repository as he was, someone able and willing to act boldly, to get the Sword of Force out of its case and into action before the threat, whatever it was, arrived.

The constriction in his throat proceeded from a fear of failure. He, a Prince of Tasavalta, should have know better, he should have known the sound of the Sword at once for what it was, he should have been alerted to the danger long minutes ago! Possibly the unthinkable had already happened, he had ignored the warning for too long, it was already too late for him to act . . . .

In the few heartbeats of time which had elapsed while those thoughts ran through his mind, Stephen's running feet had brought him to the Sword-chamber. He jolted to a stop just outside that room's single doorway, darkened now. The opening lacked any material door but was gauzed with almost invisible but effective barriers: his Great-Uncle Karel's powerful magic, spells keeping everyone out with an action like that of unseen hands.

Muttering the necessary secret password under his breath, the boy felt the hands immediately cease their opposition, the barrier of enchantment divide like a curtain to let him in.

He sprang through into the vaulted space where all of the Swords in the possession of the realm of Tasavalta, along with a few other very precious things, were ordinarily kept safe.

The low-ceilinged Sword-chamber was octagonal, and comparatively small, extending no more than about five paces between opposite walls. Two of the walls supported racks of ceremonial crowns and weapons, kept here for the sake of their jewels and gold. There were a few sword-belts and empty scabbards, there as works of art; other shelves held jewels and comparatively minor treasures. A few lamps and candles, none of them lighted at the moment, stood about on stands and ledges. The place was cool and very dim, particularly to eyes so recently accustomed to the brightness around the workbench. In fact the chief source of illumination in the Sword-chamber at the moment was the indirect glow of the Old World lamp still burning two rooms away.

Only a small handful of individuals had ever been empowered to enter this room. An even smaller number had been granted the immaterial keys required to open the inner vault and remove a Sword. The necessary secret magic, simple enough for even a non-magician to use, had not been entrusted to Stephen until very recently, on the occasion of his fourteenth birthday.

This expression of his parents' confidence had made him very proud. He had used the spell (with his mentor, Karel, looking on) for the first and only time only yesterday—actually a mere matter of hours ago, in the morning just past—to get Dragonslicer out of its case for his secret project.

* * *

Thud-thud, thud-thud, thud-thud—

Here under the low vaulting, the sound of hammering seemed notably amplified. There could now be no possible doubt about the source. The white stone walls, and Stephen's bones alike, reverberated with Shieldbreaker's pounding tocsin.

The actual place of storage for the Swords was a waist-high coffer or strongbox built into the center of the room. In this Shieldbreaker and its peers were locked away, behind a pair of carven, slanted doors of wood and metal. This coffer had been constructed of mixed materials, mostly rounded masonry, but incorporating the wood of certain exotic trees as well as several kinds of metal, ivory, and horn, all woven fast within tight nets of Karel's magic. Precious metal had been incorporated as well, gold and silver used more for their magical qualities than as mere decoration. Even rings of unidentifiable material from mysterious Old World devices had been built into the structure.

THUD, THUD-THUD, THUD—

As Stephen stretched out his hands toward the slanted doors of the inner vault, he was vaguely aware of someone behind him. Glancing back momentarily over his shoulder, he saw that the old armorer had come hurrying after him from the workroom, come as far as he could, to just outside the guarded doorway. Bazas must have acted quickly and purposefully, delayed only by the need to free Dragonslicer from the clamps which had held the Sword upon the bench. Now the elderly man, his progress stopped by the invisible hands of Karel's magic, had come to a halt. He was holding up the keen Blade in his right hand, and had his free hand raised as well, as if to test the magic sealing of the doorway, or pronounce a benediction.

The armorer called out urgently: "My prince! The Sword of Heroes must be put in a place of safety."

The words of Bazas were partially muffled by the intervening magic, but Stephen nodded his understanding. Dragonslicer was not the weapon of choice with which to repel a raid or an invasion—except in the highly unlikely event that one's foe came riding on a dragon. It was the expression on the old man's face that made the young Prince experience a sense of awe. A seasoned soldier was actually looking to him for leadership, and this realization gave Stephen the night's first moment of genuine fright.

It was not to be the last.

Nodding, the boy wordlessly turned his back on Bazas. Facing the sloping plane formed by the closed doors of the inner vault, he quickly let his right hand rest on the hard surface. There was no physical handle or knob on either door, no bolt or latch, but the guardian powers required identification of the petitioner for entrance. He started to recite the brief spell of opening—

—but before Stephen had managed to utter more than three of the seven necessary words, he choked and stumbled in his recitation. At the same time the world turned sick and strange around him, the stone floor seeming to tilt alarmingly sideways underneath his feet.

This was far more, far worse, than the choking of anxiety. Involuntarily he cried out, and heard what seemed a responding cry from just outside the room. Looking again in that direction, Stephen saw old Bazas, Dragonslicer still in his right hand, slumping to the floor. Now another figure, strange and startlingly gigantic, completely filled the doorway, its image wavering so that it looked to the young Prince both more and less than human. There was nothing about it that Stephen's mind wanted to acknowledge as a face. With a transparent appendage that was like and yet unlike a human hand it appeared to be working to put aside the defenses put up by the master-magician Karel. So far those defenses were holding back the thing, the presence, whatever it might be—

Yet already the invader could project some form of power past the barrier. Stephen was aware that he was losing consciousness, and with what shreds of sense remained he knew the cause: he was being confronted by a demon at close range. Though the young Prince had been brushed by demons' wings before—he had been in the palace during Vilkata's attack two years ago—he had never experienced anything like the force of this evil manifestation, and he found it all but completely overwhelming.

Again the world seemed to tilt crazily, wrongly around Stephen, and he clung helplessly to the rounded stonework side of the inner vault, swaying with physical illness.

In his terror Stephen involuntarily closed his eyes. But this was no help, for the monster immediately started to force its image under his eyelids.

And now a voice, a sound of dead leaves crushed that had to be the demon's voice, was calling to him. It was commanding, demanding that he do something for it.

He answered with a nearly helpless, incoherent mumbling: What was it that he had to do?

The dried leaves swirled and rustled. "You must recite for me the spell I need. Undo for me the barring of this chamber door, and let me in . . . ."

Stephen tried to think. But he couldn't think. Not beyond the knowledge that he was going to be killed—yet there remained something he *must* do.

Of course. The Swords.

For the moment his body would not move. But remembering a purpose gave him strength, and he tried to talk to the thing that was about to kill him. "Who are you? What—?"

The tones of the demon's utterance, taking form more in the mind than in the ears, were an inhuman rattling among dead bones. "You must know, child of the Prince of Scum, that I am called Akbar . . . . I say that you must open this door."

Akbar. Indeed Stephen knew the name from his father's stories, and from a hundred other tales, and that it meant overwhelming malignancy, sheer terror. He must not give way, he must not open the gate for it—no, he had to open the inner vault, recite the spell that would let him reach the Swords.

And now the demon had succeeded in forcing another part of itself—an arm that was not really an arm—partway in through Karel's barrier. One giant finger—something half-material that was not quite a finger—flicked at the young Prince.

The impact knocked Stephen off his feet, sent him rolling across the stone floor, out of reach of the doors which he must open. Scarcely aware of the bruising of his knees and elbows on the stone, he tried to scramble out of the way as the quasi-material thing came probing, reaching, after him again.

Again it struck at the young Prince, and this time a veil of darkness started to descend across his mind.

FOUR

DAZED and battered as he was, the young Prince retained enough awareness to hear Bazas screaming weakly and hoarsely, the old man lying on the floor just outside the doorway of the Sword-chamber.

Stephen himself was also sprawled on the stone pavement, but well inside the doorway where the demon's groping power had flung him. Where he ought to be protected by Karel's magic, but yet seemed to be not quite out of Akbar's reach. His knees and elbows hurt from the fall on the stone floor. The whole world felt sick and strange around him.

Drawing a deep breath, clenching his fists and his jaw as tightly as his eyelids, Stephen denied sickness. A hundred times his father had told him of the several confrontations he, Mark, had had with demons, occasions when he had been able to banish the foul creatures with a command. These were not matters of which the elder Prince ever spoke boastfully. Rather Mark described those encounters in the manner of a man still trying to understand how he had served as a conduit for powers greater than himself. And many times, Mark's younger son, when listening to the stories, had wondered whether he himself might have inherited his father's ability.

Now the boy's voice cracked again as he desperately shouted the mysterious formula which had never failed his father: "In the Emperor's name, forsake this game! Get out!"

In Stephen's own ears the slurred words sounded more like a scream of panic than a firm command. But at once the multiple foul images of the demon vanished from under the young Prince's eyelids. Some force had obviously intervened against his attacker, and the hideous thing, which a moment earlier had seemed on the point of crushing Stephen like an insect, was being forcibly separated from him. Akbar reacted with a bellow of outrage.

Raising himself on his elbows, Stephen dared to open his eyes.

His monstrous antagonist, its form still only half visible, was thrashing about as if some unseen power larger than itself had seized it and was pulling it by main force out of the doorway of the Sword-chamber, farther and farther from its intended human victims—

A moment later the demon was entirely gone.

As the young Prince scrambled back to his feet, he was dimly aware of distant screams and yells, in voices far more human than the demon's. At the moment he could not tell whether these outcries proceeded from upstairs within the palace, or from outside. But he thought it did not matter. The whole palace, the whole city, must be under attack.

Now that the demon had been ejected from the armory, Bazas, just outside the doorway of the Sword-chamber, was slowly regaining his feet. The old armorer, shaking his head and quivering in all his limbs, was still holding Dragonslicer in one hand and propping himself with the other against the wall.

Stephen turned immediately back to the task he must perform, that of opening the inner vault which held the Swords— but the moment he again began the incantation to unlock the doors, he became aware, more with his mind than with any of his physical senses, that the demon he had caused to be hurled away had not gone very far.

Howling and screaming its rage at him, its insane hatred of all humanity but the adored Master, Akbar was racing, flying back—

Again the incantation must be interrupted. Again the young Prince had only a moment in which to bark out a command. This time, heartened by the partial success of his first attempt, he managed to put more authority into his voice. Gritting his teeth, he willed and yelled his swelling anger at the beast.

Again a scream from an affronted demon—again the banishing was successful. Because the mental contact which had been established between himself and Akbar still persisted, Stephen could feel that this time his foe had been hurled to a somewhat greater distance. But the youth had no doubt that Akbar would be doggedly, relentlessly, returning yet once more to the attack. And Stephen was vaguely aware of the presence, somewhere in the background, of another demon—more likely several of them—approaching.

Meanwhile, Stephen's latest repulsion of the enemy had earned him the moment of time, the breathing space he needed.

Half leaning against one side of the inner vault, the young Prince once again reached a physical position from which he could lay his right hand on the slanted doors. Breathlessly he hurried through the few and simple words, dreading lest he stumble in his pronunciation of one of the essential syllables, and so be forced to begin yet again.

But this time Stephen managed to do the incantation properly. The vault doors of their own accord jerked open with a double slam. At once the wordless voice of the Sword of Force, no longer muffled, boomed out through the armory.

Three god-forged Swords, as well as two empty, Sword-shaped spaces, were revealed within the vault. Each meter-long blade and white-marked hilt lay nested in a velvet lining of the blue-green color of the sunlit sea. The faint wash of Old World light coming into the chamber from two rooms away touched the bright magical lines of steel, and the flat sides of the three perfect blades gave back a mottled triple reflection—Shieldbreaker, Sightblinder, and Stonecutter.

In appearance the Swords were indistinguishable from each other, save for the white symbols on their black hilts.

Three Sword-belts of fine leather, each with an empty scabbard attached, were racked separately at one side within the inner vault. The receptacle for belts, like that for the Swords, displayed two empty spaces and three filled.

Despite the immediate threat posed by the returning demon, Stephen knew a sense of awe that compelled him to a heart-beat's hesitation. These were the weapons of the gods, forged more than forty years ago by the deity Vulcan himself, with the human aid of Jord, a human smith—Jord who was also Prince Mark's foster father, and thus the grandfather of Stephen. The young Prince and his brother Adrian had grown up hearing the marvelous old stories, as often as not from their foster-grandfather's own mouth.

One of the pair of empty Sword-shaped niches within the vault was of course the usual resting place of Dragonslicer. The other space sometimes accommodated Woundhealer, which was also very often, as now, absent from this repository upon some mission of mercy. Part of Stephen's mind took note of the fact that a tiny spider was even now spinning a web in the space reserved for the Sword of Mercy.

But Stephen just now had no eyes or thought for any of the Swords but one. That one, snug in its nest, positioned a little above its fellows, was now emitting a frenzied war-drum sound. The warning boomed out louder than ever, and a verse of the Song of Swords raced through his mind.

> *I shatter Swords and splinter spears;*
> *None stands to Shieldbreaker.*
> *My point's the fount of orphans' tears*
> *My edge the widowmaker.*

The young Prince's right hand darted into the vault, ready to seize the black hilt marked with the small white image of a hammer.

—and meanwhile the demon Akbar had once more returned

*and now was rushing again upon him, sweeping from the door-
way the last shreds of protective magic—*

The Sword of Force came literally leaping up out of its
velvet casing to meet Stephen's grasping fingers. He needed no
particular skill in magic to feel the god-power surge along his
arm. Such was the effect that in that instant he gasped with
relief, as if the battle were already won.

Nor was the young Prince now required to display any skill
or strength at arms. Darting out of its case as if by its own
volition, Shieldbreaker continued its upward movement, pulling the young Prince's right arm violently with it.

Shieldbreaker, hammering thunderstrokes, lashed out violently against the demonic intruder. Stephen's right arm was
pulled helplessly forward even as his body staggered back.
Pain stabbed at his shoulder, where the movement of the
Sword twisted it.

The demon, an image of horror seeming to loom larger than
the walls of the Sword-chamber, emitted no bellow of outrage
this time, but rather a choked cry, a grating and unbreathing
sound that was to haunt the young Prince in nightmares. In
the next instant Akbar's image burst like a pricked bubble.
The sickness provoked by the demonic presence immediately
disappeared, as if it had been flushed into oblivion by cleans-
ing waves of air and light. And then Stephen was vaguely
aware that the creature which had called itself Akbar was no
longer anywhere, anywhere at all.

Relief lasted for only a moment; another ghastly scream
warned Stephen that he had no time at all for triumph. Turning with alarm, gazing toward the now-unguarded doorway,
he beheld Bazas standing in that opening with Dragonslicer in
hand. In the last few moments the old armorer's face had
undergone a ghastly transformation, had become a mask of
exalted rage and hatred.

Glaring at the young Prince, screaming Stephen's death and
the exalted name of the Dark King, Bazas leapt forward with

his Sword raised to kill—and struck, with a trained warrior's skill.

The young Prince, still reeling from the demon's onslaught, had no time to try to understand, to think, or even to react consciously. Fortunately he needed to do none of those things. As the blade of Dragonslicer swung toward Stephen's head, slicing almost horizontally under the low ceiling, Shieldbreaker of its own accord pulled his arm along at invisible speed to parry the blow.

Steel clashed with steel, both products of Vulcan's forge. With a single *thud*, monstrously loud, and a flash of light, the Sword of Heroes passed out of existence, dissolved in a burst of flying fragments that rang from stone or embedded themselves in flesh.

Stephen, his injured shoulder wrenched again, body sent staggering back against the central vault, caught one clear glimpse of the fact that Dragonslicer was gone, while the Sword in his own hand remained perfectly intact. Stephen himself was uninjured by the explosion—armed as he was now, no weapon had the power to hurt him—but he could see at once how fragments of the Sword of Heroes had torn the body of Bazas into bloody rags, dropped the old man in his tracks.

For a moment or two the consciousness of the young Prince dimmed toward faintness, then full awareness of the world came back. Breathing heavily, Stephen found himself once more slumped against the open Sword-vault, left hand clinging to the decorated stonework, right arm pulled down by the weight of the Sword of Force. His right shoulder burned with a sharp pain as if something inside it had been torn, and his palm and fingers were magically glued to Shieldbreaker's black hilt.

The weapon was almost quiet at the moment, the magical hammer-sound muted, having subsided until it seemed that the Sword might be only talking to itself.

Clutching at one of the open vault doors with his free hand, gazing with shock and horror at what was left of Bazas, Stephen fought down an impulse to vomit. He wondered what could have driven the old armorer so violently, abruptly mad. The old man had shouted something just before he swung his Sword at his young prince and died—something crazy having to do with the Dark King. . . .

At that moment the frightening truth began to dawn on Stephen: Only the Mindsword could produce such instantaneous and frightful alterations in the thoughts of good and worthy people. Skulltwister must have been once more brought into play by his father's enemies.

While struggling to cope with that idea's horrendous implications, the youth became dazedly aware that his right hand was no longer magically welded to Shieldbreaker's hilt. A lull in combat now obtained, for the moment at least, and he could if he wished put down the Sword of Force.

He actually started to do so, but then instead, despite his injured shoulder, gripped the black hilt with convulsive strength, at the same time whimpering with the thought of how near he had come to letting go—that would have meant death, or worse than death. Only Shieldbreaker could have saved him, must be saving him even now, from the same awful madness which had afflicted Bazas, almost within arm's length.

The cheering, roaring noises which now came drifting down from the upper palace confirmed Stephen's horrible suspicion that the Mindsword must be in action. This insight, along with the undoubted presence of demons in the palace, and the fact that Bazas in his madness had shouted the Dark King's name, strongly indicated that this latest attack, like that two years ago, must be led by the terrible Vilkata.

But so long as he, Stephen, had the Sword of Force in hand, so long was he protected against any other weapon, including

Skulltwister. In fact he alone ought to be able to defend the palace against any kind of attack—any kind save one.

As Prince Mark had impressed over and over again upon his sons, the only way known to defeat Shieldbreaker was to disarm oneself completely and then grapple as a wrestler with whoever held the Sword. But, as Stephen had known in theoretical terms for years, there was no way a demon could ever disarm itself; the foul creatures *were* nothing but weapons, at least as far as this Sword was concerned. Whenever they attacked its wielder directly, Shieldbreaker was capable of slashing them out of existence, as surely as if its edge could be laid against whatever material objects concealed their unclean lives.

Yesterday Stephen might have had a difficult time believing that, no matter what his teachers taught; but now that he had seen and felt the Sword of Force in action, had witnessed the virtual annihilation of another Sword and a powerful demon, he no longer felt any doubt.

And now the Dark King had come again to Sarykam, attacking, no doubt seeking frightful vengeance for his past defeats.

Stephen twisted his feet, as if he would dig the heels of his boots into the stone floor. Straightening his back, he set it firmly against the open Sword-vault. Then, ignoring the continuing pain in his right shoulder, he raised his Sword to guard position, unconsciously adopting the tactics in which he had been drilled with ordinary weapons.

Then, confident in his armament though still feeling stupid with surprise and weariness, he waited for the next attack.

Moments passed, and the suspense stretched out unbearably. Not for a moment did the young Prince believe that the danger of combat was over. Shieldbreaker, quivering with the muscles of the young Prince's right arm, muttered and stuttered to itself. Now, gradually, he could not doubt the fact, the sound was growing louder once again.

Think! he commanded himself, shaking his head in an effort
to clear it of shock and pain and horror. At the moment, as far
as he could tell, the fate of the whole realm was indeed resting
on him, and he had to think. Shieldbreaker could be, was, an
overpowering weapon. But—

But the Dark King, or any other human ally of these attacking demons, would be able to disarm himself of other weapons, and to wrestle Stephen for possession of the Sword of
Force—in such a contest the unarmed human inevitably won.
And with the Mindsword in action, Vilkata and his demons
would have a host of fanatically eager human allies, doubtless
including everyone else who had been in the palace when the
enemy struck. Bazas as a newly converted madman could have
attacked successfully unarmed, had he only waited until Stephen actually had the Sword of Force in hand.

Even as the young Prince did his best to think, to prepare,
to nerve himself to meet whatever form the attack was going
to take next, Vilkata the Dark King was dismounting from a
demonic steed which had just landed on the highest level of the
palace.

The Dark King's planning for this attack had prudently
included the caching in a secret place, the deepest recesses of
a coastal cave not inconveniently far from Sarykam, of several
of the glassy Old World spacecraft, one of which had only
hours ago completed its task of carrying the wizard back to
Earth from the distant Moon. Akbar's promise had been
made good, and the return voyage had taken no more than
two Earthly days. Much as Vilkata still distrusted *technology,*
it was plain that such devices could in many ways be useful.

Now, even as Vilkata set foot on the palace roof, he cast a
sharp glance toward a pair of bodies lying nearby. Two sentries, their useless weapons scattered at their feet, had been
silently murdered by demons within the past few minutes. The

pair of corpses, still clad in livery of Tasavaltan blue and green, now drained of blood and psychic energies, resembled dried-out, somewhat less-than-lifesize dolls.

Vilkata looked up higher. The narrow, towering eyries of the fighting birds and winged messengers, stone spires rising even above the roof where the Dark King had alighted, had been savagely raided already. Eggs had been smashed, grown birds and nestlings slaughtered, and some of the interiors of wood and straw were burning.

Vilkata nodded with satisfaction. Surprise had certainly been achieved, and at the moment no opposition to the invaders was in evidence. The Dark King had not only made sure that Prince Mark was elsewhere, but had warily planned his attack on the palace and armory so that his own personal entry should be slightly delayed. Let his demons confront the heavy counterattack, if there was to be any; he would see what happened to them before entering the fight himself.

Naturally cautious in the matter of personal risk, Vilkata had considered the possibility that he might have to face Shieldbreaker in combat today. Of course he was well acquainted with the proper way to fight against the Sword of Force; but he had two very strong objections to personally disarming himself, if and when he should be confronted with that weapon.

First, since a demon counted as a weapon, disarming would almost certainly mean giving up his demonic vision for some unknown period of time.

That would make things difficult; but the second objection, in the Dark King's estimation, was even deadlier. He clearly could not disarm himself without giving up the Mindsword, the very foundation of all his current power. He dared not hand over that weapon to any of his followers, human or demonic; nor did he doubt for a moment that, within a few heartbeats' time after he should put Skulltwister down, someone, friend or foe, would pick it up. Even if one of his loyal slaves should pick it up, having in mind some purpose tending to Vilkata's advantage, still at that moment the fierce devotion engendered in everyone else by the Sword would swing to a new object.

Most definitely unacceptable!

The Dark King could easily picture a hundred disastrous scenarios sprouting, diverging, from that point. In the worst of them his own demons, instantly converted to some fresh loyalty, pounced on him and tore him into psychic shreds—a fate infinitely more painful even than the analogous physical destruction would have been.

No, if, against his best hopes and expectations, he were confronted today by the Sword of Force, he planned to retreat, with Skulltwister still securely his. There would be time and opportunity to plot and strike again.

Having surveyed the palace rooftop and dismissed his demon-mount with orders to stay vigilantly nearby, Vilkata observed an open doorway not far ahead of him. Mindsword held before him like a torch, he approached the entrance cautiously.

For the time being he was alone, save for Pitmedden, his demonic provider of vision. This creature, hovering invisibly at the Dark King's side, was currently his sole companion and bodyguard. None of the demons who had made up the first wave of the attack had yet come back to report, and this disturbed Vilkata vaguely. In particular, he had hoped to have an almost immediate report from Akbar, who had been charged with seizing control of the room or place in which the Swords were kept, and guarding it fiercely until his Master should come to take over his new property.

Having reached the open door leading down from the rooftop, Vilkata stood gazing down the first flight of descending stairs, which were dimly, indirectly lighted by some lamp or cresset somewhere on the next lower level. Surely, he thought, the mighty Akbar could not be very far ahead of him. The creature, like its colleagues, was bound by the Mindsword to Vilkata in perfect loyalty. They were all compelled to gain for its master all the treasures of magic buried here, in particular the Sword Shieldbreaker—but under strict orders not to pick that weapon up, not even touch it. Only to keep anyone else from picking it up until Vilkata himself could reach the site and do so.

With a few brisk words to Pitmedden, the Dark King entered the palace, passing down the first stairs with confident strides. He knew that as the human beings in the rooms and passageways surrounding him were engulfed by the Mindsword's sphere of influence, every one of them without exception—each person, waking or sleeping, within an arrow-shot or so—would automatically become his fanatical ally and worshipper.

More, he felt confident that his demons would be largely unopposed—because Prince Mark was absent.

FIVE

F OR a long time, for years even before his first attack on the palace at Sarykam, Vilkata had been grimly aware of the fact that strong magical powers (quite apart from Prince Mark's special talent) were continuously on sentinel duty there. These protective forces, ordinarily quite adequate to keep demons and other malign entities at a distance, were primarily under the control of old Karel, who was Princess Kristin's uncle, and also one of the most formidable magicians on Earth. The Dark King was not sure but that that old man might not be his equal—assuming, of course, that the Mindsword was left out of the calculation.

But even without counting the Mindsword, the powers now at Vilkata's command were far greater than ordinary. When the new attack fell on the palace and the surrounding city, Karel's sentinels, human and otherwise, were able to give the inhabitants only a belated warning, and could delay the giant attacking demons only briefly.

This first line of Tasavaltan opposition was swept out of the way in a matter of moments.

Within moments after the first of his demons went bursting into the palace, Vilkata also personally entered the royal residence, determined to descend as quickly as possible into the lower regions, where he knew the armory was located, and where Prince Mark's collection of Swords was ordinarily stored. Within moments he was moving quickly downstairs, the Sword of Glory drawn cheering and roaring in his hand.

Around the invader and in advance of him there spread a murmur of mingled joy and sorrow, voiced by first one, then a dozen, then a hundred human throats. These were the voices of servants, guards, palace inhabitants of every station, all of them taken unawares, in their beds or awake, each converted in an instant into a fanatical servant and worshipper of the Dark King. Most of those falling under the Mindsword's influence were in other rooms or corridors than those through which Vilkata passed, and they failed to witness their new Master's arrival or his first passage.

Even those who had not yet seen the invader or his Sword knew exactly the name and titles of the man they were suddenly constrained to worship, and could have marshalled arguments to demonstrate that their sudden change of heart in favor of Vilkata was perfectly rational and honorable. Their joy was at his glory, their poignant sorrow at their own blind failure to acknowledge him for so long, until their lives were transformed by this moment of transcendent revelation.

The sharpest outcries came, naturally enough, from those few people who happened actually to encounter their new Master, Mindsword held before him like a bright slice of light, in his first swift passage through the palace. Trusted servants and old family retainers, who moments earlier would rather have died than betray their Prince and Princess, were bewitched into wretches stumbling and stammering in their eagerness to repent of these feelings. Their yells of joyous shock brought out from their rooms of sleep or work a steadily growing throng of new converts, men and women nightshirted or wrapped in blankets, all eager to adore Vilkata.

The invading wizard pushed his way through these where they were in a position to impede his progress. He proceeded rapidly on foot through torchlit or darkened hallways—Old World lamps were far too rare for common use.

The Dark King had now been rejoined in his progress by a close bodyguard of demons, these latter worked up and raging with fear and hatred of their enemy the Prince.

After having made doubly sure that Mark himself was absent from the palace, they lashed out at surrogate victims, even at doubly helpless converts, with murderous fury and tremendous violence.

Gleefully they reported that their colleagues outside the palace were devastating the dwellings of know enemies throughout the city.

For sport the demons now escorting Vilkata butchered in passing some of Mark's formerly faithful servants and loyal followers, an amusement for which their indulgent master granted them permission by default; but any humans who Vilkata thought might be privy to the secrets of the Tasavaltan government were forbidden as prey.

Chief among these last was Karel himself, the uncle of Princess Kristin, a stout, apple-cheeked old man who was by far the realm's most powerful wizard. Against the Mindsword, of course, the old man was as defenseless as the lowest kitchen servant. He came stumbling out of his modest palace apartment in his nightshirt, tears already streaming down his round red cheeks at the thought of how he had so long and wickedly opposed the very Master of the World.

Vilkata, remembering past defeats, would have found it very satisfying to kill Karel and certain other of his old foes, now that the opportunity had come. But he did not indulge this craving. In fact he issued strict orders to his demons to see to his old enemies' survival. Of course utilizing as many of these important people as possible in the service of his own cause was undoubtedly the more intelligent course, and that was the plan Vilkata chose to follow.

Eager as the Dark King was to reach the armory, he stopped to question and to listen to some of these freshly converted important folk. All of them were anxious to tell the Dark King (who, as any right-thinking person must understand at once, was the only being in the universe truly worthy of loyalty and worship) under what kind of protection, and approximately where in the deep central vaults of the Tasavaltan armory, Mark's trove of Swords was kept. One after another these teary-eyed defectors also hastened to inform their incomparable new Master that, to the best of their knowledge, at least a couple of Swords were still there.

The Dark King delayed his descent into the depths of the palace an instant longer to demand: "And are any of the royal family at home?"

The converts looked at one another uncertainly. All of them were desperately eager to be helpful, but at the same time in dread of inadvertently giving the Master wrong or incomplete information. It was Karel himself who finally answered: "Only the young Prince Stephen is here, great lord!"

Bad luck! But better one small fish than none. "And where is he?"

Not in his usual sleeping quarters, that was quickly reported by a scouting demon. Nor did the modest bed in Prince Stephen's room appear to have been slept in during the past few hours. The youth was old enough to have been visiting the bedroom of some maid or mistress, Vilkata supposed; or perhaps he had been taking advantage of his parents' absence to enjoy some other form of carousal.

No one had any useful suggestions to offer. Vilkata ordered an immediate and thorough search of the palace for Prince Mark's brat, and demons and converted Tasavaltans went rushing and whooping away to carry out his order. But the invading wizard was not going to spend any time on that effort himself; certainly not just now, when down in the armory there might be Swords to be had for the picking. At all stages of his planning for this attack, the Dark King had made the armory his primary target, his first concern being to seize at once whatever Swords might be available—particularly Shieldbreaker

On to the armory!

The descent of the Eyeless One continued through the many levels of the palace, becoming something of a triumphal procession. Ceaselessly the Sword of Glory worked its magic, emitting its customary roaring cheer as the Dark King bore it forward and downward like a torch.

As he advanced, descending, he wondered again what had become of Akbar, whom he had sent on ahead. At least the demon would not be up to any treachery, the holder of the Mindsword told himself—he could feel perfectly confident of that.

Down in the Sword-chamber, the young Prince at that moment was still leaning with his back against the open vault in which the Blades were customarily kept. Stephen was just emerging from a brief and successful struggle with his own fears—fear of death, and, worse just now, fear of making the wrong decision.

With the exception of his long work session with Dragonslicer, just interrupted, Stephen had never been allowed to handle any of the Swords unsupervised. But at one time or another, as part of his education, he had been given every Sword available to hold at least briefly, and had been taught the theory and something of the practice of their use. The result was that now he felt reasonably well acquainted with these weapons, whose history was so intimately intertwined with that of his own family.

It had come as no great surprise to the young Prince that Shieldbreaker had leaped up obediently to meet his touch, and then with matchless violence had disposed of a giant demon, as well as Dragonslicer and the unfortunate man who had been holding it.

But Stephen's education regarding the Swords also assured him that now, with the palace in the hands of a strong enemy force, Shieldbreaker was not going to be enough. He was well aware that if he were armed with that Sword only, it would be only too easy for a knowledgeable human attacker to overcome him.

He turned his head to look back and down into the Sword-vault, studying the two weapons still remaining in their velvet nests. Stonecutter would not help him in his present circumstances, and could be disregarded. But there was one other Sword still in the vault, and that one was quite another matter. The boy realized that his duty, and his very hope of survival, required him now to pick up Sightblinder as well as Shieldbreaker.

> The Sword of Stealth is given to
> One lowly and despised.
> Sightblinder's gifts: his eyes are keen
> His nature is disguised.

Yet Stephen hesitated. He also understood full well that the decision to hold two Swords drawn at once was not one to be taken lightly. On his recent birthday he had been allowed, very briefly and under Karel's supervision, to make the attempt with these very two. His father, Mark, had demonstrated the ability to do that effectively. (For the first time, as a boy, and then holding them only briefly, Mark had had the feeling that a great wind had arisen and was about to blow him off his feet. That the world was altering around him, or that he was being extracted from it. Then Mark had fainted; this, too, the grown Prince had told his sons.) But the effect on Stephen had been the same as it would have been on most people: confusion, mental anguish, disorientation.

Shieldbreaker and Sightblinder together, the young Prince knew, would provide anyone who held them with an almost absolutely unbeatable offense and defense. He knew of only one real flaw in this armament, but it was a daunting one—the inevitable psychic burden of carrying both Swords drawn at the same time. That would impose a disabling handicap on all but a few very capable men or women.

But he knew he was going to have to take the risk.

Shieldbreaker continued its muttering, the black hilt thump-

ing soft magical impacts against Stephen's palm. His right
arm, still hurting at the shoulder, was tiring from the weight
of the heavy Sword, and he let the arm sag again until the
unbreakable point of the Sword of Force trailed on the stone
floor; with this weapon there was no need, after all, to hold a
ready position.

And then, frightened of what he must do next, but unwilling
to put off the attempt any longer, Stephen thrust his left hand
boldly into the vault and closed his fingers around the black
hilt with the white outline of a human eye—Sightblinder.

This Sword did not come leaping up to meet his reaching
grasp. But immediately on Stephen's making contact with the
Sword of Stealth, its magic surged along his arm and through
his mind and body. A power similar to Shieldbreaker's, yet
different. This, on top of the lingering effect of the young
Prince's first brush with the demon, made him once more
dizzy, and afflicted him with deep anxiety, the fear that reality
might be about to crumble. The savage noises still drifting
down from the upper palace seemed to be swallowed up in the
sound of a great wind; it was distracting, even though the
young Prince understood that the wind really existed only
within his own mind and perception.

But Sightblinder's heavy magic worked its benefits as well.
The power of the Sword of Stealth enhanced and focused
Stephen's own perception sufficiently to let him feel assured
that the human voices he heard above were truly those of
deadly enemies—no matter that most of those who spoke and
sang had once been loyal friends—and that more demons were
indeed swarming in the near vicinity.

Feeling mentally menaced and disconnected, undergoing
sensations so peculiar he would have been unable to describe
them, threatened by impalpable winds of change, almost on
the point of fainting, Stephen was suddenly sure that he could
not, dared not, remain here in the presence of the enemy.
Armed as he now was, though, he could and would get away,

and would carry to his parents the two greatest treasures of the armory.

The great problem with this plan, as the young Prince realized even before he tried to move, was that in this state of fierce giddiness induced by double magic he would have all he could do simply to stand erect. He feared he would not be able to walk across a room, let alone travel to a distant village, holding both Swords drawn. He would have to put one of the two weapons at least into a scabbard even before he tried to climb the stairs and leave the palace.

Knowing that the Mindsword must be perilously near, Stephen did not dare to release his grip on Shieldbreaker's hilt even for a moment. Propping up Sightblinder in a position where he could grab it again instantly, he worked left-handed to extract two sword-belts from the Sword-chamber's inner rack. Working with his left hand and his right elbow, he managed, after a long struggle that at times seemed hopeless, to get the two belts fastened around his waist, so that one long leather scabbard hung at his right, the other at his left. Then he took up Sightblinder again, enduring the weight of double magic long enough to sheath the Sword at his right side, from which position he should be able to draw it handily left-handed.

Looking at the doors of the inner vault, which still stood open, Stephen made a great effort to think coherently. Stonecutter of course was still inside the vault, but it would simply have to stay there. Yes, no doubt he ought to close those doors before he left—that would set at least a small additional obstacle in the path of whoever was about to overrun the palace wholly. He grabbed one door and slammed it; the other one came with it automatically. No special closing incantation was required.

* * *

As the young Prince prepared to leave the armory, Shield-breaker in his right hand kept muttering to itself as if in eager expectation of the joys of combat. Cautiously, being very careful never to let go for an instant, he changed his grip on the black hilt from his right hand to his left, to better balance the physical weight of the sheathed Sword of Stealth. He thought that any difficulty he could eliminate, even the most minor, might make the difference for him between success and failure.

On his way to the door he had to detour slightly to avoid stepping right over the old man's body. But before setting foot out of the Sword-chamber the young Prince paused, fascinated against his will, to take one more horrified look at Bazas.

Almost straddling the corpse, which lay sprawled upon its back, Stephen for the first time took note of the ruined hilt of Dragonslicer, black wood splintered and still smoldering, still clutched in the old man's hand.

At that sight, another thought went fluttering through the youth's shocked, half-disconnected mind: *But how now was he ever going to be able to complete his father's gift—?*

Shaking his head in an attempt to clear it, the young Prince shuffled past the dead man and stepped through the doorway. He turned his back on the Sword-vault chamber, and started automatically for the nearest stair. He had done very little conscious planning, but was holding to the fixed idea that his parents several days ago had gone to the village of Voronina, some sixty kilometers away, and that he must reach them there with the two important Swords.

If only, Stephen prayed, circumstances did not compel him to travel any distance with both Swords drawn. And if only he could decide correctly which one he had to have drawn at any moment. . . .

Walking with a persistent slight unsteadiness, he was half-way across the room in which the abandoned workbench stood holding its neat and meaningless pile of dragonscales, and where the Old World lamp now burned unheeded, when what seemed a better plan of action struck him with the force of inspiration.

The house of Stephen's grandparents, of Mark's mother, Mala, and foster-father, Jord, was right here in Sarykam, at no enormous distance from the palace. Surely he, Stephen, would be able to carry his two Swords on foot successfully at least that far. In the house of Jord and Mala he would be able to get help.

But now more demons were coming toward him. The vile creatures were moving somewhere near. . . .

Hastily Stephen snatched Sightblinder lefthanded from its sheath. Once more his head went spinning with the force of double magic, but now he could see, feel, exactly where the foul things were. Still more than a hundred meters distant, they were no immediate threat, but at any moment that might change.

Restricted by his burden to a staggering and seriously uneven progress, the young Prince went forward carrying both Swords drawn. He would continue to do so, he told himself, at least until he could get out of the palace.

Experiencing recurring waves of a feeling that the world was twisting itself into knots around him, a sensation unpleasantly reminiscent of the night last winter when he'd secretly experimented with drinking too much wine, Stephen kept going.

He had gained no more than a couple of rooms' distance from the Sword-vault, traversing with difficulty the darkened armory on a course for the nearest ascending stairs, when through a concentric pair of doorways on his left he observed movement, that of one person walking.

The enhanced perception granted the young Prince by Sightblinder showed him the single figure clearly: that of a man bearing in front of him a Sword raised like a torch, who had just now descended to the level of the armory by another stair, several rooms away.

For a moment Stephen could not react. The mental strain of carrying the two Swords was growing worse, not lessening. Invisible surges of power seemed to blend inside his nervous system, with unpredictable effect. Nevertheless Sightblinder still augmented the boy's sight sufficiently to allow him to become aware of the invader before the invader saw him; and it also enabled Stephen to identify the Dark King with certainty, even from several rooms away. That man had just come hurrying—alone, except for the one demon which clung to him like an incubus, and functioned as his eyes—down, down into the dimly lighted armory.

Not that this towering, eyeless albino, in the ordinary course of events, would have been very difficult to identify.

Stephen tensed, and in his sudden concentration even came close to forgetting for the moment that he was carrying two drawn Swords.

Vilkata. The Dark King.

This was the man—say, rather, the monster—who, two years ago, had almost killed Stephen's mother, inflicting upon her months of physical and mental agony. The evil magician who was the deadly enemy of Stephen's father. The fiend who preferred the society of demons to that of people, and who had wrought great havoc upon the whole world—the realm of Tasavalta in particular.

The boy's naturally combative nature, and his princely training in the theory and practice of war, asserted themselves, and he was ready to attack.

SIX

AT once, without the need to pause or think, the young Prince turned away from the stairs he had been about to climb and began to retrace his steps toward the Sword-chamber. He was moving to intercept the invader. Scarcely conscious of the continuing pain in his shoulder or the bruises on his knees and elbows, Stephen stalked his hated enemy. Shieldbreaker was once more in his right hand, drumming softly as he held it ready for a thrust. In the left hand of the young Prince, Sightblinder continued to exert its silent power; with the help of the Sword of Stealth the youth was able vaguely to perceive the demon accompanying his foe, a half-transparent cloud of something in the air beside the wizard's head.

Meanwhile the eyeless magician had satisfied himself that he was now on the deepest level of the palace. The bright image of the Tyrant's Blade, gripped fiercely in the Dark King's right fist, emitted a muted roaring, to itself and to the world, the sound of a fire started by some enthusiastic mob.

Unaware of Stephen watching him from three rooms away, Vilkata paused briefly at the foot of the stairs to gaze about him with his unnatural vision. In the next moment the Dark King, without looking back, beckoned to someone or something above and behind him, at the top of the stone stairs; then the man turned his back on the stairs, and turning away from Stephen also, strode forward purposefully.

In response to the Master's commanding gesture, a small squad of demons, fanatical and protective, came pouring after Vilkata down the stairs, to take up their positions swirling behind him like an evil mist. None of these creatures darted ahead to scout, because the Eyeless One had already warned them that he must be first to enter the room where the Tasavaltan Swords were kept. The Dark King walked at the head of his powers alone—except, of course, for Pitmedden, who continued to provide his sight.

Yes, Vilkata was thinking, the weapons and tools arrayed here in profusion left no doubt that he had reached the armory. Now, to locate the room of Swords . . .

Holding the murmuring, faintly roaring steel of Skull-twister—in his own demonic vision a towering spear of pale fire—raised before him as he advanced toward the Sword-vault through the lowest level of the palace, Vilkata sighted from the corner of his eye a movement on his left which was not demonic. To his surprise he became aware that someone else, a single human figure, was walking there in the dim light, indeed was steadily approaching him.

A moment later, scowling doubtfully, the Dark King felt an inward chill as he identified the newcomer as the newly-converted Karel. Yes, Princess Kristin's wizard-uncle, the same almost-tearful convert who just a minute ago, up on one of the higher levels of the palace, had informed Vilkata of the words of the incantation necessary to open both inner and outer sealings of the Sword-vault.

As Pitmedden's vision presented the image of the Tasavaltan magician, the old man's hands, slightly upraised, were empty. Karel's mien was humble, his smile gentle and apologetic, as befitted a convert in the full flush of his enthusiasm.

Vilkata was vaguely puzzled. Only moments ago he had left Karel behind him, at the head of the last flight of descending stairs. Had the Tasavaltan wizard so quickly disobeyed orders and followed him downstairs out of some irrational concern for Vilkata's welfare? Or did Karel perhaps come bearing urgent information? Some fresh news of Prince Mark? Or—?

"What is it now?" the Dark King snapped at the approaching one. Meanwhile his swarm of demons hung over his head, snarling and droning among themselves, like poison bees around his ears. However Vilkata's bodyguard perceived this human walking toward them, the figure caused them no alarm.

Stephen, having closed now within a few paces of his enemy, seeing the tall man's pale face with its scarred and empty sockets turn toward him, felt a chill of fear, despite his intellectual confidence in Sightblinder's protection. When the villain snapped a question at him, the young Prince, suffering another wave of confusion, hardly understood what the man was saying.

Under the continuing burden of the two Swords' double magic, Stephen wondered who the Dark King took him for . . . a moment passed before the lad realized that it hardly mattered. Vilkata was not alarmed or alerted. There was no need for him, Stephen, to pretend anything. The Sword of Stealth would do all the necessary pretending for him.

But duration and reality were crumbling. His next step toward the Dark King seemed to take forever. The young Prince tried to steel his nerves by reminding himself that his father, even as a boy, had held two Swords simultaneously and had survived the experience.

Stephen advanced another pace toward his foe, and yet another. In fact he was walking almost at normal speed, yet each stride seemed to be protracted through endless time. It seemed to be taking him minutes, hours, just to get from one room of the armory to the next.

The tall, hideous figure of his enemy shrugged, and turned away from him again . . . but the double magic of the Swords was roaring in Stephen's ears, and now, whatever else happened, he was going to have to stop, for just a moment, to try to organize his thoughts . . . .

Brutal, physical noise cleared the cobwebs of magic from his mind, and momentarily shocked the young Prince back to full awareness. Ever louder and more savage had grown the sounds of disturbance drifting in through the high, barred windows of the lower levels of the palace. The cheering, roaring tumult issuing from the Mindsword itself was being drowned out, swallowed up in the rush of similar sounds from human throats. It sounded as if a joyous crowd was pouring out into the streets around the palace to welcome the arrival of their glorious new Master. The conversion had overtaken hundreds, perhaps thousands of the citizens of Sarykam in their sleep, had engulfed everyone within the palace and the houses on the nearby streets, all who had been within an arrow's flight of the Sword of Madness along whatever route its bearer had used to enter the city.

Now the roaring had become more raucous. Individual screams and challenges testified that something like all-out war had erupted in the precincts of the city surrounding the palace. Of course, besides the possible thousands of new converts, there would still be an even greater number who had remained outside the Mindsword's sharply defined range. The fanatical converts could not but see the latter now as deadly enemies, no matter that they might have been close relatives or friends an hour ago—and the converts were ready to strike for their Master in deadly earnest, and with the full advantage of surprise.

Stephen blinked and looked around, to find himself alone. Now where had Vilkata got to? He must be up ahead, he must by now have reached the repository of the Swords. Now the young Prince, still doubly armed, clinging to his sanity and alertness as best he could, forced himself to follow.

The Dark King had already forgotten for the moment the perfect image of a nodding, smiling, speechless Karel, approaching him obsequiously, because Vilkata was sure that he had now reached the Sword-chamber itself. Still holding the Mindsword raised before him like a torch, he had arrived at the doorway of a vaulted room which, if the directions he'd been given were correct, must be the very one he wanted.

The wizard placed a sensitive hand high on the stone wall, fingers delicately stroking. Shreds of old Karel's protective magic clinging to the doorway, ineffective now but still perceptible, assured the invader that he had come to the right place—and supporting evidence, tending to confirm that this was no ordinary room, was visible in the form of a dead body, physically mangled, on the floor inside.

Vilkata paused, scowling. Just here and now, he could not interpret the presence of a corpse as a sign that things were going well.

His escort of demons, droning almost mindlessly, still filled the air around him.

Using the glowing point of Skulltwister, the tool readiest to hand, the Dark King quite easily, almost absent-mindedly, put aside whatever bits of Karel's handiwork still survived about the doorway. Taking note of the nature of these remnants of enchantment as he did so, and of how completely their fabric had been torn apart, he thought: *Akbar has certainly been here.* That senior demon, and few other beings, human or demonic, could have shredded Karel's defensive handiwork in such a way. But then the question persisted: Where was Akbar now?

After stepping across the threshold of the Sword-chamber, Vilkata paused again before approaching the inner vault, whose doors he saw were closed. He delayed a moment to study more closely the body on the floor. With faint disappointment the Dark King saw that the dead man was no one he could recognize as an enemy.

Particularly the intruder now took note of the blasted Sword-hilt in the corpse's hand.

Vilkata bent to investigate further; even without touching this relic he thought he could identify it, even drained of magic as it was. There was no doubt that these scorched wooden splinters, no gram of metal left, had once been part of the Sword Dragonslicer.

No doubt at all?

"Pitmedden."

"Master?"

"Do you pry his fingers open. I want to get a better look at that black wood, to make absolutely sure."

Some part of the vision-demon's nature took on the form of a dwarfish, malignant-looking human child, unnaturally hairy, crouched by the dead man's outflung right arm. In a moment the dead fingers loosed their grip.

The white dragon-symbol, offering a final confirmation of the smashed weapon's identity, was still visible upon the hilt.

A shattered Sword just now was even a worse sign than a dead body, because it was a sure indication that Shieldbreaker had already been brought into action.

Vilkata, scowling at this discovery, was suddenly no longer sanguine about his chances of finding the Sword of Force available when the inner Sword-vault—obviously this construction standing in the center of the chamber—should be opened.

In another moment he had employed the secret incantation given him by Karel, and the two doors thudded back.

Vilkata frowned to find the vault already emptied of its best treasure.

Only one Sword, obviously Stonecutter, was still in its rack. For the time being, Vilkata let it stay there. Above and below the single occupant, four empty velvet spaces yawned.

A moment later Karel appeared—for the second time in a few moments, as Vilkata thought. Princess Kristin's mighty uncle, as helpless in the Mindsword's grip as the humblest of servants, having now in great concern for his Master's welfare followed him downstairs, caught up with the Dark King in the Sword-chamber, discovered in his turn the body of Bazas, recognized the man, and expressed grief over the loss.

"What loss is that?" demanded the Eyeless One.

Karel murmured something to the effect that it was to be

hoped that Bazas before dying had also seen the light, the glorious truth about Vilkata.

Vilkata mumbled viciously. "Old idiot, are you going to prove as useless as you look? What does it matter what a dead man thought or felt? The real loss is here; the most important Swords are gone. I want to know who has them."

Karel obediently turned his attention to the inner vault. He was clearly surprised, and every bit as chagrined as Vilkata, by the absence of Sightblinder and Shieldbreaker. "I do not know who has them, Master," he admitted sadly.

Vilkata shook his head impatiently at this evidence of ineptitude. "Well, where was Shieldbreaker when you saw it last? And Sightblinder? Surely they *are* customarily kept here?"

"Yes, sire. I had thought they would be here now." The old wizard continued to look stricken at the loss.

"Well, find them! You know the people here, the lay of the land. Use your vaunted powers!"

The elder wizard looked gently pained. "Master, if whoever now possesses those two Swords does not wish to be found, neither my powers nor any others will search effectively." And the graybeard made a helpless gesture.

Of course he was right. The Dark King gestured too, and muttered, summoning into the armory more demons, who rolled down the stairs like so many billows of smoke. A moment later, fearing Shieldbreaker in the hands of some unknown enemy, he shouted to bring more human converts to his side as well, potential unarmed champions and defenders if he should need them.

To the young Prince, who had been brought to a virtual halt two rooms away, these additional demons, which would ordinarily have sickened him to the point of disability, now seemed no more than storm-wraiths passing at a distance. Armed as the boy was, they could neither harm him nor even really see him; each demon, Stephen supposed, must be perceiving him as one of their own kind, or as the wizard whom they worshipped, no matter that the real wizard was visible only a few paces distant. Such was the power of the Sword of Stealth . . . .

Stephen's mind was for the moment clear again, though he had to struggle to keep his perceptions and his balance steady. Once more his feet were carrying him relentlessly, almost silently, toward the Sword-room, and in each hand he still held a heavy weapon poised.

Whatever conscious fear he had experienced a few moments ago was now completely gone, and even his dizziness and disorientation were now abated, swallowed up in a burst of murderous rage directed at this intruder. Shieldbreaker's steady, muffled hammering sounded no louder than the beating of his own heart.

When he saw who stood beside the Dark King in the pose of an adviser, Stephen's rage, unreasonably enough, extended to Karel. But Karel at the moment was in no danger; he was not the one who had to be struck down.

The young Prince's quarry, a powerful man, an almost matchless wizard, seemed unable to hear or see the doom which was coming upon him. This tall creature before Stephen, pale and eyeless as a cave-worm, repulsively malignant and at the same time helpless, was the evil man who two years ago had almost killed Stephen's mother and had come near bringing disaster upon the whole realm.

Yet again the moment of final confrontation was postponed. One of the flock of circling demons, evidently caught up in an ecstatic urge to worship the figure it perceived as its true Master, came flitting toward Stephen—then, at the last moment, turned in terror, on the point of flight from whatever sudden alteration it now saw in the shape before it.

In a spasm of hatred and revulsion the youth armed with the two Swords killed the demon. An effortless flick of the young

Prince's right wrist, a single drumbeat from the Sword of Force, and the hideous thing was gone—he wondered why the man who was going to be his next victim should not at least have heard that much warning? Because, the demon-killer quickly understood, Sightblinder muffled and transformed everything. . . .

Yet perhaps the Dark King had heard something after all. His demeanor changed; he was almost alert. Warned by his powers that some new violence had occurred, but unable to pinpoint precisely what had taken place or where, he looked about him nervously . . . .

The magical and physical searches of the armory and lower palace, which moments ago Vilkata had commanded certain demons to perform, had already been carried out. Helpless against the Sword of Stealth, the searching demons had discovered no human presence unaccounted for—none save their Master's own, and that of his loyal converts.

The searchers were once more swirling round him even now, reporting. "There is no one here who means you harm, great Master, no enemy at all. . . ."

But of course, the Dark King thought, cursing suspiciously, such a negative result was all one would expect in the case of an enemy working under Sightblinder's protection—the searchers however diligent and clever, would be unable to perceive—

In the next moment, just as Stephen with weapons raised approached the door to the Sword-chamber, Karel, the real Karel standing just inside, turned an astonished countenance to confront him briefly.

"Master?" the old man asked, in wild bewilderment. Then, turning from Stephen to the genuine Vilkata standing just beside him, he uttered the same word once more.

"Master?" And with that the helpless old magician, befuddled like all Sightblinder's victims, fell down in a near-trance

of terror or worship, and was for the moment forgotten by the
dueling powers that were about to come crashing into conflict.

Vilkata's thought on the subject had no chance to develop
further. Stark terror gripped the Dark King's guts and seemed
to stop his heart.

Because a figure of utter and abysmal terror had just
stepped from somewhere into the very room where he was
standing. This entity came seemingly from nowhere, and immediately the Dark King knew in his bones that this confrontation meant his doom.

Facing him now was Prince Mark, in full battle gear, smiling a terrible smile of triumph, and lifting Shieldbreaker for
the killing blow—*or was the truth yet worse than that?*

The fact that the approaching figure was being transformed
even as Vilkata watched it made the apparition more terrible
rather than less—the truly powerful were often capable of
appearing in any guise they chose. The Eyeless One now perceived with merciless clarity, he was for a moment utterly
convinced, that he was confronted by Orcus, the king demon,
archfoe of Ardneh.

Not Mark. Still worse even than a triumphant Mark.

Orcus of old legend, the equal at least of Arridu in strength,
peerless even among demons in sheer malignity, and somehow
now rendered immune to Sightblinder's control . . .

But in the next moment the figure was transformed again,
and the Dark King beheld Ardneh himself, a body looking
squarish and half-mechanical, ancient and utterly terrible to
demons; the implacable enemy as well of wizards who preferred demons to humanity.

And yet again, repeatedly, Vilkata's perception of the figure
changed. Flickering in rapid succession, there came an image,
more an intimation, of Vilkata's own archrival in evil magic,
Wood—then he was certain he was seeing Wood, pretending
to be Orcus. Then vice-versa.

And now once more he beheld Prince Mark, fully armed with the Sword of Force, immune to any influence Skulltwister could exert . . . .

Whipsawed by these various possibilities, the Dark King was left in a state of terror beyond thought, worse than what could have been evoked by any single, simple presence. His instinctive reaction was to pull a trigger of enchantment, to activate a long-prepared reflex of flight.

He knew that his Enemy, whatever mask It wore, whatever powers It wielded, was One. Certainly someone, a single being, had slipped inside Vilkata's ring of ferocious demonic bodyguards, had confused and blinded them, neutralized them, with such ease and strength that they might as well not have been there at all.

And in these moments of Vilkata's freezing terror, the young Prince approaching, his deliberate strides now bringing him almost within Sword's-length of his foe, his own perception now feverishly enhanced by holding Sightblinder, was able to do more than recognize with absolute certainty his father's great and almost lifelong enemy the Dark King.

Now Stephen found himself empowered, even compelled, to study the man, in the most chilling and disgusting detail.

The face strongly featured, except for the ghastly empty eyesockets—a face looking neither young nor old—the clothing, rather nondescript for a great king and wizard—the pallid, powerful body.

With a feeling of unutterable loathing, the young Prince stepped forward and willed to strike with the Sword in his right hand.

And, at the same time, the thought existing simultaneously, Stephen consciously reminded himself that he must be ready to try to rid himself of Shieldbreaker on short notice, should his enemy at the last instant be unarmed. Then he, Stephen, would have to use the weapon in his other hand instead; use

Sightblinder as a simple piece of sharpened, weighty steel, a physical killing device like any other sword. The Swords were all of them, save Woundhealer, effective in that simple deadly way.

And Vilkata in that same instant, overwhelmed by a mind-bending agony of fear, instinctively raised his own weapon, and at the same time willed with all his soul his magical escape . . . .

The man's body was almost completely dematerialized in flight before metal clashed on metal and one phase of the gods' great magic broke against another.

In the almost instantaneous surge of combat, the Sword of Force responded at once to the movement of Vilkata's Sword, and simultaneously to Stephen's will to kill. There was a jar of opposition, an instant of overwhelming violence—the Mindsword was blasted into splinters.

A stunning explosion accompanied the clash, an echo in the ears of Stephen of the recent blast in which Dragonslicer had perished. This latest detonation stung at Karel's helpless, fallen body, and wounded more than one of the converted people who happened to be standing near. The demons nearby too felt pain from the passage of those smoking fragments.

Stephen, as in his earlier encounter with Bazas, felt his arm pulled violently through a hacking motion. Fresh pain shot through his shoulder.

The young Prince assumed for a moment that his enemy must be dead. Then, when he could see clearly again, he realized that none of the bodies he could now see on the stone floor was that of the Dark King.

Vilkata had been slightly injured by the Sword-blast, but not enough to interfere with his escape. He continued instinctively to concentrate all his remaining energies upon the magical retreat he had already willed.

The Dark King's vanishing, to somewhere outside the palace walls, was magically swift, quick enough to save him from most but not all of the Sword-fragments.

Had Vilkata's flight been an eyeblink slower Stephen could have and would have killed him on the spot, thrusting Sightblinder awkwardly, left-handed, into the guts of the suddenly unarmed man.

That thrust was ready, but it was never made.

SEVEN

WITH a crash that resounded in his own ears like a minor thunderclap, Vilkata's body arrived—somewhere.

So rapid had been his magical escape from the underground armory that he had even been separated from Pitmedden, the demon who provided him with vision, thus rendering himself at least temporarily sightless. Still, the flight-spell had succeeded admirably, and the Dark King felt reasonably sure that for the moment at least he was physically safe.

The utter, weak-kneed terror induced by his confrontation with the ultimate horror in the armory was gone. He had escaped, and for the moment he was alone . . . .

But where was he now?

All he could be certain of was that he was lying awkwardly facedown upon a curved surface that felt like wet stone, his body caressed by a whispery breeze that suggested outdoor air, amid invisible surroundings which smelled like a mudpuddle. This place, wherever it was, was quiet, shockingly so after the abrupt termination of the Mindsword's cheering noise. But somewhere nearby water was trickling audibly.

Against the power of the spell Vilkata had just uttered, mere stone walls, regardless of their thickness, could have had little or no constraining effect, and he had no doubt that he was now outside the palace walls.

But where?

A quick groping about him with both hands provided no very helpful information. His body was draped, in what occurred to him must be a most undignified manner, over a hard, wet surface curved, now that he thought about it, like the rim of one of the fountains in the central plaza of Sarykam—certainly the shape felt more like a fountain than a watering trough. He remembered a number of each located in the plaza before the palace, and along the adjoining streets.

And the Dark King could still feel, clutched in his right hand but emptied of all magic, the Mindsword's hilt. Reflexively he passed the fingers of his left hand over the raw, splintered end, making absolutely sure that all the Blade with all its power was really gone.

Long moments passed in which the Dark King continued probing his immediate environment by groping around him with both hands and listening intently. He learned very little by these means, but did get his body into a less awkward position. He was sitting now on the fountain's rim, his booted feet on some kind of pavement. Wherever he was, his sight-demon still had not caught up with him.

Another thing to worry about. Suppose the creature had not survived the encounter with Shieldbreaker? That was a distinct possibility. And could Pitmedden's fellows, the Dark King's entire force of demons, have been scattered or destroyed as well?

He, Vilkata, continued to be utterly alone and Swordless. Gradually his body reassumed the crouched defensive posture he had instinctively adopted as his magic shot him like a spirit out of the armory.

Muttering spells, he loaded and surrounded his own sightless body with further protective magic. Afraid to move, he crouched where he was, and continued to concentrate upon his hearing.

Below a variety of other sounds, he could detect those of nearby crickets, cheerful elementary creatures remarkably unperturbed by human and demonic travail and violence. Farther off were a couple of barking dogs, and a distant outcry of human voices. And, at the moment, very little else.

Vilkata grunted as he came to realize—somewhat belatedly because of the general wetness of his surroundings—that he was bleeding from several small wounds, tears and punctures in his arms and legs. The wounds called themselves to his attention by starting to grow painful—inordinately so, it seemed, for their size. Gingerly he probed them, one after another, with a finger. They were throbbing as if they might have been made by some poisoned weapon. After a moment's thought the Dark King realized that these injuries had very likely been made by tiny fragments of the shattered Mindsword.

He muttered curses to himself, and waited. Another seemingly endless interval—it was really only the space of a breath or two—passed before the demon Pitmedden managed to catch up with his angry Master and, apologizing abjectly for the delay, magically reattached itself to his very brain.

The Dark King's sight immediately came back, his anger weakened with his relief, and he could see that his first thought about a fountain in the plaza had been correct. His trousers and boots and half of his upper garment were dripping wet. Now he disentangled himself completely from the low stone structure and stood erect, glaring about him into the night.

Looming almost over him, less than a hundred meters distant, was the bulk of the Tasavaltan palace; his swift escape had carried him a lesser distance than he had thought. Behind many of the huge building's windows lights were coming alive and moving about uncertainly. From those same apertures there issued the sounds of exotic human ecstasies and sufferings, results of Skulltwister's recent passage, making the Dark King smile.

Only now, having regained his sight and determined his location, did the Dark King slowly unclench his fingers from the dead hilt of what had been the Mindsword. He stared, with borrowed vision and gradually growing understanding of the implications, at the lifeless fragment on his broad white palm.

Meanwhile his servant-demon Pitmedden had not only restored the Dark King's sight, but in quick response to his urgent commands had started trying to heal his freshly bleeding wounds and relieve their pain.

Soon this unlikely physician reported that the injuries resisted the usual methods of magical treatment. The patient only snarled in response; the wounds were not vital, his tolerance for physical pain was high, and he had greater matters to worry about just now.

Along some of the main streets converging on the plaza, there burned gaslights, famed for their decorative effect; other main thoroughfares in Sarykam, like the plaza itself, were lit by magically-enhanced torches set on metal poles at regular intervals. Even as the demon finished its attempt at healing, Vilkata was distracted from his various problems by the sight of human movement nearby. A single passing stranger, a man of nondescript appearance simply garbed in gray, definitely a commoner by the look of him, had just turned onto the plaza from one of the adjoining streets and was now crossing the paved and planted area as if on his way to some early morning job. The fellow was carrying in a bag what might have been a set of gardener's tools, as well as a spade or shovel over his shoulder.

Whether the briskly moving gardener—or perhaps a gravedigger, out on some early job—walked through darkness or through light, in the shadows from the plaza's lamps or under their direct illumination, Vilkata could see part of him—not much more than an outline—equally well. The details of his person, perceived only through demonic vision, came out poorly—attempts to see certain things by that means were doomed to failure.

Beholding the man through the demon's often selectively distorted perception, Vilkata thought at first that he appeared to be wearing a simple mask—and a minute later that the fellow had no face at all. The Dark King growled at Pitmedden, and the demon squealed in anguish, but the seeing got no better.

Meanwhile the man in gray was behaving as if he could see just as well as the Dark King could, or better, though Vilkata thought the place where he himself was standing must appear to normal human eyesight to be in heavy shadow.

This passing gardener, sexton, or whoever he was, favored the now-Swordless conqueror with a little saluting gesture. His voice was brisk and cheerful. "Good evening, sir. Or should I say good morning?"

Vilkata only stared back at this workman who sounded courteous, though not at all like one freshly enslaved by the Mindsword. No doubt the fellow had been just beyond Skulltwister's reach before the Sword was destroyed, and had no idea of his narrow escape. Even now the increasing uproar of the converts in and around the palace was spilling out into the streets; but the workman, as if deaf, was totally ignoring it.

Before going on his way, the other paused to add: "The choice, I think, is up to you."

No more than a few breaths after the arrival of his vision-demon Pitmedden, within the short interval of time after the workman had walked on but before any other human had yet discovered him, the now-Swordless Dark King with an effort of will managed to recover a large measure of his self-possession.

Suddenly his spirits rose. Here came Arridu, whistling down out of the night, a giant subdued and harnessed, compelled by the even greater power of the Mindsword to feel anxiety for the welfare of his human Master.

And here at last came a small handful and then a score of converted humans, including Karel himself, running across the plaza, as joyful as so many demons to see Vilkata alive and not seriously injured. Raising his voice to speak to all of them at once, Vilkata related to his followers a condensed and unemotional version of the confrontation in the Sword-vault, and his own hair's-breadth escape. He mentioned nothing of his own abysmal terror.

On hearing of the Dark King's close call, Arridu, inflamed with the need to protect his Master and avenge his injuries, screamed demonic outrage and flew back into the palace to scout. Arridu returned a few moments later to say that the enemy, whoever it had been, was no longer in the armory.

Vilkata only grunted. The demons freshly come from the Moon perhaps did not fully grasp the power of the Mindsword yet.

Arridu stood before him in the shape of a titanic warrior, armored all in black. "But who was it who attacked you, Master?"

"I—could not be sure." He paused, looking about him at the rest of his retinue. "Understand, all of you, that this enemy is probably equipped with the Sword of Stealth. Perhaps I will have to explain more fully just what that means." Vilkata himself had needed long moments after his escape to come belatedly to understand that the being he thought he had seen down there must have been only a phantom generated by Sightblinder, the deceptive image of some real person who not only enjoyed the powers of the Sword of Stealth, but worse, who struck with Shieldbreaker . . . .

And only now, when he began to try to put the event into words, did full comprehension dawn. Vilkata's first sensation on realizing the deception was one of shuddering relief; he had faced only some well-armed human; *that being* was not coming after him. But then . . .

"Shieldbreaker," the Dark King breathed aloud.

Pitmedden and Arridu were concerned, as was Karel and other converted humans; the number gathered around Vilkata was steadily increasing. "My great lord?"

"Nothing."

Whoever his real opponent in the armory had been, he, the

Dark King, had survived an armed encounter with the Sword of Force, a feat few men or gods or demons ever had accomplished . . . and those only when they had been able to break the skirmish off.

But even Shieldbreaker was not the whole story. He had actually, Vilkata now realized, survived a simultaneous confrontation with Shieldbreaker *and* Sightblinder. The figure which had terrified him so had not in fact been Orcus or Wood, but someone, some human enemy, not only armed with two Swords but able to use them both virtually simultaneously.

Vilkata realized that his arms were trembling. He was *very* lucky indeed to be alive.

Again he briefly studied the Mindsword's dead hilt, and having done so started to hide the piece of useless wreckage in a pocket of his clothing—then he abruptly changed his mind and cast it violently away from him.

At least, he thought suddenly, he now had a good explanation for what had happened to Akbar.

For years Vilkata had been carrying that demon's life around with him. Now he reached into a pocket with trembling fingers, brought out and unwrapped the object—like many chosen abodes of demons' lives, it was in itself a simple, homely thing, in this case a small mirror of quite ordinary appearance.

Inside its untouched wrappings, the mirror had been diced, not broken, into a hundred fragments, as if by some steel edge keen enough to deal with glass like paper.

The time elapsed since the Dark King's arrival at the palace did not yet amount to half an hour.

He threw away the glittering bits of what had been the demon's life-object; no magical virtue of any kind remained to it.

Over the next minute or so Vilkata was distracted from the contemplation of his various problems, and somewhat heartened, by the continued arrival from the direction of the palace of still more of his demons, howling their joy to find him safe; and, within moments, more dozens, scores, hundreds of people, all rejoicing loudly in his living presence and outraged by his wounds. These starry-eyed folk came running up to gather round him at a respectful distance in the predawn darkness.

The numbers of these human worshippers seeking him out continued to increase. The thought occurred to the Dark King, bringing with it a wave of bitterness, that these folk were certainly the last converts the Sword of Glory would ever make.

Karel was far from being the only high-ranking defector from the palace. A number of others could claim with justification to have been quite high in Tasavaltan councils. These important people in particular kept trying to get closer to Vilkata, though with violent gestures he did his best to keep them all at a little distance. With touching remorse they tried to plead with him for his forgiveness for their own evil deeds, their years of support of that vile renegade Prince Mark, for their protracted and stubborn and incomprehensible opposition to the Dark King's beneficent rule.

Now that their eyes had been opened by the glorious Sword of Glory—so some of them now loudly assured their new Master—they could see the light of truth, appreciate the proper and natural order that ought to hold in human affairs.

Karel himself was among the first converts to locate his new Master outside the palace. The fat old man ran up gasping and wheezing, then knelt down trembling, to give thanks for the Dark King's survival; the fact that he prayed to Ardneh evidently did not strike his convert's mind as inconsistent; Vilkata himself was faintly amused.

And then Karel began to do his best magically to heal the sting of the wounds made by the Sword-fragments. In this he was soon more successful than any of the demons had been.

But dominating Vilkata's thoughts amid the prayerful babble of this swelling human mob was the realization of how soon these turncoats were going to turn on him again. With his empty sockets the Dark King glared balefully at them all, Karel included. Nothing was more certain than that, with the Mindsword gone, most of these contemptible scum would be his mortal enemies again in a matter of only a few days—in some cases only hours would pass before there was reversion.

That posed a grim prospect for him and his plans; but there was one aspect of it which he could enjoy in anticipation: When the time of their recovery came, these sycophants would regard their present behavior with a loathing as great as that they now expressed for their own supposed sins in helping Mark.

Vilkata questioned Karel about General Rostov, Prince Mark's chief military commander, and learned that Rostov could not be immediately accounted for. The General had been on an inspection tour of the northern provinces, and, like the Prince and Princess, would have to be dealt with somehow later.

The Dark King's next question was about Ben of Purkinje.

With the exception of Mark himself, Ben was undoubtedly the individual whose appearance in an enslaved state would have most gladdened the conqueror's heart—but Vilkata had already been told, and had received independent confirmation of the fact from several sources, that Ben also had been out of town when the attack struck. Karel gave assurances, and Vilkata's other informants agreed, that Ben had gone with the Prince and Princess, and was most likely with them still. His home in town had already been visited, and he was not there.

By this time Vilkata, now surrounded by a thick swarm of anxiously protective demons and a cheering mob of human converts, had almost completely recovered his wits and his nerve. His usually savage temper was returning too.

What to do with these eagerly worshipful humans? In his

sullen anger the elder wizard considered ordering them, while their fanaticism was still at its height, to kill each other off—but, on the verge of issuing that command, he had what struck him as a much better idea.

Presently, with the idea of deriving as much benefit as possible from their enthusiasm before it faded, Vilkata ordered the creation, from the ranks of the palace's converted soldiers, of several assassination squads. These were to sally out into the countryside, targeting whatever unconverted Tasavaltan leaders they might find there, especially Prince Mark. There was at least a fair chance, the Dark King supposed, that before the Sword-based conversion of these troops wore off one of them might actually manage to destroy Mark. At worst, they would be scattered, and at a considerable distance from himself, when their current adoration began to turn to hatred.

Vilkata found he was still unable to free himself totally of the lingering notion that, despite his logical deductions regarding Sightblinder, despite the reassurances of Karel and of Arridu and others, his opponent in the armory might after all, somehow, have been Wood—or one of the other possibilities, which bore thinking about even less. Shuddering with the recent memory of that awesome presence, the Dark King could not connect it with any mere sniveling Tasavaltan princeling.

But when Vilkata questioned his retinue on the subject of Wood, he soon learned from one of his demon aides, or from some converted soldier or magician, that about a year ago that master wizard had fallen to his doom and death before the power of Shieldbreaker in the hands of Prince Mark's nephew Zoltan.

Had Vilkata still retained the state of mind in which he had begun the attack, had he not been obsessed by the fresh loss of the Mindsword, the news of Wood's death would have been reason for celebration—one important competitor eliminated.

Vilkata also heard, with some satisfaction, that the Sword Wayfinder had been destroyed by the Sword of Force at the same time that Wood fell.

An hour ago the news of that destruction, too, would have afforded the Dark King satisfaction, because that recently it had still been his ambitious plan eventually to acquire and somehow eliminate all of the Swords except the Mindsword.

If the report concerning Wayfinder were true, then he now had good evidence that five of the original Twelve Blades had already been destroyed—Townsaver and Doomgiver some years ago, and now Wayfinder, Dragonslicer, and the Mindsword. Yet seven more—Shieldbreaker, Sightblinder, Coinspinner, Farslayer, Woundhealer, Stonecutter, and Soulcutter—were still in existence somewhere.

Of course it was Shieldbreaker which Vilkata most dreaded, and most craved to possess—as would any prudent man in his current position. He could still feel the shock of that Sword-smashing impact running up his arm. His minor wounds still stung despite the demon's, and even Karel's, ministrations.

But there was hope. Now a human convert physician, the latest to have served the royal family in the palace, was in attendance on the Master. The woman was putting on salves and urging patience.

. . . Yes, when one was setting out to subdue the world, Shieldbreaker had to be one's Sword of choice, even beyond such fearful tools as Sightblinder and Soulcutter. As had just been so violently demonstrated, the Sword of Force was quite capable of nullifying any other weapon, magical or physical, that might be used against its owner. Even the Sword of Vengeance, which otherwise, launched from the hands of a determined enemy anywhere in the world, could end his own much-hated life at any moment. Meanwhile, the ugliest weapon of all, the Tyrant's Blade, was a wild card with the potential of overthrowing all the calculations of Vilkata or any other human.

Ultimately the Sword of Force was going to present a special problem, even after Vilkata came into control of it, as he thought he eventually must do if he was ever going to rule the world—a special case, because so far he had been able to conceive of no way in which Shieldbreaker itself could ever be destroyed. Even had he eventually been able, by means of the Mindsword, to perfect his mastery over the thoughts and bodies of every thinking being on the Earth, yet the Sword of Force, however he might attempt to hide or bury it, would present a perpetual danger to his rule.

There might be discoverable some method, though, by which it would be possible to eliminate Shieldbreaker. He did not consider the matter hopeless—but at the moment, of course, he was a totally Swordless man, and had to make his plans under all the disadvantages being in that state entailed.

For a minute or two he had been thinking about Swords, concentrating on the problems they posed to distract himself from the pain whilst his small wounds were cauterized by the palace physician, with Karel's help.

Presently Vilkata, now thoroughly and protectively surrounded by a clamorous escort of outraged demons and human converts—those of his human worshippers who could best tolerate being near the demons—decided that, Swords or not, he should delay no longer his re-entry of the palace. Certainly he was not going to conquer Tasavalta, or prevail against his superbly armed assailant of the armory, by huddling indecisively out here in the street.

But before he passed into the building again, the Dark King dispatched a small army of human converts ahead of him—he was determined to get as much use as possible out of these people while he could—to scout and act as a temporary occupying force.

* * *

Of course, since Sightblinder was missing from the Sword-vault and presumably had already been taken up and used by an enemy, no one could be sure that the same enemy was not still lurking nearby somewhere.

The demon Arridu and the great converted wizard commiserated with their lord and Master.

It was Karel who came up with the suggestion that any one person armed with two Swords, especially Shieldbreaker and Sightblinder, must almost certainly be undergoing psychic difficulties from the strain; the problem would be worse if the simultaneous use of the Blades continued for any length of time.

This was faint comfort to the Dark King. "But who was it, really, old man? Can you tell me that?"

The old wizard discounted the idea that Mark himself could actually be near, in the palace or even in the city; the royal couple were known to be at some little distance.

Then Karel suggested that Vilkata's sole opponent in the armory had very likely been young Prince Stephen. Who else known to have been present would have been able to gain access to the Swords? Rostov had been away.

The fact of Stephen seemed inevitable.

Karel went on: "The Mindsword having been so unfortunately denied us, as you say, great and dear Master, we must try to find some other way to make plain to the lad the truth of your superior nature. Failing that, of course, we must find some way to get those Swords away from him. He is badly misguided, but there must be some way."

"I eagerly await your discovery of an effective method." Vilkata looked round him in all directions. "Meanwhile, I am not going to be kept out here on the street because of the mere possibility of trouble."

Even as Vilkata re-entered the palace, this time going in

through the main entrance from the street, he was met by a minor demon bearing electrifying news: the confirmation that at least one intact Sword, Stonecutter, was still available in the deep armory. This information was whispered in the Dark King's ear by a messenger sent out by Arridu, who himself was mounting jealous guard upon the find.

This was no news to the Dark King, but now he decided that he had better pick up at once the Sword which was available.

That the enemy had not taken Stonecutter was shrewdly regarded as evidence that the enemy might already be having trouble carrying Swords. This in turn argued for the young Prince rather than some more experienced and capable wizard or warrior.

Despite his eagerness to return to the underground storeroom of the Swords, the Dark King thoughtfully took care to disarm himself completely before doing so. He would rely upon his escort to deal with any problem that needed weaponry to solve. Now, let any enemy armed with Shieldbreaker dare to threaten him!

No enemy could be detected when the Dark King again descended to the level of the armory. No Sword-phantom appeared—at least he thought not. Of course, with Sightblinder one could never be sure.

Vilkata, on being welcomed and escorted back into the conquered palace of his enemies by a horde of joyous converts, was soon able to bring Stonecutter peacefully under his control.

Bitterly, Vilkata again cursed his failure to seize Shieldbreaker, or at least Sightblinder, in the first rush of his surprise attack.

Having opened the vault in the Sword chamber unmolested, the Dark King stood staring earnestly at the sole intact Blade before him—yes, this was undoubtedly Stonecutter. He pulled the Sword of Siege unceremoniously out of its rack, looked at the small white wedge-sign on the hilt, and hacked a notch or two in floor and wall, just by way of final demonstration. Stone slid and crumbled away like butter before the Blade, which in action made its own hammering noise, heavier and slower than that of Shieldbreaker.

Vilkata tried to think whether there was any way in which this remaining Sword could be of notable benefit to him. Karel and Arridu, when consulted, could suggest nothing. Rather regretfully, the Dark King had to concede that Stonecutter had no immediate use. For the time being the Sword of Siege could stay here, under close guard and protection.

Meanwhile, other problems demanded the Dark King's immediate attention. Chief among these were the implications of the loss of the Mindsword. He understood that he had to put on a bold front in the presence of his subordinates, many of whom probably did not yet realize that Skulltwister was gone. Those who did were themselves still under the dazzling influence of its power, and so Vilkata thought they might not be able to grasp the importance of the loss. And, by the time they did, they would be tempted to rebellion.

Still staring into Prince Mark's Sword-vault, which was now empty but for the Sword of Siege, it occurred to Vilkata to wonder whether he ought to try to deceive his adversaries, and the world at large, into thinking he still wore the Mindsword at his side. Certainly it would be beyond his art to replicate the powers of Skulltwister, but he was quite a good enough magician to be able to create a visual simulacrum good enough to deceive the world, or almost all the world, for some time.

Then the Dark King was struck by a simpler idea. If deception was truly desirable, he could carry Stonecutter sheathed at his side in lieu of the Mindsword, letting others glimpse only the black hilt with its white symbol concealed.

EIGHT

MOMENTS after the explosion, Stephen came stumbling his way out of the Sword-chamber, leaving it for the second time in a few minutes. He felt half dead with exhaustion. The overwhelming challenge of the surprise attack had fallen upon him at the end of a long and wearying day of physical work, and in the first moments of that onslaught his body had been injured and his mind twisted. He had been allowed no time to recover from his skirmish with the demon before being subjected to the psychic burden of carrying the two Swords.

Now the young Prince had undergone the shock of combat with a mighty wizard, a clash in which the Mindsword had almost certainly been destroyed—the young Prince wanted desperately to believe that, but in his dazed state at the moment felt he could take nothing for granted. And his chief enemy, a man he considered worse than any demon, had been repulsed, if not killed. Vilkata had certainly disappeared, perhaps was dead.

The burdens of ongoing responsibility, and of the two Swords' magic, would not allow Stephen the luxury of triumph. At the moment he could think of little else but the sanctuary and help awaiting him in the house of his grandparents.

With regard to Jord and Mala, a horrifying possibility had already crossed their grandson's mind—suppose they had become the Mindsword's converts too? The youth would not, could not, allow himself to consider that possibility seriously. He told himself that most of the city must have escaped. The Dark King's attack must have been aimed first and primarily at the palace, with the objective of seizing the Tasavaltan Swords before an alarm could be sounded. But if, as seemed probable, the Mindsword had been destroyed before the area of its evil influence could be expanded, then the great majority of the city's population, all those more than a long bowshot from the palace, should have retained the mastery of their own minds and souls—and this majority should have included Stephen's grandparents. Fiercely the young Prince assured himself that it must be so.

A few of the Mindsword's final converts, servants and soldiers and palace functionaries so recently loyal to Tasavalta, now shrieking and crying their concern for their new Master's welfare, had come belatedly following Vilkata down to the lower level of the palace. Now these people had been thrown into panic by the Dark King's sudden disappearance, and were raising an alarm.

Stephen, his right shoulder and his bruises aching, all the muscles of his body weary, heard these folk, many of whom had been his friends, babbling their concerns for the fiend's welfare. The young Prince ignored them as he had ignored Karel after the most recent Sword-blast. Stephen went on dragging Shieldbreaker and Sightblinder, the bare blades trailing, up a broad flight of stairs to the ground floor of the palace. The two Swords seemed too heavy now for him to carry in any normal way.

On the stairs and above them, turmoil continued. Demons and shrieking human converts seemed to be everywhere, on the ground level of the huge building as well as in the basement. Most of the faces of Skulltwister's victims were familiar to Stephen. Others he would have known, but did not, because their ecstasies of hate, rage, and devotion transformed them into strangers.

Since leaving the Sword-chamber, the young Prince had not dared to sheathe either of his deadly Blades. He could only assume that Sightblinder was working effectively as always, because so far none of the enemies surrounding him on every side had challenged him, but rather were promptly giving way.

Most went hurrying past him on the stair with averted faces. On the rare occasion when one came near, Stephen drove the man or woman away with a sharp gesture, a wave of one of his Swords. What Sightblinder made the other see when he did this, he did not know, but the method was effective.

So far Stephen had been able to overhear only disconnected odds and ends of speech from the strange beings, converts and demons, among whom he was suddenly an isolated stranger. And still he had no way of determining whether his family's archenemy Vilkata had survived the Mindsword's negation or not. Those around Stephen who were chanting Vilkata's name in ecstasy said nothing to indicate that he might be dead.

Well, supposing that the Dark King still lived, the young Prince just now had neither the means nor the intention to seek him out. Not while Stephen's own soul felt as bleak and exhausted as it did just now, his battered body aching, and his head spinning with Sword-magic until he feared that he would faint.

The young Prince came to a pause, body swaying slightly. He had, without quite realizing it, reached the top of the long flight of stairs. He now stood on the ground floor, in one of the many rooms of the old palace whose original purpose had never been quite clear to him. But this room and its furnishings were perfectly familiar, and from here it was an easy task to choose a passage through the building which brought him quickly to one of the small side doors. A moment later Stephen was outside, and a minute after that he was opening an iron gate, leaving the palace grounds.

At every step, the young Prince kept hoping to catch some hint of a place nearby, a sanctuary where he might find a moment's safety, a chance to rest. But so far he had seen no hint that anything of the kind existed. He had only the Swords, and his own will, to depend on.

The city, or at least this portion of it, was as hectic as the palace itself had been. Screaming converts, some waving weapons and torches, some divesting themselves of their Tasavaltan livery of green and blue, seemed to be everywhere, indoors and out. Out in the street, just as in the palace, the dark night air seemed filled with demons. Shieldbreaker effectively warded off any sickening or other untoward effect caused by the presence of the foul creatures, but still Stephen was aware of the vast forms moving above him and around him, like ominous shadows behind thick glass.

Even after the youth had distanced himself by a full block from the palace grounds, he did not dare to sheathe either of his Swords. As a result, the psychic strain upon him continued to mount.

Only after he had dragged his double burden two full blocks from the palace did the number of visible enemies around him begin to diminish noticeably. But it seemed he had been wrong, the city away from the palace had not been spared by the attack. Horror, in several forms of human death and ruin, continued to dominate the streets around him.

Here Stephen walked among the blood and havoc those sounds of distant fighting had produced. His mind, already reeling with shock, took in the dead and wounded people, the smashed windows—a number of the shops and houses close to the palace boasted real glass—the wantonly slaughtered work-animals and pets, and general destruction. Here was a building totally destroyed, crushed like a toy by some wanton child, the ruins sprouting greedy flames. No one was paying any attention to the wreckage or the fire.

Several times during these first minutes of Stephen's struggle through the city he considered sheathing Shieldbreaker—but he could not be completely sure that Skulltwister was really gone. The Sword of Force intermittently muttered drumbeats of warning, and he dared not take the chance. Even had he been willing to put the Sword of Force away, it sporadically adhered by magic to his palm and fingers.

Neither could the young Prince nerve himself to muffle the power of Sightblinder. The Sword of Stealth, gripped tightly in his left hand, continued its silent and effective service. People and demons alike, whether individuals or roving bands, took one look at the image shown them by Sightblinder and silently, unanimously, gave Stephen a wide berth. To judge by the expressions on the human converts' faces, many or all of them must have been convinced that they were face-to-face with one of Vilkata's nastier demons. As long as Sightblinder continued to do its job, he might hope to avoid more shoulder-wrenching exercise with Shieldbreaker.

The young Prince struggled on, squeezing the hilts of both his god-forged weapons, as if by that means he might moderate the dizzying currents of their power. But when he had progressed a little more than two blocks from the palace, he had to pause, gasping, and sit down on the curb. He was forced to concede that he could not long sustain the unremitting struggle with this double burden of magic.

Still, for the moment at least, there could be no thought of abandoning the struggle. Sternly Stephen put from him all thoughts of failure. Briskly he got to his feet and tried again. But his steps wavered, and before he had gone twenty paces more, dizziness and a feeling of mental fragmentation compelled him to stop again, to try to rest, and try to think. The trouble was that the Swords gave him no rest, no, not a moment's.

This time the young Prince had seated himself—almost he had collapsed—on a carriage block in front of the wrought-iron fence of one of the tall, elegant houses which here lined the avenue. Gritting his teeth, he continued to clutch the two black hilts. In the absence of any direct threat, his right hand at the moment had the power to sheathe and release the Sword of Force; but now Stephen was afraid that if he sheathed either Sword, or even put one of the pair down in search of a moment's relief, he would find it impossible to resume the double burden.

The strain was being intensified by the physical injuries the boy had suffered before coming under the protection of the Sword of Force, as well as by the shoulder damage inflicted by that very weapon. In his dazed and terrorized state immediately following his first encounter with a demonic foe, these hurts had passed almost unnoticed; but now they were making themselves felt.

Stephen, trying very awkwardly to rub his sore shoulder with the back of the hand still holding Sightblinder, realized with sudden insight that one weapon against which the Sword of Force could never protect him was itself. In his dazed condition, trying to rub his bruised left elbow with the back of his right hand, he cut his shirt, and came near wounding himself, with Shieldbreaker.

After trying without much success to rest and think, the young Prince again got to his feet—this time it cost him even more of a struggle than before—and resumed his effort to do what he knew that he must do. Every instinct shrieked that only disaster lay ahead unless he could find help, and soon.

Only a few more blocks, he told himself. Only a few hundred meters. He told himself that he ought to be able to run that far, and back again, in the time he'd already spent on this slow struggle.

Then he thought that trying to deceive himself, to make the matter sound easy, was a childish trick, and it wasn't going to work. He might as well tell himself it was kilometers instead of meters; the one was going to be as impossible as the other.

But no, it wasn't impossible. He was a Prince of Tasavalta, and his father's son, and he could do it, because there was no other choice. He'd just rest here another minute, or try to rest, and then . . .

The direction and location of his goal both remained clear in the mind of the young Prince. Jord, Stephen's grandfather, knew how to deal with Swords as well as any man alive could be said to do so—perhaps Jord, though he was no magician, really understood better than anyone else, because he had been the only human actually present and directly involved in the Twelve Blades' forging, more than forty years ago.

No longer, Stephen decided, were most of the people converts who came hurrying past him in the street. In this neighborhood the faces and the voices were different, terrorized but not fanatical. The great majority, like Stephen himself, were heading away from the palace, and a considerable number were actually fleeing in a panic. There were women with small children, a man trundling his household belongings in a cart. Even in their haste and fright they continued to give Stephen plenty of room, as did every demon swirling past him overhead. Demons were much scarcer here, and, as far as the young Prince could tell, those which appeared were not attacking the population now, but seemed rather to be continually patrolling, searching . . . more than likely, he realized, he himself was the object of their search.

On top of all Stephen's other difficulties a sense of guilt began to nag at him. Even armed as he was, almost invincibly, he was retreating and leaving the enemy in possession of the palace. Now and again he looked back over his shoulder. Sturdily he clung to the thought that his first instinct, to save the great treasure of the two Swords, had been correct: It would be impossible for him to vanquish or even seek for his hereditary enemy now, while he himself was so nearly incapacitated.

In fact the young Prince was being forced to a bleak decision: If the stress of magic continued as it was much longer, he might be compelled to abandon one of the Swords before he could get as far as his grandparents' house.

Jord and Mala's modest cottage had been built some years ago in a neighborhood of roughly similar homes, each with a small plot of grass and garden and a few shady trees. Through the darkest time of the late night the young Prince struggled on, holding in his mind a vision of that grassy shade where he had so often played as a small child.

Here was the street at last, and Stephen eagerly increased his pace. But as he turned the last corner his heart sank at the fresh signals of disaster. Straight ahead in the pre-dawn darkness he saw the glow of fire, and smelled fresh smoke.

Did he have the right street after all? Yes, there were landmarks—a shop where Mala had bought him candy, a tree girdled by a circular bench—to give grim confirmation.

The young Prince rubbed his weary eyes with the back of one Sword-bearing hand. But no, his eyes were not at fault. There was smoldering fire ahead where there ought to have been no fire; low flames flickering up, trying to gain strength to consume an entire building, provided illumination enough for him to confirm that there was only a collapsed and smoldering ruin where the familiar house had stood.

NINE

DIMLY Stephen was conscious of the fact that the houses on either side of his grandparents' had also suffered heavy damage, though neither was as badly off as the cottage he had so often visited. One of the adjoining buildings was also smoking, as if it might soon start to burn; and two or three additional fires were visible at some distance in the neighborhood.

But just now the young Prince had no time or thought to spare for neighbors. He ran forward, still convulsively gripping a black hilt in each hand, though for the moment he had almost forgotten why it was essential to retain the Swords. Stephen's weary arms were allowing the two unbreakable points to drag, god-forged steel striking sparks from the cobblestones of the street.

Three or four neighbors, in nightshirts and hastily thrown-on clothing, had been standing within a few meters of the smoldering ruins. However these folk perceived the bearer of the Sword of Stealth, they at once drew back to give him plenty of room. One of the onlookers, getting a close look at Sightblinder's version of Stephen's approaching figure, screamed and ran away.

The other bystanders had not taken to their heels, at least not yet. For the moment the young Prince ignored them all, keeping his attention riveted on the jumbled ruins before him. Maybe, he thought wildly, Jord and Mala hadn't been home in their bed when disaster struck. Maybe . . .

Gasping, his whole body burning and aching with strain and weariness, Stephen halted under a fruit tree in what had once been his grandparents' grassy yard. It was all sickeningly unfamiliar now. A few meters ahead of him, small flames snapped avidly at freshly splintered wood, illuminating ruin.

The fire seemed eager to establish a solid foothold in the timbers and siding which lay tumbled and broken among the shattered masonry and tiles.

"Grandfather! Grandmother!"

There was no reply.

Once more Stephen called upon his tired arms to lift his Swords so that the long blades ceased to drag. So armed, he edged closer to the ruin. The flames were not big enough—not yet—to force him back, nor were they growing swiftly. Intermingled in the wreckage with the broken and burned pieces of the building's structure were household items: pots, pans, furniture—there was a padded chair he thought he recognized—bundles of old clothes . . .

The gaze of the young Prince moved on, came back. In a moment he realized with horror that what he had thought for a moment were two bundles of old clothes, three-quarters buried in the rubble, were really the bodies of his grandparents, clad in nightshirt and nightgown. Gray hair was visible, exposed pale arms and legs.

Suddenly all of the night's horror, which had been starting to seem dreamlike, regained immediate reality. The grandson of Mala and Jord noted that the couple lay almost side by side, as if they had been together when the walls of their home crashed in around them—or possibly one had come to try to help the other . . . .

"Prince? Prince Mark?" Someone was pulling tentatively on Stephen's arm, speaking to him in a voice he dimly recognized. Turning, Stephen came face to face with a nextdoor neighbor, a man whose name he could not remember at the moment, but whom the boy had sometimes seen and spoken with on visits. The neighbor's face was altered, and he, like Stephen himself, seemed almost paralyzed by horror.

"Prince Mark?" the man repeated.

That name administered a shock of hope. The young Prince looked around dazedly, to see if his father might indeed be present. He needed a moment to realize that Sightblinder must be presenting him to the neighbor in his father's image.

"What is it?" Stephen at last responded to the man who stood beside him.

"May all the gods defend us, Prince Mark, the demons have done it. Killed the old people, knocked down their house and ours, too. The rest of the neighborhood is damaged, as you see. But now that you're here, you can shout the demons away again—you can do that, can't you? You must!"

For the moment, Stephen could only stare helplessly at the man.

The neighbor gazed back, pleadingly, his eyes now focused just over the top of Stephen's head—no doubt where Sightblinder was showing him the face of the taller Mark.

"Prince? We're going to win now, aren't we?" The man's voice cracked. "The army's coming?"

The moaning sound was slight at first, and Stephen almost failed to hear it over the background of nibbling flames and distant uproar in the streets. But it brought his eyes back to the crushed bundles under the rubble, and a moment later he saw movement in one of them. The moaning grew.

Though he could not be sure of the exact source of the sound, it testified that at least one of Stephen's grandparents— he could not tell who—still breathed.

"They're alive—!"

Upon making this discovery the young Prince cried out incoherently and gestured awkwardly, with Sword-filled hands. Realizing that he would need his hands free to save his grandparents from the slowly growing fire, he sheathed both Swords, an operation that seemed nightmarishly slow and awkward—he had to thrust several times with each steel tip to find the narrow opening in its respective sheath.

When Stephen released Sightblinder's hilt, the neighbor standing beside him recoiled, startled.

"Prince Stephen—but where's your father? He was just here." The man was blinking and stammering in confusion.

Stephen mumbled some kind of answer, even as he turned his back on the man to go climbing awkwardly into what was left of the ruined building, scratching his legs and ankles in the process. Reaching for Grandfather and Grandmother, whose bodies, partially buried, both lay just below reach, he started to dig into the rubble with his bare hands.

The long scabbards hanging on each side of Stephen's waist got in his way with every movement when he crouched to attack the wreckage. With feverish haste he slipped both Sword-belts off, setting them down within reach.

Grabbing a long, thick beam in an attempt to lift and move it, the young Prince succeeded only in burning his fingers, and discovering that his strength was not equal to the task.

The neighbor who had been talking to Stephen now climbed energetically into the rubble beside him and did his best to help. With that example before them, two more people, who had evidently been watching from a little distance, now came to give assistance.

With four pairs of hands to dig and lift, there appeared to be some chance of getting the two old people out of the wreckage—but one long beam was still wedged in place, preventing the rescue.

Even the united strength of everyone on hand was not going to be enough. The beam was held down at both ends.

The lad promptly turned to his Swords again, and slid the long blade of Sightblinder from its sheath. With the other rescuers standing back to give him room, he dug other pieces of wreckage out of the way, then braced his feet and swung the Sword like a long axe, chopping at the beam.

As soon as he took up the Sword of Stealth again, his image once more changed in the eyes of everyone watching.

As Stephen had expected, a Sword's indestructible blade proved a good digging tool, an excellent chopper, an unbreakable pry bar. You had to be careful, of course, about stabbing or slicing the victims you were trying to rescue. In this case, fortunately, there was adequate clearance, and the bodies plainly visible.

It occurred to Stephen that, if the rules of Sword-magic worked as he had reason to believe they did, Shieldbreaker used as a digging or cutting implement ought not to hurt the flesh of an unarmed victim buried in the wreckage. But it crossed his mind also that either Jord or Mala could be armed, having grabbed up some weapon when an alarm was sounded.

Letting the Sword of Force rest in its scabbard, he continued chopping with the Sword of Stealth.

Stephen labored on, using the keen, indestructible edge to sever the fallen roof beam which at first had frustrated the rescue efforts. The seasoned wood was as thick as his leg; but the weighty sharpness of the steel made the Sword at least as good as an axe for this mundane purpose.

One of the neighbors, seeing what good success Stephen was having, grabbed up Shieldbreaker and used it to chop with too—the young Prince noted distinctly how the Sword of Force remained silent at this mundane task, like some proud warrior forced into routine, supposedly less heroic, labor.

As soon as the beam had been chopped through in two places, the helpful neighbor put Shieldbreaker awkwardly, but almost reverently, back in its sheath.

Now that the beam was cut, Stephen used Sightblinder as a lever, leaning his weight on the Sword to force up the remaining length of timber while others pulled the bodies free. Moments later, the bodies of Jord and Mala had been dragged and lifted as carefully as possible out of the smoldering rubble and laid gently on the grass.

This latest effort left the young Prince swaying on his feet with weariness. Tears of grief, anger, and fatigue were running down his cheeks, even as he looked down on the bodies of his grandparents. Mala and Jord were quiet now, and motionless.

Stephen could not be certain for the moment that either of the old folk still breathed; but neither was he absolutely sure as yet that either one was dead. Both were marked with blood.

Sightblinder was still in the right hand of the young Prince when he bent anxiously over the old people to try to talk with them. Now he could be sure that his grandmother was dead; but Jord was muttering, trying to say something clearly.

Some helpful neighbor had gone to get water. Coming back, he tried to give the old man a drink.

Jord's eyes focused slowly on Stephen crouching beside him. In a moment the old man muttered: "Don't leave me, Mark."

Stephen hesitated, then retained his grip on the black hilt. He would let his grandfather see Mark, if that was what Jord wanted.

"I ought not to have kept a Sword on the wall, son. . . ."

Stephen had heard the story, from his father, often enough. It came from Mark's childhood. "It's all right, gr—. It's all right."

The old man let out a feeble breath. He had almost no voice left. "I shouldn't have forged Swords. Not that Vulcan gave me much choice."

And presently Stephen realized that those were the last words Jord was ever going to speak.

Stephen, preoccupied with grief, was still holding Sightblinder, unsheathed, when the great demon Arridu came swooping down upon the scene. The distraught young Prince did not even notice the wave of sickness brought by the demon until the foul thing was very near, until the neighbors had either scattered in blind terror, or fallen down in fear and demon-sickness . . . .

When Stephen turned his head at last, to his horror he beheld the figure, larger than humanity, of a man in black armor, bending to grab up the sheathed Sword of Force from the place where the Sword's last user had set it down.

A demon, an ungodly great demon by the look of it, had Shieldbreaker; though the Sword of Force was still undrawn, inactive in the enemy's hand—

The monster turned an almost paralyzing gaze on Stephen, and spoke. Nearly frozen in terror, the boy could scarcely hear or understand the words of its soft, rumbling voice; nor did he realize that they were uttered in humility: "The great Sword lay unattended here, dear Master. Any of these human beasts might have grabbed it up. I hold it for you—"

On the verge of fainting, Stephen lashed out at Arridu as best he could.

"In the Emperor's name, forsake this game—!" The young Prince thought he could feel the veins standing out upon his forehead as he yelled.

And the Sword of Force and its hideous bearer were both gone, whirled aloft and out of sight in an instant.

Not until the demon had been banished, and a measure of sanity and stability had returned to the locality, did the young Prince realize the extent of his own blunder—*Shieldbreaker must have gone with the demon!*

Now that it was too late, the horrible memory came clear: his glimpsing the undrawn Sword of Force in Arridu's grip . . .

Stephen knew tremendous horror and guilt at the great loss . . . and fear that at any moment the demon, invincibly armed, would be coming back to eat him alive.

Meanwhile the last terrorized neighbor had crawled away somewhere. Stephen was alone in the night, with the crackling fire and the howls of riot and murder coming from the distant reaches of the city.

There was no disputing the fact that now both his grandparents were dead. There was no disputing either that the loss of Shieldbreaker was, for the moment at least, irretrievable. The doom of its return was hanging over him, and over all the Earth.

Staring numbly at the dead bodies of his grandparents, listening to the disorder and the horror of Sarykam around him—Arridu's brief presence had stirred up new tumult over an area of several square blocks—Stephen swayed on his feet with weariness.

Where now? What now? From somewhere in the back of his mind a simple, natural suggestion presented itself: He might try going to the house of Ben of Purkinje. Conscious planning might well have rejected that idea: If the enemy had sought out people as far removed from power as Jord and Mala, surely the home of Ben and his family would have received much more intense attention; if that house survived at all it would be watched.

Stephen started walking, seeking sanctuary, without being aware that he had made any decision about where he ought to go. Already the thought of Ben's house had slipped from his conscious awareness.

At least Sightblinder was still his—his hand still gripped, unconsciously, the hilt of the sheathed Blade—and he was vaguely aware that, unless an enemy armed with Shieldbreaker came against him first, the Sword of Stealth would get him safely out of the city and to his parents.

But first he must find a place where he could rest.

Walking slowly, still moving without a conscious plan, the young Prince felt himself in the grip of bitter guilt over the fact that he'd lost Shieldbreaker. Stumbling, he felt himself abruptly overwhelmed by tiredness. There were moments when the world turned gray, and he came near fainting on his feet.

Before traveling very far away from the ruins of his grandparents' house, without even getting anywhere near the city gates—even before deciding what his next move had to be—he left the street, seeking some shelter where he could rest.

Turning from the noise of the street to pass through the open gate, he found himself behind high stone walls, in the garden of Ben's half-wrecked and freshly deserted house. This was definitely a more elegant neighborhood than Jord's and Mala's . . . .

Only after he had entered the grounds surrounding the big house did he consciously recognize this as the home of Ben of Purkinje and his family. It was not a place that Stephen had often visited. The roof had been smashed in, but here, too, the enemy had come and gone. Perhaps that meant it would be a safe place, for a little while, in which to rest. He'd rest for only a moment, relying on the Sword of Stealth, and then he'd move on . . . .

The young Prince stretched out in a grassy place under some bushes . . . but for the time being, sleep refused to come. The horned Moon, lately risen, and the stars provided all the light he needed. He lay directly on top of the naked Blade of Sightblinder, the fingers of both his hands interlaced around the hilt . . . he would rest for just a moment . . . he supposed there was nothing for it now but to make his way to Voronina, the village where his parents were—or where they had been. As soon as they got the news of the attack, they'd be on the move . . . somewhere.

But he'd find them. He could still bring them Sightblinder, and while he had that Sword and no other to carry, the journey ought to be quite feasible.

One Sword he still had—and that one he was not going to let go of. His life, and likely much more than his own life, depended on his ability to retain the Sword of Stealth.

Now, if he could only rest, close his eyes for a few moments, he would be able to push on again.

* * *

Vilkata, tightening his grip on the palace in the last hour before dawn, had secreted himself in one of the upper chambers, from which he kept issuing a stream of orders to demons and converts, patiently establishing his new base of operations in rooms which only hours ago had belonged to his great enemy.

Meanwhile the Dark King was steadily recalculating, reconsidering his situation. Like other people on both sides of the conflict, dwellers within the city as well as outside its walls, he was profoundly interested in what interference, if any, could be expected from the Swords still remaining in the world, or what advantage gained from them.

He assumed that Shieldbreaker and Sightblinder were still in the hands of his lone enemy of the recent confrontation. The locations of Soulcutter, Farslayer, and Coinspinner remained unknown as far as the Dark King was concerned; and each of these weapons in its own way was capable of completely turning the balance of the great game.

Grimly, Vilkata had determined that the loss of the Mindsword was not going to plunge him into a panic. His enemies were reeling too, and badly hurt; he had struck a hard blow at their leadership by converting Karel and others, he had slaughtered a number of their proud and stiff-necked populace, and occupied their capital.

Mark, he supposed, and the surviving Tasavaltan military, would need a day or two at least to make preparation for some attempt at striking back. In about that time, also, the converts' zeal would be starting to turn to ashes. So it was plain to the Dark King that in one or two days he might well have to retreat—unless in the meantime he somehow managed to acquire substantial human help, of some kind not dependent upon the Mindsword.

He considered the option of retreating now. He could summon his loyal demons, declare that he had intended nothing more than a raid on Sarykam, and withdraw from the city, perhaps to the seacoast caves where he had secreted the Old World spacecraft. But the idea of retreating at the first setback, sharp though it had been, rankled; and the Dark King quickly decided that to withdraw, now, at least, would be premature.

Also Vilkata tried to formulate some way to pursue or entrap Mark, who, on leaving the city a few days ago, had evidently taken with him from his special armory no other weapon besides the Sword of Healing. Karel and other converts had amply confirmed that fact.

The idea of a massive hostage-taking was beginning to grow in Vilkata's thoughts. Whatever problems might be about to confront him, having a few thousand hostages on hand would be a good idea.

He snapped out decisive orders to get the process started. Let a thousand or more of the city's people, without any particular selection, be rounded up, disarmed, and herded into the palace complex. Converts good for nothing else would do perfectly well as hostages, and would be as fanatically eager to assume that role as any other.

The elder magician Karel, with all a convert's eagerness to be of help, had volunteered to be Vilkata's counselor, and appeared with an offer to send a treacherous message to Prince Mark.

Vilkata, raising an eyebrow in approval, listened judiciously.

Kristin's uncle was eager to do all he could for his new lord. "The best tactic, Master, might be to persuade the Prince that I, Karel, have not been converted after all."

"You think you could convince him?"

"I think the tactic worth considering. If we can thus get Mark, and my dear niece—ultimately for their own good, of course—"

"Of course."

"To give up this foolish and unequal struggle."

Vilkata had grave doubts that any such plan to work. But he asked the old wizard to work out the details.

When informed of the plan to take hostages, Karel was not so enthusiastic. But, in his converted opinion, if people refused to see the light, they really deserved no better than a miserable death. Of course it was too bad about the children; but their fate could hardly be blamed upon the glorious Dark King, who never did anything wrong.

The Dark King, having now ordered repeated searches of the palace and its grounds, believed that his recent opponent in the armory had been no one but the young Princeling, Stephen. That puppy had gotten away with two of the most dangerous Swords.

Karel offered firm assurances that the stripling would never be able to carry such a double burden of magic very far.

Then, quite unexpectedly, the wizards' conversation was interrupted. One of the Dark King's new human slaves, still strongly under the Mindsword's lingering influence, came running in with word that Arridu was clamoring to be admitted to Vilkata's presence. The great demon was announcing his intention to give the Dark King a great gift.

Vilkata, having had no report from the monster demon for several hours, had begun to fear that Arridu had gone the way of Akbar, had become a victim of Shieldbreaker in the Tasavaltan Princeling's hands.

In a moment the gigantic fiend, in the guise of a black-clad warrior, was entering his Master's presence, one hand outstretched and far from empty. Arridu was making a present to his beloved Master of a sheathed and belted Sword, its power for the moment safely muffled.

One glance at the black hilt showed Vilkata that the weapon

being put into his hands was no less than Shieldbreaker itself.

The Dark King cried out with joy, with near-disbelief at his own good fortune.

The loyal one, the great demon Arridu, stood back in silence. Quickly recovering from the Mindsword's influence, he might already be starting to have second thoughts about the wisdom of turning over this Sword—but those thoughts came at least a minute too late.

Vilkata waved the Sword of Force, and roared with triumphant laughter.

TEN

THE news of the attack on Sarykam reached Princess Kristin and Prince Mark in the sleeping village of Voronina just before sunrise. These first disjointed signals of the horror arrived in confused and fragmentary form, borne in the small brains and uncertain speech of two half-intelligent bird-messengers, the only creatures of their kind who had succeeded in escaping the demons' onslaught on the palace.

Actually it was Ben of Purkinje, sleeping in his blanket-roll under the stars, who was first awakened by the beastmaster; and it was Ben, huge and ugly Ben, who then, grumbling and blaspheming all the gods that he could think of, came bringing the unwelcome tidings on to Mark and Kristin, in the yeoman's cottage where the royal couple were being housed during their visit.

Prince Mark was jarred out of some dream that was very strange, skirting a strange borderland between beauty and ugliness, by a knocking on the yeoman's door. Mark was in general a lighter sleeper than his wife, or any member of the farmer's family.

Working himself out from under the light cover, and then from under the outflung right arm of his sleeping wife, Mark, a tall, strong man now forty years of age, stood beside the bed and reached for some clothing. He had made his way downstairs and was listening to the news before anyone else in the house was properly awake.

He had had time to hear Ben's message before blond Kristin, four years younger than her husband but looking younger still, followed Mark downstairs with a blanket wrapped around her, to join her husband where he was standing with

Ben and the beastmaster in the morning twilight at the front door of the little house.

Kristin stood beside the three men listening carefully, grasping swiftly many of the implications of what was being said, herself having little to say at first. Shortly after she arrived, the farmer himself, next to be awakened, came to stand with his extraordinary visitors, listening too, holding a flaring brand from the hearth that gave at least uncertain light.

None of those who listened had much to say at first. The news of the attack came as a ghastly shock to all who heard it. Could there be any possibility of a mistake?

"Where are the birds now?" the Princess presently asked. "I want to hear directly from them whatever they can tell me."

"Yes, let's see them," Mark agreed.

Ben bowed lightly, a graceful gesture in so huge a man, and turned and led the way across the darkness of the farmyard. Mark and Kristin followed him to where a lantern was burning in the barn. Here the beastmaster had established himself with his little squadron of messengers. Bird-eyes glowed down in pairs from the high loft.

The two feathered creatures who had just arrived with the black news from Sarykam were of the species of giant night-flying owls. One of these messengers had arrived wounded and with its feathers scorched—ominous confirmation of the ghastly news. The uninjured owl had been flying half a kilometer from the city when the attack came; the other had somehow managed against all odds to make its escape from the ravaged aeries and blunder its way through the cloudy night to Voronina.

This bird, the smaller of the pair, speaking in its halting, half-intelligent small voice, could give few actual details of the attack. But it reported the presence in Sarykam of many demons, which strongly tended to confirm Mark's and Kristin's immediate suspicion that the Dark King was involved.

The Princess, listening, sighed and said: "Well, let us rouse our squad of soldiers."

But there was no need, most of the men had been sleeping outdoors near the barn and were already stirring. A small military guard, some fifteen or twenty mounted troops under the command of a captain, had accompanied the Prince and Princess on what had been expected to be a relatively uneventful trip.

In fact, at least half of the small village now seemed to be awake. Perhaps, the Princess suggested to her farmer-host, everyone should be awakened, since all had a right to know the situation.

The commanding officer of the small military squad, Captain Miyagi, came up to find Prince and Princess scanning the lightening skies, concerned about a possible attack on the village by demons or flying reptiles.

The Master of Beasts was also part of the military detachment who had come out from the capital. Fortunately, as a routine measure, he had brought along a complement of messenger-birds, intended to keep the royal couple in touch with all the relatively far-flung portions of their realm.

Now the Prince and Princess gave the beastmaster explicit orders. He saluted and moved briskly away.

Kristin looked at Mark. "Stephen," she said. All her concern and hope were audible in the one word.

Ben was standing by, muttering words of counsel when requested. At the same time he was privately and intensely worried about his family left back in the city, though he acknowledged that by his own choice he'd seen neither wife nor daughter for some months.

Following a night of violence and terror unprecedented in Sarykam, the early stages of a summer's dawn, heralded by the traditional signs of cockcrow, fresh dew, and a changing sky, were now overtaking the normally bustling outskirts of the city.

This morn was unusually quiet for an area so populous and ordinarily so filled with activity. At the moment the main road approaching the capital from the west carried almost no traffic. Conspicuous was a single rider, mounted on a large, magnificent riding-beast. This animal was bearing the rider's considerable weight toward the city at a brisk pace, even after laboring under the same burden through most of the night.

This close to the city the road was broad and smoothly paved, and a recent shower had left the pavement wet. The rider sniffed the heavy, smoky air and seemed to grant the morning his approval. He was a bulky, gray-haired man in his early sixties. His powerfully built body, scarred by a hundred fights, was wrapped in a gray cape, which in the eyes of naive observers would have identified him as a pilgrim. A more accurate reading would have been that he preferred just now to be anonymous.

The Moon, a waning crescent with horns aimed approximately toward the zenith, hung in the eastern sky, where it had just emerged from behind a tatter of cloud. A morning star was visible as well, Venus, to the east beyond the city and above the sea, a planet so round and lustrous that many people seeing it on that morning took it as an omen. The weary rider had little faith in omens, as a rule. But something in which he did have faith rode at his side in a long sheath, under his gray cape. Half-consciously he touched the black hilt with a large hand, as if to make sure it was still there.

When he had come within half a kilometer of the city walls, the traveler reined in his mount slightly, slowing his progress the better to observe a certain gray-clad man on foot who was carrying what looked like garden tools, notably a shovel, over his shoulder. This fellow was plodding along, coming from the direction of the main gate, and evidently bound for the loop of road that would take him to the coastal highway heading south. On becoming aware of the mounted man's inspection, the man on foot returned his glance and waved, without breaking stride, as if to some fellow pilgrim.

The mounted traveler waved back, without really giving the gesture any thought. Then he faced east and urged his riding-beast forward once more.

As the bulky man on his strong mount entered the area of practically continuous settlement just outside the city walls, he took note of half a dozen columns of smoke, each of a steady thickness, all together far in excess of what might have been expected from morning kitchens or other common activities. These smoke-plumes, ascending from unseen sources within the walls, blended at high altitude into a sooty cloud smeared by the morning breeze all across the lightening eastern sky. The sight suggested to the traveler that in the city several buildings, perhaps a great many, must be burning. Indeed, the volume of smoke suggested that no one in Sarykam was making much of an effort to put the fires out.

The traveler was not particularly worried that the whole city ahead of him was going to go up in flames. For one thing, there had been the recent rain to wet things down. For another, he was familiar with Sarykam, and recalled that most of the buildings inside the walls were constructed of stone and tile. A third and more fundamental reason for the traveler's equanimity was that he personally did not really care whether or not the city and everyone in it might be burned to cinders.

Steadily he pushed on, approaching the main inland gate of the Tasavaltan capital.

Just before he reached that tall portal the visitor turned once more, frowning, to look after that other supposed pilgrim—there had been something odd about that man and his tools—but the road behind was empty now.

With a shrug the mounted man proceeded about his business.

* * *

When the mounted traveler's methodical pace had brought him right up to the main gate where the high road went through the walls, he paused again to look the situation over. The gate, as a rule alertly guarded, now stood wide open, and there were no lookouts visible on the high city walls. These were ominous signs, even on such a superficially peaceful morning as this.

Even as the traveler sat in his saddle watching, there emerged from the gate a very young man wearing only a nightshirt, tall and thin to the point of fragility, looking both distressed and dazed. Blood that seemed to have run down from a recent untended scalp injury was drying on his forehead. This youth came wandering out of the open gate and along the high road for a couple of dozen paces, then off the road into an adjoining ditch. There he stood, staring at nothing, pulling thoughtfully at his lower lip like a scholar trying to remember the answers to a test. When the mounted traveler hailed him, the tall youth did not respond.

Well, thought the man in the saddle to himself, *I certainly cannot say that I have not been warned.*

But he had business here. He was not about to be turned back by warnings so indirect and impersonal as these.

Again the mounted traveler moved on slowly. By listening carefully he could hear, coming from somewhere inside the gate, a distant roaring, as of a crowd or mob, acting at least roughly in unison. The traveler's riding-beast, which seemed to be listening too, pawed the stones of the road and snorted.

Taking into account the several indications he had now been given, the observer decided that something in Sarykam was seriously amiss. He felt no great surprise at the discovery.

And now, even as the visitor watched from his saddle, he observed a new banner, of gold and black, being hoisted on the watchtower beside the gate, replacing the accustomed blue and green of Tasavalta. The latter banner was now hurled rudely to the ground by soldiers—if they were soldiers—of ragtag appearance, at least half out of uniform.

The observer thought the new emblem's stripes were somewhat uneven, as if the flag had been hastily sewn together. And looking in through the open gate he was able to catch a glimpse of another such flag going up on the tallest mast of the towering palace, well in beyond the walls.

The rider nodded; it was a brisk and private gesture of satisfaction, that of a man having a prediction confirmed. In the hues of the new banner he recognized the livery colors of the Dark King.

Whenever the traveler's gray cape moved aside a little on the left, the sword at his waist once more became visible. Harder to make out was the fact that this was no ordinary weapon, but a Sword, the Sword of Chance.

Before definitely deciding on his next move he partially drew Coinspinner and consulted the Sword, making the pommel point one way and then another, observing a vibration in the blade and feeling it through the black hilt.

Then briskly he dug heels into the ribs of his tired mount, and once more confidently rode forward, straight in through the main gate.

As the journeying rider entered the city the indications became even more obvious that here remarkable and violent events had very recently taken place.

At frequent intervals Coinspinner's wearer guardedly drew, or half-drew, the weapon. Each time the Sword cleared enough of the sheath to allow the owner to feel the surge of magical power, indicating to him which turning he should take next. The course thus mapped by Coinspinner was about as straight as the streets would allow, and took him in the direction of the palace.

From time to time during the intervals when he was not actually consulting the Sword, its owner repeatedly looked down at the black hilt, or felt for it to make sure that it was still there. Each time he was reassured; but with the Sword of Chance, one could never be really certain from one moment to the next where in the world it was going to be.

Coinspinner, uniquely among the Twelve, had always been fundamentally its own master. Following its usual pattern of moving itself about mysteriously, magically, the Sword of Chance had some months ago come into the hands of the adventurer Baron Amintor.

Having ample experience with the Swords, enough to trust their powers implicitly when Fate granted him the privilege of doing so, Amintor had been overjoyed at his good fortune. He had wasted no mental effort or energy trying to account for such a blessing, but had followed Coinspinner enthusiastically.

Firm in his expectation that Coinspinner would continue to provide good luck, Amintor now continued to follow the Sword's guidance through the maze of streets. It was leading him in the general direction of the palace.

The sky over Sarykam had changed again, getting past the stage of dawn, assuming now the colorless glow of very early daylight. The sun was still obscured in fog, somewhere above the eastern sea. The streets of the capital were quiet at the moment, but the visitor decided that this hush must have been a very recent development. A brace of dead bodies lying unattended in the middle of the thoroughfare testified with silent eloquence to an exciting night just past.

The traveler was not one to be dismayed by a few dead bodies; no stranger, he, to either war or civil tumult. And at present he felt comfortably well armed. Alertly he allowed his Sword to guide him forward. His riding-beast, also a veteran campaigner, pricked up its ears as it stepped past the bodies, but the animal betrayed no great excitement either.

As the bulky man in pilgrim gray continued along one of the main streets, still being guided by his Sword in the general direction of the palace, the signs of recent disturbance and violence were multiplied. In the distance many voices were chanting something. They were human voices, he felt quite sure, not the utterance of beasts or demons, but he could not make out the words. The Baron saw no reason to assume that all the violence was over—quite the opposite—but he had always been ready to accept a reasonable amount of risk when he thought there was also a good chance that a profit of some kind could be made.

He rode past several more dead bodies lying in the street, and another hanging halfway out of a second-story window. Here was a building upon whose sides someone had scrawled, in red paint that was still fresh, gigantic words. These might have been in some way helpful to the seeker after knowledge, but unfortunately the building had collapsed soon after being thus decorated—in fact it appeared to have been flattened by some superhuman power, which was perhaps the fact—reducing the messages to gibberish. No way for anyone to read those fractured, crumbled slogans now.

Amintor's methodical, Sword-guided advance was now bringing him very near to the main plaza and the palace. He detoured, without stopping, closely around a building that was burning fiercely, while a handful of people with buckets made an effort, only desultory, to wet down the neighboring structures.

But the fire had not drawn a crowd. It was attracting no more attention than did the bodies of the victims of violence. Plainly, on this strange morning the majority of the good citizens of Sarykam—presumably a majority still survived—had little thought or emotion to spare for the death and destruction which had been wrought among them overnight. Looking into the glittering eyes of some of the survivors, the visitor thought that another and transcendent excitement consumed their minds and spirits.

At least half of the people he had seen so far, living and dead, were still in night-dress, and one or two stark naked, with no one paying much attention. A number of other folk, the traveler noted, had hastily improvised a livery of black and gold for themselves to wear. Many had been marked by the night's festivities with soot and ashes, and some with blood. Not just your city riff-raff either. To judge by their generally well-fed appearance and neat barbering, they might have been until very recently among the city's most prosperous and reasonable inhabitants. Now the good burghers marched and chanted, even while some of their houses stood freshly ruined and others were burning down before their eyes. Folk of the Blue Temple (although the Blue Temple had only a very modest foothold in this city), the Red Temple, and the White, were all behaving uncharacteristically.

On one streetcorner stood a group of a dozen people singing, or trying to sing. The syllables they were chanting so hoarsely rang plainly in the visitor's ears. They made up a man's name and title, and they, like the livery of gold and black, belonged to an individual he recognized. Nay, one he thought he knew quite well.

Hand on his Sword-hilt, his own eyes now glittering with hopeful ambition, Amintor advanced. Now the palace was only two blocks ahead.

He had been less than half an hour in the city, but that was more time than the Baron needed to realize that in his long and far from sheltered life he had several times before seen conduct very similar to that now being displayed by the citizens of Sarykam. These people around him, engaging in such uncommon behavior, reminded him less of drug-overdosed devotees of the Red Temple than they did of folk fresh-caught by the Mindsword's spell.

A loud shout made the new arrival turn his head. He reined in his mount when he discovered that the cry had been directed at him. A group of six or eight young people, mounted upon a motley collection of loadbeasts and riding-beasts, was trotting toward him down a side street. All were wearing armbands of gold and black. The stocky youth who rode at the head of this small armed band now shouted another challenge at Amintor.

As they came up to him, the leader declared in a loud, raucous voice that they were seizing Amintor's riding-beast.

"Our glorious new King, Vilkata, will have need of many servants and many soldiers, of cavalry and messengers!" As he reached out to take the reins from Amintor, the stout youth glared at the visitor as if daring him to dispute the fact.

For just a moment as the Baron considered this demand, his broad, lined face was utterly blank of any expression. But an instant later he was smiling broadly as he swung himself down from the saddle. With a gesture at once proud and commanding he handed over the reins to his challenger, making the donation into a personal accomplishment.

In the circumstances Amintor was perfectly ready to abandon his tired riding-beast—let someone else feed the animal and care for it. He was confident that Coinspinner would find another mount for him whenever one was needed.

The Baron walked with a moderate limp, noticeable as soon as he alighted from his mount.

The little band of youths, a couple of them girls, all their faces slack, sat blinking down at him from their saddles or bareback mounts. Obviously they had been put somewhat off balance by the apparent enthusiasm of Amintor's compliance. It was equally obvious that they remained suspicious of this stranger, and that they wanted to be sure of his complete devotion to their great and glorious leader, the rightful ruler of the entire world, Vilkata the Dark King.

Certainly no doubt remained in the Baron's mind about the identity of the man who must have descended on this city during the night, bearing the drawn Mindsword and thus creating his own apotheosis.

Vilkata. Yes, indeed.

Amintor, rubbing his chin thoughtfully, remembered a great deal of that potentate's long history. The most recent highlight in that saga had been Vilkata's magical banishment, along with a flock of his demons, about two years ago, from this very metropolis. Since that time, as far as the Baron was aware, the world had heard nothing from the Dark King.

But now . . . yes indeed, the Dark King's demons. Amintor thought that he could smell them in the air. Vilkata always had demons with him.

While the fanatical youths were muttering among themselves, trying to decide what they ought to demand of him next, the Baron looked around the sky apprehensively.

He was recalled from this concentration on what he considered more serious matters by a fresh challenge from the stocky youth, who now sat holding the reins of Amintor's riding-beast as if uncertain what to do with them.

The Baron glowered at him. "What did you say?"

"We insist upon an oath of loyalty," the youth repeated grimly.

It was Amintor's turn to blink. But then he laughed. "An oath? Why not? Have you a formula devised, or would you like me to create one for the purpose?"

This provoked open disagreement among the self-appointed committee of conformity.

The Baron let them argue for a time among themselves. Then, interrupting further fervent, quasi-religious babble, he inquired of them firmly: "And just where, at this moment, is that flawless divinity, the Dark King we all adore?"

None of the young enthusiasts seemed to detect the mockery in their elder's tone. They looked at one other with helpless expressions; it seemed that no one in the small group had any real idea of where their divine leader could be found, or what he might be doing.

One of the band finally suggested, humbly, that their great Master might be in the palace.

Amintor, casting a wary glance in the direction of that tall building, made a face of disgust upon noting that Vilkata's bodyguard of demons were at least intermittently in evidence. Half a dozen or so of their half-material shapes could be seen flitting in and out of the upper windows. He decided that he would rather not go there just now—unless the Sword of Chance advised him to do so.

Yet again he drew and tried his Sword, half expecting the magic of the gods to warn him to move in the opposite direction from the palace; but Coinspinner was quiet in his grip. Doubtless, Amintor thought, the demons were relatively harmless just now. After a few buildings had been flattened in sheer demonic exuberance, and some key prisoners taken if that proved possible, the Mindsword's holder had doubtless given orders that his new and soon-to-be-useful human subjects and other property were not to be molested.

A new clamor jarred him from his private thoughts. Now several of the little band of youths, their faces alight with sudden inspiration, were daring to demand of him his Sword—now that he had called their attention to it.

Again, the Baron's mind had been elsewhere, and he had to ask for the demand to be repeated. "What?"

"I said, that looks like a good sword you have there. Hand it over, in the name of the Most High King."

The Baron favored with a mirthless smile the one who made this demand. "No, my Sword you will have to take from me by force." Doubting that any of this slack-jawed crew had yet recognized the true nature of his weapon, he added: "But in fairness I warn you, making any such attempt would be a serious mistake."

Only one persisted in demanding that he give up the Sword. And Coinspinner, working more silently than dice, saw to it that the offender was punished for his temerity without any effort on Amintor's part. A loose stone bigger than a fist came tumbling from the parapet of a half-ruined building to strike the fellow's head a glancing blow, and bang his shoulder. When he lurched in his saddle and cried out, his riding-beast reared up and threw him to the street.

Disregarding this warning—or perhaps unaware of cause and effect—the stout youth, utterly intent and sincere in his fanaticism, persisted in his attempt to challenge Amintor. At this the old man boldly claimed acquaintance, even hinted at strong friendship, with these people's new god.

"I enjoy already the privilege of acquaintance with the magnificent, the, the indescribable—how shall I put it?—the ineffable Vilkata."

A claim so bold caused the last challenger's companions to withdraw a little from him, looking worried.

Amintor in a firm voice dared them, if they really doubted he knew Vilkata, to put the matter to the test.

That overawed, even if it did not entirely satisfy, the last fanatic. The Baron knew that if they were really convinced he was a danger, a menace to their new god, they would have fought him and his magic Sword to the death, to the last man or woman; and in that event Amintor had no doubt that, despite the odds and his advancing age, Coinspinner would see to it that he was still unscratched when none of the others were still on their feet.

But in the end matters did not come to that. The Baron's arguments, as usual, proved convincing. Presently the little band moved on and allowed Amintor to do the same.

As soon as he was free to move about again without harassment, the Baron's own demeanor changed, with a facility worthy of a skilled diplomat.

For the next half hour or a little more—while the sun finally cleared its high eastern horizon of oceanic fogbanks, to glare down pitilessly upon the wounded capital and its dead bodies—Amintor wandered the city. When he thought himself about to be once more challenged as a stranger, he went into an act, contorting his face and waving his arms like one in ecstasy, pretending to be enthralled like the most ardent of those he beheld around him.

Slowly, traversing a zigzag course through several nearby streets, he completed an entire circuit of the palace and its grounds. The uneven new flag of black and gold hung limply from the highest tower. The great stone edifice itself, now plainly visible from every angle, appeared to have suffered more from the attack than most of the rest of the city. Baron Amintor could see where some of the bars protecting the lower windows had been torn aside. Structural damage was apparent, a forcible entry had been made upon one of the higher levels, as by something that could fly and was heroically destructive.

He smiled thinly, wondering if any of the royal folk inside had survived the night to become the Dark King's prisoners. Whatever else was happening, there would be real satisfaction in seeing the proud rulers of this land brought low.

At this point Amintor observed some of the first gatherings of Vilkata's hostages, a ragged formation of a few score folk, largely women and children, being rounded up by a demon and herded, shuffling and limping, toward the palace.

It was obvious that a sizable minority of the group were converts, for they were going willingly, in fact were earnestly singing some improvised hymn in praise of their transcendent Master, even as they flinched, averting their faces from the stalking figure of the demon who had them in his charge. The majority were helpless captives, herded by demons and by stern convert guards.

The Baron stood motionless, watching the ragged little procession out of sight. He wondered for precisely what purpose these Tasavaltans had been conscripted. Not for labor, for there were many poor specimens among them, and a number of powerful demons available if Vilkata wanted heavy work accomplished. It would seem that he wanted hostages.

And now there was no doubt that demon-smell, far more psychic than physical, hung in the air. Amintor sniffed, and shivered.

Demons aplenty, but no great number of human soldiers. In fact the visitor could see none at all but Sword-converts of passionate but precarious loyalty.

Opportunity waited in this city, Amintor was more than ever convinced of that—Coinspinner would not have led him here for nothing. He would have a lot to offer in a partnership with the Dark King. And Vilkata, if his power here was to have any permanence, would soon have to base it upon something more than magic and demons.

ELEVEN

A S the sun burned its way through the last of the morning's high fog, Amintor wandered rather aimlessly about the city, getting no clear direction from Coinspinner, remaining in sight of the palace but not approaching it closely. He told himself that his Sword's seeming indifference, the fact that it was giving him no advice and arranging no meaningful chance encounters, simply meant that he was in the right place. All he needed to do for the time being was wait.

His saddlebags had gone with his riding-beast, but at the moment he had no need for any of their meager contents. When a need for anything arose, Coinspinner would provide.

Presently, feeling somewhat tired and hungry after his long ride, Amintor seated himself on a bench, hailed a street vendor whose enterprise had not been totally discouraged by recent events, and ordered some breakfast: hot tea, fried bread, and broiled fish, the latter fresh-caught here in this seaport.

The vendor's pushcart shop-on-wheels was not the only business establishment now open. There were increasing signs that at least an imitation of normal economic activity was getting under way. Also the Baron observed that an improvised body-wagon was beginning to make the rounds, staffed by white-robed acolytes of Ardneh—it would be interesting to see what the Dark King tried to do with the White Temple—picking up the casualties of the hours just past. A Red Temple, a tall, narrow brick building with hedonistic statues writhing and posturing across its façade, was also among the first businesses to open, the click and whirr of gaming wheels starting to sound from inside the main room on the ground floor.

All in all, the city was now giving an impression of starting to come awake from its nightmare, of pulling itself together—to some extent. Not that conditions were back to normal, or anywhere close to that. Still, the Baron saw many people putting aside weapons, beginning what must be their daily routines, despite the glazed and wary look in their eyes. Probably, thought Amintor, observing carefully, some who were not really Mindsword-converts were pretending that they were, thinking thus to protect themselves against attack. And perhaps real converts were playing the game the other way, as *agents provocateurs.*

Hundreds, it seemed, were discarding and burning garments and flags of blue and green, making up new ones out of black cloth and any yellow fabric that might pass for gold.

Still other folk, as if exhausted by noisy demonstration or activities still more energetic, sat quietly now, their hands and garments sometimes smeared with blood, their faces numb and blank, as if they might be considering the inner meaning of their lives.

The Baron, while munching on his bread and broiled fish, made use of his time to do some thoughtful considering of his own. Looming large was the fact that he himself had been in the city for a couple of hours now but was still unbewitched. The most likely explanation of that, of course, was that the Mindsword's influence had only passed over these people and moved on elsewhere; Skulltwister was no longer on the scene, or at least no longer drawn and active.

Another possible explanation, one Amintor considered much more unlikely, was that he was being individually protected by some magic of a potency equal to that of Shieldbreaker—if any such equality could be imagined.

Had Coinspinner somehow, without his knowledge, obtained for him immunity to Skulltwister? The Baron shook his head. He thought the chance of that extremely remote, though he could not rule it out absolutely. In general the Sword of Chance provided protection by keeping its possessor away from danger. Coinspinner had brought him here to Sarykam, and so here he ought to stand in no great peril.

The thought of Shieldbreaker reminded Amintor that the Sword of Force was, or had been, generally thought to be in Sarykam, under the control of Prince Mark. Well, if so, the Prince had obviously not been able to get his hands on it in time to save his city. If several Swords had really been kept here in the palace armory, as was popularly believed, a successful surprise attack might have captured one or more of them.

The Baron's thoughts drifted. What he had always wanted, really wanted in his heart of hearts, was the chance to be a general—better yet, a field marshal; to command a victorious human army, to win or at least have a fighting chance of winning the great game of power, the struggle in which for forty years all the Swords had played such a central part.

And over the past several months the Sword of Chance, coming suddenly into his possession like an answer to his prayers—not that he had really offered any prayers—had allowed him to realize his dream, at least as far as forming the army he had wanted.

As for being able to lead his army into battle, well, he supposed that wish would be granted him, in the Sword's good time.

It occurred to the watching Baron that other travelers must be approaching the city this morning, as on any other morning, and that a few of these, at least those with the strongest reasons for doing so, must be actually entering, despite all the obvious signs of disaster.

In fact he was soon able to observe some of these, who with evident trepidation were making their way to a place near the central square. The Baron watched with measured interest as at that point they came to grief through not being quick enough to emulate the fanaticism by which they now found themselves surrounded.

Amintor's natural disinclination to interfere with whatever

was happening to the victims was not disturbed by any counsel of his Sword. Coinspinner lay inert at his side.

Sipping tea from the vendor's cracked mug and trying to better understand the situation, the Baron made an effort to mentally reconstruct last night's events here in the capital. It seemed to him that Vilkata, armed with the Mindsword and doubtless accompanied by his usual swarm of demons, must have launched his sneak attack upon Sarykam no more than a few hours ago. Then the Dark King, having quickly secured the palace and achieved his own apotheosis in the hearts of a key segment of the population, must have given orders to take hostages. Having taken that precaution he had himself moved on, no doubt in pursuit of Mark or other enemies. And, of course, Vilkata would have taken Skulltwister with him.

It seemed likely that the conqueror would be returning to his conquered city fairly soon. Certainly the Dark King knew as well as anyone how impermanent were the Mindsword's spells; unless they were renewed every couple of days, Vilkata would stand in serious danger of losing his grip upon the capital.

With these facts in mind, Amintor looked up at the skies, frowning, alert for the sight of demon or griffin with the Dark King on its back, the rider with a gleaming, cheering Sword in hand. Skulltwister bothered him. The Baron was ready to accept risks, even high risks sometimes, but he had a chronic terror of falling under the Mindsword's spell. Often enough he had seen what that weapon did to others.

He turned his head sharply to study a new disturbance at ground level. Here came another little mob of chanting fanatics, marching down the street right past his bench. The Baron stared back at them coldly as they went by. He shivered slightly, and felt for the reassuring black hilt at his side.

Well, he supposed he could continue to rely on his own Sword for indirect protection—and for more than that. Coinspinner had guided him to Sarykam, and he thought it must have done so to help him achieve more than mere survival.

Everything the Baron knew about the Sword of Chance suggested to him that opportunity for great gain or advancement, perhaps of several kinds, abounded here in this conquered city. Now, if only he could determine how best to take advantage of the occasion . . . .

But naturally Coinspinner would show him how, if he only gave it the chance.

Amintor started to sip his tea again, then impulsively threw half a cup of the vile stuff away. Getting to his feet, he limped about again. He felt it was time to be moving.

Several times in the space of the next half hour he consulted his Sword, trying to attract as little attention as possible in the process. Each time he frowned at the negative result and strolled on. In his own perception he was doing little more than killing time; but as far as he could tell, the Sword of Fortune, giving him only slight indications or none at all, was advising him to continue.

An hour or so after breakfasting, the Baron was sitting in a sidewalk shop, imbibing still more hot tea—this of slightly better quality—and waiting for opportunity to present itself. The state of keyed-up alertness in which he had entered the city had long since faded; nature was asserting herself, and he was beginning to get sleepy, having been in the saddle most of the night. The tea at least was helping him to keep his eyelids open.

Then abruptly Amintor was jarred to full wakefulness. The voices around him had suddenly taken on a new tone. He became aware of an accelerated swarming and gathering in the streets, a concerted movement finally involving thousands of people, all converging upon the central square before the palace. The normal business of the day, tentatively begun, was once more being put aside.

Amintor reacted decisively, getting swiftly to his feet and moving with the crowd. Proceeding at a fast limp, sometimes almost running, he wondered whether he should draw his Sword again. But he decided that was unnecessary for the moment, as Coinspinner had certainly brought him here. He allowed himself to be carried along.

The stream of people in which he moved joined other streams, from other streets, all eddying in a great pool across the central plaza. The Baron drew in his breath sharply upon recognizing, despite the distance, the virtually unmistakable figure of the Dark King. The tall, blind albino had come out on one of the second- or third-level balconies on the high palace of gray stone. There was the usual half-visible blurring of demonic presence in a small cloud above the wizard's head, and Amintor thought—though it was difficult to be sure at that distance—that he could see small bandages in several places on Vilkata's body.

Rapidly the enthusiastic crowd—if Amintor's private calculations regarding the number of converts were correct, the throng must be heavily augmented by folk only pretending to be converts—pressed forward, gathering as closely as possible underneath the balcony. There were thousands or tens of thousands of people now, looking up with evident awe and worship. When Vilkata's distant figure gestured that they should be still, they fell for the most part into reverent silence.

Amintor, cheering and falling silent in tune with those around him, felt somewhat uneasy, despite his own firm grip on the hilt of the Sword of Chance. He considered prudently working his way back through the crowd to the far side of the square; but surely the Mindsword's power, if it should be drawn, would extend that far.

He took some comfort from the fact at the moment neither of Vilkata's pale hands were holding any Sword, though there might well be one sheathed at the man's side.

Vilkata soon began an oration, of which Amintor could

hear no more than a few isolated words because of the fresh outbreak of screaming the speech provoked among the multitude—until the people's god once again, more sternly this time, commanded silence. Once he was perceived as being serious on that point, a deathlike hush fell over the assemblage.

With relative quiet established, Vilkata in his smooth, deep voice at first complimented the mass of his followers on the zeal they had so recently displayed in hunting down and killing anyone suspected of still adhering to the cause of the old royal family. But in the next breath the Dark King sounded a different note, saying that the time for such random slaughter had now passed—all the citizens of Sarykam were to be considered valuable assets in his cause, except, of course, for any unregenerate scoundrels who proved unwilling to serve.

Turning from side to side upon his balcony, waving both arms to acknowledge the renewed cheering of his worshippers, Vilkata from time to time revealed the dark hilt of a Sword at his side.

Now the speaker let his hand rest on that dark hilt. The crowd roared anew. Amintor, watching, nervously continued to assume that this was the Mindsword.

The Baron knew a chill of fear. *If he should draw Skulltwister again right now, I'm lost . . . .*

But Coinspinner, by whatever means, was evidently still doing an adequate job of looking after its owner; or else some other tremendous power was on the Baron's side. For though Vilkata's hand stayed resting on the dark hilt, he did not draw his Blade.

The Baron, forcing himself to relax again, mused that Coinspinner might very well have brought him here for the very purpose of becoming the Dark King's partner; what he had told the fanatics earlier had contained more than a grain of truth. The two men had in fact worked together in the past.

And the Sword of Chance seemed to confirm this idea as

soon as Amintor tested it. The magic-laden tip of Coinspinner twitched decisively in the direction of Vilkata on his distant balcony.

Granted this seeming encouragement, trying to put thoughts of Skulltwister out of his mind, Amintor began to use his bulk to work his way in that direction.

Meanwhile Vilkata, even as he stood looking out over the adoring throng, found himself obsessed by the idea that every one of these folk now offering him such frenzied adoration would very shortly be starting to come out of the Mindsword-fog. A few of them—and the thought was enough to give him chills—might be already faking their devotion. The very first defections, he surmised, had occurred already. They would have begun within a few hours of Skulltwister's smashing, an event now some eight hours in the past.

Perhaps the most urgent problem that he faced was that there were very few humans whom he could even begin to trust on any basis other than enslavement—and, at the moment, none of those people were within a hundred kilometers. Demons were useful in many ways, sometimes invaluable, but that race certainly had its limitations.

The Baron, having managed to consult his own Sword once again as he kept pushing his way through the crowd—his actions with that formidable weapon earned him a few suspicious looks from people around him—persevered in his bold effort to approach the Dark King.

The closer Amintor got to the balcony, the more his progress was disputed. Trying to elbow one's way through a throng of jealous worshippers was inherently dangerous. A murmur went up, then an outcry, at last enough of a disturbance to attract the attention of the Eyeless One upon his balcony. The Baron gestured with his free hand, and called out. A guardian demon, watchful, came buzzing overhead.

Vilkata's demonic vision was evidently acute, for a moment

later he had recognized Amintor and was shouting orders for
the crowd to make way; and once the Master's will was made
known to the crowd, they instantly complied. Very quickly the
Baron was pushed and drawn into the palace, then, after some
further delay marked by arguments among converts, he was
conducted to Vilkata's side.

It was unnecessary for Amintor to climb all the way to the
balcony, for Vilkata in his eagerness had come down from it
to meet him in an intermediate room. On first coming into
each other's presence, the two men hailed and greeted each
other warily, though with considerable show of good fellow-
ship and enthusiasm.

Vilkata at once felt confident that Amintor was not under
the Mindsword's influence; certainly the Baron's manner,
while respectful, was vastly different from the adoring attitude
of those by whom the two men were surrounded.

The Baron, as if he could deduce what thoughts were running through the Dark King's mind, stated the fact explicitly.
"I am here by my own decision, Majesty."

"I am glad to hear it . . . some years have passed since we
have seen each other. You look healthy and prosperous."

"Indeed, too many years, Your Majesty."

Vilkata's eyeless gaze fell to the black hilt at the other's side,
which Amintor was making no effort to conceal. "What brings
you to Tasavalta, and to this city, Baron, at this auspicious
time?"

"With your permission?" Amintor—taking care to move
his hand very slowly and cautiously—drew Coinspinner, just
enough to let the Eyeless One have a good look at the hilt.

The pale brows above the empty sockets rose. "Aha! So the
Sword of Chance has counseled you to come this way—I take
it that your arrival in the city was quite recent?"

"Shortly before dawn, Majesty." Amintor was wincing involuntarily, making a not entirely successful effort to ignore the close proximity of the Dark King's demons.

The Dark King smiled in amusement, then scowled fiercely. "Do they bother you, my little pets? Hey there, Arridu, Pitmedden—all the rest of you—stand back a little! Give this, my partner, room to breathe."

At once the noisome cloud of demons, their looming presence, became, gratefully, less obtrusive.

Amintor raised a not completely steady hand to wipe his forehead. "My thanks," he said sincerely, "and my apologies for any inconvenience. But such creatures inevitably make me feel a little sickish." He did not mention the other side of his concern, which was not directly for his own personal welfare, rather that one of the pets out of sheer exuberant malignity would attempt to play some prank upon him, and Coinspinner, active at his side, would somehow blot the foul thing out of existence in a twinkling. Which would not endear the Baron to the Dark King.

Vilkata shrugged, dismissing the subject of his pets and guardians. He stood waiting, evidently considering something very thoughtfully.

The Baron seized what seemed to be an opportunity. "Your Majesty, I have never been one to hide my intentions in clouds of rhetoric. With all respect, I propose that you and I form a partnership—you, of course, to be the senior."

The Dark King did not appear to be at all surprised by the offer. Better, from Amintor's point of view, he was immediately receptive to the plan, spreading his arms wide in a slow gesture, as if to say: It is accomplished! Not bothering with any coy pretense of reluctance. He confessed that he stood in need of relatively trustworthy human assistance.

Not that the Dark King gave the impression of begging for help. Far from it. Vilkata's willingness to take a partner was surely the confident seizing of an opportunity, not an act of desperation. A sixth sense warned Amintor that something in the situation remained unexplained. "But, Majesty, if you have the Mindsword, surely recruiting people to serve you is no problem?"

All human onlookers, prodded by demons, had withdrawn to a distance of a room or two. Vilkata, taking the Baron by the arm familiarly, began to stroll with him along a marble hallway. Their boots clopped almost in unison, drawing rich echoes from the stone.

The Dark King said quietly: "Since we are partners now, I'll keep no secrets from you. Alas, I have it no longer."

"The Mindsword? Ah!" Amintor stopped in his tracks.

"The fact is that no one does." And Vilkata related in a few terse words the basic facts of his skirmish in the armory— leaving out, of course, the great fact of the abject terror he had experienced.

He concluded: "At this moment I am in possession of perhaps a thousand enthusiastic human converts, for a few days more—perhaps for no longer than a few hours, in some cases. You know, Baron, how these things work."

"Indeed, I have some passing acquaintance with the effects of all the Swords. And your demons? To what degree, if I may ask, will your control of them be altered?"

The Dark King shrugged, then explained that it was not the fact that his demons would soon be free of Skulltwister's spells that worried him the most. Vilkata had been dealing with demons almost all of his long life, and he considered himself magician enough to handle his present crew, even without the Mindsword in hand to set the ultimate seal on his authority.

But controlling people was in many ways more difficult.

Amintor nodded. Then he asked: "If Skulltwister has been smashed, Your Majesty, then what Sword is it that you now wear at your side?"

Vilkata smiled faintly. "Another reason we may hope for ultimate success." And he allowed the Baron to see the small white hammer on the hilt, and gave some indication of how he had so recently come into possession of Shieldbreaker.

Now Amintor could understand the confidence.

When some minor details of the partnership had been concluded by mutual agreement, the Dark King—naturally confirmed in his expectation to be senior partner—now in effect getting his hands on Coinspinner, began to consider out loud whether it might be better to smash it right away.

When the suggestion was made, Amintor was horrified.

The Dark King yielded the point. He admitted that it seemed preferable, almost essential, at this stage of affairs, to get all the help the Sword of Chance was capable of giving. For one thing, it could be an invaluable help in finding the other Swords and eventually getting them all out of circulation. Not to mention Coinspinner's usefulness for other purposes as well—for example, in finally disposing of Prince Mark.

The partners quickly agreed that Coinspinner's first assigned task ought to be tracking down Prince Stephen—or whoever else the lonely warrior in the armory might possibly have been.

Amintor, struck by what he considered inspiration, drew a deep breath and announced that he was presenting Coinspinner freely to his new senior partner as a gift. With a dramatic gesture he actually unbuckled the swordbelt and held it out.

Vilkata was immediately wary of such generosity; the hideously smooth, pale face, eyeless but very far from blind, pressed a silent and suspicious query.

The Baron was smoothly reassuring, and disarmingly frank. "In the first place, Your Majesty, I could not, even supposing that I wanted to, use this weapon against you, armed as you now are. And in the second place, the Sword of Chance has been with me now for many months; as you know at least as well as I, there's no telling when it might fly away of its own accord. Therefore it seems to me that the best use I can make of it right now is to cement our bargain."

And he handed over the sheathed weapon.

He was right, suspicion had not been allayed. Vilkata, reaching out as if to accept the great gift, gave it only a symbolic touch, then pushed the Sword of Chance right back to the giver.

Both partners considered themselves to be in a position of great strength, armed with Shieldbreaker and soon to have available Amintor's army, which was still offstage—now Amintor had to tell his new partner about that asset as well.

Just like the old days, Vilkata commented, smiling. Amintor agreed. The old days when they had sometimes worked together.

Neither man chose to remind the other that in the old days the relationship had sometimes been far from smooth.

TWELVE

T HE partnership agreement was soon concluded with a
formal oath, a vow of mutual loyalty rather hastily and
mechanically recited by both parties, and solemnized by the
sacrifice of the small child of a servant, willingly donated by
its convert parent. The formalities being thus concluded, the
Dark King called his new colleague into a private conference,
inviting him to breakfast on the least damaged of the palace's
rooftop terraces. The Baron, still faintly belching the street
vendor's fried bread and broiled fish, accepted automatically.

No more than half an hour after Amintor had entered the
palace, the two men, quite alone except for the ubiquitous
demon Pitmedden, were comfortably seated under a summery
arbor of grapevines, on an architectural elevation which gave
them a view of the ocean beyond the red rooftops of Sarykam.
It seemed plain now that the surrounding city was not going
to burn after all, in any wholesale way, though here and there
a diminishing column of smoke still rose from among the
roofs.

The Dark King gave orders to his guardian demons, and to
his new human aides, that he and his new colleague were not
to be disturbed at their conference, save for the most serious
emergency.

Vilkata had also seen to it that the convert servants waiting
on table were magically rendered deaf, in a selective fashion,
that they might hear table orders and yet learn nothing of
importance—just in case they survived long enough to be
deconverted.

These details out of the way, Vilkata settled himself in his
chair at the head of the table. "Now, Baron. Tell me about this
army you claim to have. Where is it now, and how strong?"

"No mere claim, Majesty." Amintor began to explain in

circumstantial detail about the current disposition of his forces, just where and how his people were encamped, in certain well-watered meadows not far outside the borders of Tasavalta. There were some five thousand fighting men, plus auxiliary magicians, and several hundred flying reptiles of diverse sizes and subspecies.

Vilkata did not appear to be entirely convinced. Amintor was aware that his former associate cultivated an attitude of rarely approving anything enthusiastically, of never really trusting anything that he was told. The Dark King said: "Such a force must have been difficult for any individual, no matter how wealthy and talented, to raise—and it must be hard to maintain in the field."

"Oh, quite impossible, Your Majesty—except for this." And the Baron tapped the black hilt of Coinspinner, now so luckily restored to his side.

"Of course." The Dark King went on to wax somewhat enthusiastic about all he was going to be able to achieve, in the way of further conquests, with a reasonably reliable army at his disposal. "With Shieldbreaker here, and Coinspinner now as well, I think we may say conservatively that we have good grounds for optimism."

"Indeed we do." And Amintor raised his fruit juice in something like a toast. Suddenly he had to struggle to keep from yawning. He had spent a long night in the saddle, and was now well into what promised to be a long and busy day.

Not that Vilkata was openly discussing all his assets. He continued to keep secret one he considered among the most important—the Old World spacecraft he had ridden from the Moon and now had stowed and waiting in a certain cave little more than an hour's ride south from Sarykam along the coast.

Amintor, of course, did not suspect anything of the kind. But in the privacy of his own thoughts he was congratulating himself on his success in keeping a certain secret of his own.

* * *

Having indulged briefly in mutual congratulations, the partners turned urgently to planning.

Vilkata seemed to consider seriously the possibility of leaving Amintor in charge in the city while he himself took personal command of the pursuit of Mark's young cub, Prince Stephen. It was important that the enemy not be allowed to retain Sightblinder.

His junior partner inquired: "This lone opponent you faced down in the armory—that must have been Mark's offspring Stephen, hey?"

"So it seems."

The two men were casting back in their respective memories, calculating how old Mark's younger son must be by now. The result was not complimentary to the Dark King's image as a conqueror. "A mere stripling—you are sure that he's the one?"

All the evidence pointed that way. Karel, still trembling with a convert's emotions, almost weeping, was called in to testify again about the current whereabouts, as far as they were known, of the members of the Tasavaltan royal family. Yes, all the available evidence indicated that the Dark King's anonymous opponent in the armory must have been young Prince Stephen.

Arridu—who was still safely under the Mindsword's influence, the Dark King was sure—was also called in for consultation. This time, on joining the two men, the demon took for himself the image of an elderly and grave enchantress.

Arridu stoutly denied that anyone answering the description of young Prince Stephen had been near when the demon picked up Shieldbreaker. There had been only a few inconsequential citizens of the neighborhood—"and, of course, the person of Your Glorious Majesty."

There was a little silence before the Dark King reacted. *"You thought I was there?* I assure you I was not."

A complete explanation of the powers of Sightblinder, followed by lengthy persuasion, was needed to convince Arridu that his glorious Master had certainly not been on the scene when the Sword of Force was captured.

The Dark King rubbed his temples, and said for the fourth time: "I tell you, you did not see me—you saw an image cast by the Sword of Stealth."

Amintor interrupted to point out that, whatever images had been seen, Stephen's presence at the demolished house of his grandparents seemed to be confirmed by the fact that the demon's banishment had been effected at that place—only the Emperor's children, and, apparently, grandchildren, could hurl away demons with such authority. And it appeared highly unlikely that Mark himself had been there.

Another problem loomed, seeming at least equally as pressing as the search for Sightblinder. Within twenty-four hours Amintor, assuming he was still present, would be the only human being within a hundred kilometers who was not the Dark King's bitter enemy.

Vilkata, toying with the black hilt of Shieldbreaker at his side, cast a sardonic eye at the figure of the elder convert standing patiently beside the table. "How soon will you become my enemy again, old Karel? Another three or four hours perhaps, before your faith begins to weaken? Another entire day, before you are completely apostate?"

The stout old man was shaken, hurt, insulted. "Never, Master! I had rather die first. And I refuse to believe that our people will turn on you, now that it has finally been given to them to know the truth."

"Your confidence is touching," the Dark King remarked drily. "See that you do die before you waver—I will make sure of that—but it occurs to me that I will have another mission for you to accomplish before your loyalty begins to flag."

* * *

In fact, as Amintor now remarked, the two of them and Vilkata's thousand or so converts were already surrounded by swarming enemies—all of Tasavalta who had managed to remain out of the Mindsword's range before that weapon was destroyed. These people would soon recover from the effects of the lightning attack and begin again to be effectively organized. Moreover, the great majority of the converts, however fanatical in the Dark King's cause they might be at this moment, were, within a matter of a day or so, going to become his bitterest enemies of all.

After brief discussion King and Baron had to agree that Amintor would almost certainly find it impossible to hold the city without Coinspinner. The Baron's army was still more than a hundred kilometers away and could not possibly arrive in Sarykam before the majority of the converts relapsed. Add to this the difficulty that Amintor had no skill in the control of demons. If the Dark King were to proclaim this man his regent in command of Sarykam, surely what remained of the city's population, hostages or not, would revolt and murder him long before Amintor's own force could reach the city.

On the other hand, if Amintor were allowed to keep Coinspinner, he would probably succeed at holding the city or at practically any other task—the Sword of Chance could work miracles of good luck. But then Coinspinner would not be available to help run down the escaping Prince.

Arridu or other demons could not very well be sent in pursuit of Stephen, because Stephen had already demonstrated his power of exiling their kind. Of course, if Arridu were given the loan of Coinspinner for the task, then unlucky things might be expected to start happening to Stephen at once, to arrest his flight or at least slow him down.

Vilkata soon came to one firm decision: that he himself had better stay in Sarykam. With Shieldbreaker in hand, and his demons and a large number of hostages all at his disposal, he felt confident of being able to maintain his grip upon the capital. Baron Amintor would be allowed to retain the Sword of Chance, and to him would go the job of running down the Princeling.

Amintor agreed that this was probably the best way to manage things. Privately he was well pleased with this arrangement, because it allowed him to keep the Sword of Chance. His intention, as soon as he should be alone again, was to consult Coinspinner once more, with an exclusive view to his own self-interest.

Still mulling over the problem of how best to achieve his own advantage, the Dark King nibbled absently at his elaborate breakfast while he continued his conference with the Baron. Meanwhile the selectively deafened palace servants, naturally all converts desperate to please, plied their god and his new second-in-command with hot tea, fruit juices, and the finest viands from the palace cellars. There was also some fine wine on the table, but both men sipped it only sparingly.

When the Baron got to his feet to stretch and stroll about the vine-shaded terrace, he found himself overlooking one of the palace courtyards into which the thousand or more hostages had been crammed. The murmurous voices of these victims rose; Amintor could hear some of them still singing the hymn to their new god. Well, in a day or two, that at least was going to change rather drastically.

All exits from these courtyards had been blocked off—some magical provision for sanitation had probably been made—and above each of the enclosed spaces a minor demon crouched like a stone gargoyle, sleepy-eyed but watchful.

Staring at the table before him, Vilkata remarked almost wistfully that this would probably be the last peaceful meal either of them would be able to enjoy for a while. The burdens of leadership were immense.

"Immense!" Amintor agreed, matching his senior partner's mood.

They toasted each other and their joint enterprise, sipping some of Prince Mark's fine wine.

During this time old Karel was kept in silent attendance, like one of the table-servants—except that his hearing was left intact.

"What are we to do with this one?" the Baron asked, after a while.

The Eyeless One smiled faintly. "Something special, I think—there's no great hurry we have many hours yet before his faith could possibly begin to waver. Perhaps he should go with you on your search. With Coinspinner at your side, that should not take you many hours."

Amintor nodded. And yawned. He had been in the saddle all night, and his first breakfast had not entirely agreed with him. He fought against yawning and remarked that he wanted to get a couple of hours' sleep before setting out to hunt the enemy who seemed still to be equipped with Sightblinder. He was far too experienced a campaigner not to prepare methodically, even when time was pressing.

"Anyway, there's no great hurry. He'll not be making very good time out of the city."

The Dark King looked a question.

Amintor smiled faintly and tapped the dark hilt of the Sword of Chance.

"Oh. But of course."

When Vilkata, a moment later, wanted to know whether the Baron had yet formed any plans for the search, Amintor pushed back his chair from the table and drew and consulted his Sword. Coinspinner gave him a northwesterly direction in which to begin his search for Sightblinder and the youth who was presumably still carrying it.

Amintor would have liked to consult the Sword on another matter—what direction his army should take, on its forthcoming march to Sarykam—but could not think of a way to frame the question so Coinspinner would answer it.

Vilkata, when informed of this difficulty, only shrugged. "Actually there are several questions I would like to put to the Sword, but I cannot think of any way to do so." Of course, it was hopeless to try to obtain guidance, beyond the indication of some physical direction, from the Sword of Chance. In that respect the weapon shared largely the same virtues and limitations as its fellow Sword, the late lamented Wayfinder.

The Dark King frowned when Amintor, now yawning helplessly, repeated his suggestion that he really ought to get some rest before starting after Stephen. Still, the fact that Amintor, no longer young, had been up all night could not be ignored.

"I have a better idea," his senior partner stated.

He, Vilkata, would treat his junior partner to a magical stimulus; privately Vilkata thought that the spell would probably wear the old man out in a few days, but ought to spur his aging body to two or three days of quasi-youthful vigor.

The administration of a powerful wake-up spell was simple as child's play for a magician of the Dark King's caliber. The business was conducted with little ceremony, and with no need for additional sacrifice, right at the breakfast table. Vilkata gave his subject no information about possible long-term effects, but Amintor wondered privately if this stimulation was good for his no-longer-youthful heart.

While the conqueror of Sarykam and his new partner continued their business on the palace roof, Prince Stephen was awakening—the feeling was more like that of regaining consciousness after an injury—under a hedge in the garden of Ben of Purkinje's house, the heat of midday sunlight on his back.

He had not rolled over, indeed he had hardly moved a muscle, in the course of his badly-needed sleep.

Now, slowly, he did turn over, and presently sat up. Stretching stiffened joints and muscles, he looked for, and soon found, some water to drink—there was a garden fountain still burbling merrily, as if the peaceful world had not turned upside down.

Close around him birds sang, and a squirrel climbed a tree in summer foliage. Although this grander house, like his grandparents' cottage, had been smashed, the world was still here, it still had peaceful parts, and he was in it. Remembering last night's events, Stephen felt confident that the Mindsword must have been truly destroyed. And as for Shieldbreaker, perhaps the enemy really did not have it yet. Maybe in his swelling anger he'd hurled that demon to a year's distance, or two years', as his father had. That would at least give people who were demons' enemies time to prepare.

Casting an eye at the elevation of the sun behind a barrier of leaves, the young Prince knew a lesser twinge of guilt for having slept so long, and determined that if possible he would not rest again until he had reached his parents.

Also, he was ravenously hungry. He realized now that he hadn't even eaten very much yesterday, during his long work session in the armory.

Stephen understood it would be necessary to provide himself with transportation before he went outside the city walls, and also to acquire some provisions for the journey.

Trusting in Sightblinder's power, knowing that unless he should run directly into Shieldbreaker in the enemy's hands he had little to worry about, the young Prince had no difficulty in moving freely about the streets to obtain what he needed.

Back in the street, he appropriated a fine riding-beast from a joy-screaming convert who could not get himself out of the saddle quickly enough once Stephen, no doubt perceived as the great Dark King himself, had indicated an interest in the animal.

After this acquisition—while the former owner accommodatingly held his new mount for him in the street—Stephen entered shops untended in the city's chaos, where he helped himself to some food and a water-skin. He felt in his pocket for coins to leave in payment, realized he had no money, and decided that in the circumstances it did not matter. Coming out of the last shop, he filled the skin with water at a public fountain.

Meanwhile he continued to observe the condition of the city around him, and his mind raced in an effort to assess the situation clearly. Though still nagged by the minor physical injuries he had sustained in his first skirmish with a demon, the young Prince had been recovering mentally ever since he had been separated from Shieldbreaker.

Stephen remembered from his father's teaching that the effect of the Mindsword dissipated only gradually. The young Prince realized that, even if his belief that the Mindsword had been demolished was correct, all of the humans recently brought under its influence would probably remain in that hideous condition for at least a day, more likely several days to come. In some cases, where the person was naturally susceptible, the madness might persist much longer or even become permanent.

Remembering last night's confrontation in the armory, he felt sure now that at least no one need ever again fear falling under the Mindsword's control. He was sure now that Skulltwister was gone; and whatever else might happen, he would feel proud to the end of his days that his hand had dealt the blow of its destruction.

Before Stephen could travel more than a few blocks from the house of Ben of Purkinje, his riding-beast pulled up lame.

Bad luck, he thought, bad luck. Well, it should be easy enough to obtain another animal.

As Stephen got down from the saddle, he stepped accidentally upon a pebble in the street, twisting his ankle painfully.

Meanwhile, the roof-top conference, where Amintor sat thinking about Stephen and toying with the hilt of the Sword of Chance, was not yet over. The two partners still sat at the table, old Karel standing beside them, the elder's helpless eyes fixed with an expression of seeming contentment upon something in the far distance.

Vilkata was saying that it was imperative that Amintor, even before beginning his search for Stephen, dispatch marching orders to his army.

"My swiftest demon will convey them—I presume you have some capable wizard in your camp? At least one who can hold intelligent converse with a demon without retching or fainting?"

The junior partner assented meekly. "I am served by several who are more than merely capable, Majesty—though, of course, none of them approach your stature."

The Baron went on to assure his partner that his army was waiting for orders, that it was ready to march, to fight lustily, to conquer, in whatever cause he might choose to assign it. The five thousand or so fighting men and male and female enchanters, and those commanding their associated beasts of war, were purely mercenaries.

The need to continue to feed, maintain, and inspire this army provided a strong argument that Amintor ought to be allowed to retain the Sword of Chance.

A force of only five thousand men would be ineffective if scattered around the countryside. Both men agreed that Amintor's army, or the bulk of it, ought to stay together and march to Sarykam as quickly as it could—doubtless it would prove necessary for the men to fight their way in across the Tasavaltan frontier. At the moment there were no large Tasavaltan units known to be in position to block such an invasion, but certainly spirited resistance could be expected, especially after word reached the frontier patrols of the disaster at Sarykam. Therefore the success of the invasion could not be automatically guaranteed.

Vilkata spoke of being ready to employ his demons more energetically and of devising further schemes to get as much use as possible out of his converts before their usefulness should turn to treachery. At the proper moment he would dispatch such a ground-air force to join with the reinforcements soon to be approaching in the form of Baron Amintor's army.

And Amintor voiced his approval of Vilkata's gathering thousands of hostages.

Within a matter of a few minutes, the new partners had dispatched a demonic messenger carrying a handwritten and personally identified note from Amintor, complete with personal token, to the experienced officer the Baron had left in command of his five thousand or so men when he himself had gone following Coinspinner off to Sarykam. Acknowledgment of the message could be expected within the hour, if all went well.

Amintor was gone to prepare for his Sword-hunt. The Dark King, still seated at the table, with crushed husks of fruit around him, turned his eyeless countenance up to Karel, who still stood by faithfully. "Well, old man?"

"Sire?"

"Tell me something—profound—about the Swords. You are still loyal to me, for a little while as yet, and you know as much or more than any human about this handiwork of Vulcan. I am interested in how you foresee the course of the Great Game."

Karel hesitated. Then, gazing into the distance, his voice grown vaguer and softer than ever, he stated that anyone keeping track of such things must realize that if this recent rate of Sword-destruction should persist, the time was fast approaching when a majority of the gods' weapons would have perished from the Earth.

Karel noted also that the balance between destroyed and active Swords was now approaching the point of even numbers. Townsaver, Doomgiver, Dragonslicer, Wayfinder, and the Mindsword all were gone. But there still endured Stonecutter, Woundhealer, Shieldbreaker, Coinspinner, Farslayer, Soulcutter, and Sightblinder to tempt and afflict humanity.

Vilkata in turn revealed to the helpless Karel his plan ultimately to gather all the remaining Swords, acquiring them by one means or another, one by one, and as soon as possible destroy them, retaining only Shieldbreaker, the maximum weapon, for himself.

"Destroy them all," the uncle of Princess Kristin muttered. "Destroy the Swords."

"Yes, old man. I tell you it seems impossible to impose true order on the world as long as they exist."

Vilkata's long-range plan, on his return from the Moon, had been to do his best to conquer and rule the world with one Sword—preferably the Mindsword, which he had then possessed. But now, with a smile of satisfaction, he said to Karel that it was probably just as well things had worked out as they had. Shieldbreaker was superior to Skulltwister. Because, among other things, having the Sword of Force made possible a systematic attempt to annihilate the rest of the output of Vulcan's forge.

THIRTEEN

A MINTOR, energized by the powerful stay-awake magic so efficiently administered by his senior partner, paced the alley and yard behind the palace stables in a swift restless limp, barking impatiently at nearby converts, damning their clumsiness, demanding they bring him a totally acceptable mount—he'd already rejected two riding-beasts as looking spiritless. In some ways the stay-awake spell had made the Baron feel twenty years younger, but in other ways he had retained his age; his joints still ached, and he found himself puffing when he began to pace too rapidly.

It was now around midday, the sun as close as it was going to get to overhead, and the Baron had not slept for approximately twenty-four hours. He could remember this fact clearly, but the lack of sleep seemed to carry no mental or physical impact. At the moment weariness and rest were among the farthest things from his mind.

Foremost in his thoughts at the moment was the impression that the Dark King's convert and demon forces, despite their relatively small numbers, were tightening his grip on the city with fair efficiency. From where the Baron paced, he could both see and hear the hundreds of hostages crammed into one of the sealed-off courtyards nearby. More prison-voices came floating up out of the heavily barred ground-level windows behind which a dungeon had been improvised. More hostages were constantly being brought in, and Amintor wondered vaguely where Vilkata thought he was going to put them all.

At this moment old Karel, who had been detailed to accompany Amintor on the hunt for Stephen, came stalking out of the palace to talk to the Baron while they both waited for the routine stable preparations to be completed. Amintor was eager to bring Karel with him on the search for Prince Stephen. Certainly the old wizard, Princess Kristin's uncle, was well acquainted with Prince Stephen and with the city. Also he probably knew as much about Sword-magic as anyone in the world—except, of course, the inimitable Master. It would be a pity to waste that knowledge. The Baron thought that in the remaining hours of the old man's life, before Karel's conversion began to wear off and it became necessary to dispose of him, his help could be invaluable.

Now a fresh sound of hooves echoed sharply from the walls of stone enclosing the stable-yard. With glad cries a lackey announced that the Baron's own riding-beast had just been located, and now it was being brought back to him.

Amintor, a vein swelling in his forehead, waved away this gracious present with an oath, startling and upsetting the convert who'd hoped ardently to be helpful to one so exalted as the Master's partner. The Baron, hand on Swordhilt, shouted to the convert lackeys that he wanted a fresh animal, not one already run half to death. Surely the Tasavaltan stables offered a number of good choices?

Attendants scurried to satisfy his demands.

Now Amintor and Karel both flinched, as there came an unwelcome swirling of nauseating presences about their heads; both were well aware that the Dark King had assigned a pair of demons to accompany them on their search. The announced purpose of having the creatures on the search for Prince Stephen was to provide a swift means of communication with Vilkata; but Amintor had no doubt that they were also under orders to keep an eye on him for their Master. There appeared to be no good way for the men to get rid of the unwelcome creatures.

At least, Amintor supposed, the foul things ought to be constrained to obey his orders, or most of his orders, and he could keep them from hanging over him like poison mist. "Take some approximation of human form!" he snapped.

In a moment the poisonous-looking mist had coalesced into shapes of solid appearance. The foul fiends now appeared as a rather ugly manservant and his wife, standing beside the humans in the stableyard. The Baron was relieved to find that they obeyed him.

Now the last members of the search party arrived—an escort of human converts armed mundanely. These were a squad of regular Tasavaltan soldiers, augmented by a few civilian volunteers. Mounts were soon provided in sufficient number— even for the demons, though they certainly could have kept up on foot—and all was at last in readiness.

The search party, the Baron leading with Coinspinner in hand and vibrating, cantered out through one of the great gates of the palace.

Stephen, meanwhile, had been unable to make any headway at all in his effort to return Sightblinder to his parents. A series of unlucky happenings had prevented the young Prince from even leaving the neighborhood of Ben's house.

The bad luck had been so pervasive that the fugitive had already begun to suspect strongly that the Sword of Chance must be in action against him. The second mount obtained by Stephen had run away, and the third had also been disabled before it could be ridden any meaningful distance. Fortunately he himself had suffered no additional injury; evidently whatever individual enemy was being served by Coinspinner did not want the young Prince dead, or seriously hurt—the idea, simply and ominously, must be to keep him where he was.

Exhaustion soon set in, and Stephen slept again, once more lightly concealed among the bushes of Ben's garden, stretched out upon the flat of Sightblinder's blade.

Stephen awakened from this second sleep to find that his most recently lamed riding-beast was nuzzling at the back of his neck. He turned over and began a mumbled protest, then suddenly pushed the animal's head aside and sat up straight. Ten meters away, a small band of mounted men—two of them looked to be more or less than men—had come riding into the extensive walled garden of Ben's house. They were halted now, ten meters away, shifting uneasily in their saddles and looking at the young Prince with expressions he could not immediately interpret.

In the next moment Stephen realized that one of the mounted men was Karel. Another of them, who looked as old as the Tasavaltan wizard, held a Sword half-drawn from the scabbard at his side. *Coinspinner,* the young Prince realized suddenly, his perception sharpened by the magic of his own Sword. He could only hope that the Sword of Chance, powerful as it was, could not recognize Sightblinder as an opposing factor, and would not be able to deal with it effectively.

Amintor and those with him, led to this spot by the Sword of Chance, had reined in sharply on catching sight of the figure among the bushes. Looking toward Stephen, the members of the search party saw—never doubted they were seeing—the Dark King himself, Vilkata, now rising from an inexplicable prone position to his feet, then swinging himself up into the saddle of a restive griffin.

The pursuers, gazing at a collective image of Vilkata— whom they visualized as holding in his hand the Sword of Force—were taken aback, perturbed, to see that the Master had evidently got ahead of them somehow to this unlikely place, and even gave the impression that he had been waiting for them.

"Master?" Karel called tentatively.

The young Prince experienced a moment or two of hideous fright before that word reassured him, informed him of exactly who his discoverers thought he was.

* * *

. More than one of the searchers were thinking it odd that Vilkata, with a whole palace and its people now at his disposal, had chosen to come into an enemy's garden and lie down alone under a hedge—but still it did not occur to any of them to doubt for an instant that they were really looking at Vilkata.

Amintor, wishing to hold converse with his senior partner, moved as if to urge his riding-beast a little closer.

But instantly, to his amazement, the Baron's own Sword, twitching and tugging in his hand, warned him sternly not to advance.

Warily Amintor reined in his mount. Then he began, from a respectful distance, to issue a hopeful report on the progress of the pursuit of Stephen, with some additional remarks on the gathering of hostages.

In the eyes of those hunting him Stephen's lamed riding-beast still appeared to be a saddled demon or griffin; but now the animal moved uneasily, and the lad hopped down from the saddle briskly before he could be thrown. It seemed to the beholders that their Master was now minded to stay with them for some serious discussion.

Meanwhile the young Prince was doing his best to think what his next move should be. He understood with a pang that Karel was still under Skulltwister's spell. Stephen had heard of the adventurer Baron Amintor, though never actually laid eyes on him before, and, aided by Sightblinder's enhanced perception, he thought he recognized the Baron now. This identification was confirmed when Stephen heard Karel address the scoundrel by name, in tones of respect that Stephen found sickening.

When Amintor momentarily urged his mount forward, Stephen made ready to stab the man as soon as he came close enough—after making as sure as possible that this enemy wasn't armed with Shieldbreaker.

For a moment Stephen hovered on the brink of swirling away the two demonic members of the search party—but he held back, fearing to reveal his own identity and accomplish nothing. It would be better, much better, to kill the Baron if he could . . . and there was Karel. If only he could find some way to set the powerful wizard free . . . .

Of course, as Stephen fully realized, great caution was necessary in opposing, let along trying to kill, anyone who was holding Coinspinner. Until now, the bad luck inflicted upon him by the Sword of Chance had been minimal, a mere holding action sufficient to prevent his escape. One of the facts that had been drilled into the young Prince during his lifelong education in the matter of Swords was that killing someone armed with the Sword of Chance was well-nigh impossible, and trying to do so was a good way to attain an early end oneself.

Meanwhile Coinspinner in the hunter's hand was continuing to behave erratically. That weapon was now signalling its owner to keep back, remove himself to an even greater distance from the dangerous illusion that he faced all unaware. The rest of Amintor's party started uncertainly to move with him.

Stephen called: "What are you doing?"

The Baron, hearing the words in the Dark King's commanding voice, hesitated briefly. But then the obvious explanation for his own Sword's peculiar behavior occurred to him.

He replied as calmly as he could. "Of course Your Majesty is armed with Shieldbreaker—I suppose that's why Coinspinner here is giving me erratic signals." Patting his black hilt, Amintor peered more closely at the figure before him. Still, no suspicion that he was not looking at Vilkata found room in his thoughts.

The young Prince was silent, thinking furiously of what he

ought to say and do. He was afraid, but not so much of men or demons as of failure, of losing another Sword as he had lost Shieldbreaker . . . .

The guilt of that loss now struck Stephen with renewed force. Now he knew beyond any doubt that Vilkata—who was, fortunately, not here—must indeed have been given Shieldbreaker by the demon.

The Baron meanwhile had begun to deliver a kind of non-report, in respectful tones, from the back of his riding-beast, and from a timid, rather inconvenient distance.

Stephen, listening, soon had confirmation, if any were needed, that he himself was being eagerly sought by the enemy.

But he could see that Coinspinner was even now urging its owner to retreat. Why—?

And then, in a flash of revelation, Stephen understood.

"Baron!" He tried to make his voice that of a tyrant who tolerated nothing less than instant obedience—he could only trust that Sightblinder would help him to succeed. "You will hand over Coinspinner to me. Now."

Amintor's mouth fell open at this belated acceptance of his earlier gift, even as the Sword of Chance redoubled its signals advising him to beat a swift retreat—but the Baron, totally convinced that he was confronted by Vilkata with Shield-breaker, this once did not take his own Sword's advice.

He had planned no specific treachery against Vilkata—as yet there had hardly been an opportunity to do so. And now it might well be that he was doomed. The Baron concealed his own rage and desperation behind a smile. It would be useless to disarm himself and try to leap upon the Dark King—one of the fanatical converts watching jealously would skewer him in an instant, or a demon's claws would find his flesh . . . .

As for the Dark King's demand, the Baron had no choice but to comply, swallowing his own anger, for the time being, as best he could. With shaking fingers Amintor began to unbuckle his swordbelt. Then he dismounted and carried the treasure to his lord.

Feeling the double burden of Sword-magic once more come upon him as he did so, Stephen grasped the black hilt of the Sword of Chance, letting sheath and belt fall free. He needed guidance, required all the help that he could get. His brain once more buzzing and swirling with the psychic burden of two Swords, he decided uncertainly that he ought to kill this man—though it was going to be hard to do that in cold blood.

He was given an even better reason to hold back. The Sword of Chance itself, as soon as the young Prince began to raise the heavy steel to deliver a killing blow, tugged at Stephen's arm, unambiguously directing him to let Amintor live.

Obeying this tugging indication by the Gods' Counselor, the young Prince pondered what he ought to do with the Baron and his unpleasant cohort, if he was not to endeavor to wipe them out.

Roughly he demanded of their leader: "So, you have not found the young Prince yet?"

The shaken Amintor had rejoined his party and was climbing back into his saddle. "No, sire. We have hardly started—"

"Never mind. Abandon that pursuit. I have new orders for you."

Stephen had the satisfaction of seeing Baron Amintor's assurance crack momentarily, this elder warrior blink at him in astonishment and poorly concealed fear. After a moment the Baron ventured: "But Majesty, what of the Sword the young Prince Stephen still carries?"

"Do not dispute my orders!"

"Of course, you are the senior partner. But—" Then Amintor quailed. "What are the new orders?"

Again imagination flagged, and Stephen was momentarily

stuck. Then inspiration flashed again. "What would you expect them to be? Use your head, man!"

"I—I— to rejoin my army. To see that my forces reach and
occupy Sarykam as swiftly as possible."

"Clever. Good thinking, Baron. Would you like me to provide demonic transportation for you?"

The Baron declined that offer.

"One more thing, Baron. The wizard Karel will stay here
with me."

"As you wish, sir. Of course."

Karel, delighted to be allowed to serve his new god directly,
stood worshipfully beside the image of his Master, while Amintor and his remaining escort rode out of the garden and out
of sight, starting on the new mission.

Back in the palace, the Dark King was pondering intensely
his problems and his opportunities. He understood that Arridu, as well as his squadron of lesser demons, were likely to
remain under the Mindsword's lingering influence for only a
few more hours at most. His only prudent course from now on
would be to assume that all his demons had thrown off Skulltwister's yoke.

Fortunately for himself, Vilkata had never been forced to
depend entirely on the Mindsword when dealing with Arridu's
race. He had taken care to establish an independent magical
control over his demonic cadre. Even after the Mindsword's
influence had faded, the vicious creatures would still be constrained to serve him, as many another mighty member of
their race had been in the past.

The Dark King thought that, of course, the difference between demons in an ordinary tamed condition and those
under the Mindsword's bondage was that in the former case
it was not totally unthinkable that the foul creatures should
turn treacherous. In fact it was almost certain that, sooner or

later, one of Arridu's strength would make the attempt to do so.

Vilkata's thin lips smiled faintly. He, the Dark King, if anyone, knew how to manage demons.

And he judged that an opportunity had now arrived for him to satisfy at least in part his curiosity about the Swords.

The fact was that Arridu, until very recently a stranger to the Swords, was still not totally convinced of just how incomparably strong those weapons were. In fact Arridu, going along with his Master's wish to rid the world of most of them, announced that he could manage that.

"You? Are you saying that you by your own powers can break a Sword that was forged by the gods themselves?"

Arridu, projecting an image of serene power, was quietly self-assured. "I see no gods about me now."

"They have been vanquished. Exterminated."

"But I have not." Truly it seemed that the great demon did not believe that any mere artifact of metal and magic, whether forged by a god or not, could resist his strength.

The Dark King, staring at his most powerful vassal, nodded slowly. He was in a mood to accept this challenge. He thought he could be certain of the outcome.

Vilkata considered that there had always been difficulties, certainly, in the way of any plan to destroy all the Swords. Not the least of these obstacles being that the only known means of permanently eliminating any Sword, the only method by which any had yet been demolished, was by bringing the Blade of lesser strength into violent opposition with Shieldbreaker.

At least that was the consensus of knowledgeable opinion. Vilkata, wavering somewhat in his assurance, questioned on the point by the confident demon, had to admit that he wasn't at all sure how often Sword-smashing had seriously been *tried*.

* * *

Descending into the airy cellars of the Tasavaltan armory to try it now, Vilkata gave Arridu full permission, nay, commanded him, to do his best to obliterate or at least damage Stonecutter. To swing a heavy blacksmith's hammer right at the keen edge, with superhuman strength.

For the purpose of this test, Vilkata ordered the Sword of Siege to be set up in a vise on a handy workbench, under an Old World light. Arridu selected a hammer, the biggest and hardest available from the armorers' shop in an adjoining room, and, after warning his Master to take cover, wielded the tool with all his strength.

This effort produced impressive pyrotechnics, a stunning blast and a ruined hammer, but no detectable damage to the Sword.

Arridu in baffled rage, and his Master in restored confidence, inspected the result carefully. Not the finest chip or nick marred even the very thinnest edge of Blade.

"Let it stay there, in the clamps." And Vilkata raised Shieldbreaker, whose muttering drumbeat swelled. In another moment, Stonecutter had perished, in a blast whose flying fragments left the Dark King totally unscathed.

In the course of their subsequent discussion about the surviving Swords, Arridu calmly assured his master that he knew where the Tyrant's Blade was to be found.

Vilkata became very still, staring at the great demon, who had now assumed the likeness of an elder sorceress. Pitmedden buzzed like a great fly beside the wizard's head. Vilkata demanded: "Soulcutter? Do you know what you are saying?"

"Oh, indeed, Master, indeed I do. Now that you have taught me about the Swords, Master, I can understand certain events on the Moon which for the past twenty years have puzzled me."

"And what events were these?"

"Those surrounding the visit, to a site near our place of

imprisonment, of a man whom I can now identify. It was he who is called the Emperor, and he brought with him a certain object, and he caused that object to be there buried, deep, deep in lunar rock, where once volcanoes flowed; and he sealed the burial with mighty spells and other sealings."

Vilkata demanded more details, and Arridu was ready to provide them. Though, of course, the demon could not answer every question, Soulcutter, it indeed appeared, had somehow been carried to the Moon. Piecing together what Arridu now told him with certain facts he had long known, Vilkata decided that the deadly toy must have been put away there by the Emperor some twenty years ago.

Still Vilkata had scarcely moved since Arridu's claim, and promise, first fell upon his ears. The human wizard mused: "Aye, that would have been like him—the Great Clown, the matchless hypocrite. Saving Despair to use it, for his own advantage, later." Vilkata chewed his pale lower lip.

The speech of the elegant, gray-haired lady's image was soft, utterly reassuring. "And I know where it is, great Master. Say the word, and that weapon shall be yours."

The Dark King thought for some time. Suspiciously he at last replied: "When the time comes, you will return there with me and show me where that Sword is buried, and help me remove such obstacles as may keep me from it; but it will be my hand alone that takes control of that Sword, or any other we may find."

"It is easy to see, great Lord, how that Sword might be of inestimable value to your cause."

"Indeed."

Whenever the Dark King perceived the Sword of Despair, in reality or in imagination, the symbolism of his special vision presented that weapon to him as a narrow pillar of darkness, radiating tendrils of negation, stifling light and movement, hope and purpose, everywhere nearby. So, in his mind's eye, he visualized Soulcutter now . . . .

Yes, that Sword was what he needed to set in motion the perfect plan for domination.

It would, of course, be folly *for anyone not armed as well with Shieldbreaker* to simply draw Soulcutter, thus exposing oneself to its deadly, corrosive power, along with all other humans, beasts, and demons within a long bowshot. But Vilkata *was* armed with the protective Sword of Force. He could walk unharmed, untouched, amid despairing armies.

And there would, of course, be other ways to use the Sword of Despair intelligently. For example, to arrange for it to be unsheathed in the midst of an enemy army. For example, give Soulcutter to Mark or his associates, to some person among them who could be fooled or persuaded into drawing Despair at the right moment . . . .

Oh yes, the tactical details would all have to be calculated very carefully. But the Dark King had no doubt at all that he could manage them.

An hour after Vilkata had dismissed Arridu from his presence, another conference took place, this one between Arridu and Amintor. It happened in the latter's tent, while the Baron was resting, somewhere well outside the city, after the first few hours of the wild-goose chase he had been sent on by Stephen.

Outside, around the tent, Amintor's escort, all unaware of his visitor's arrival, were going on about the routine chores of camp. The Baron felt seriously sickened by the close presence of this thing which had intruded its presence upon him.

The demon, becoming aware of this reaction, caused itself to be perceived as having withdrawn to a somewhat more comfortable distance—the tent having apparently elongated itself rather strangely. Also, Arridu took the non-threatening appearance of a simple peasant, some prosperous small farmer who might have come to discuss the sale of an allotment of potatoes.

"Thank you." Amintor wiped sweat from his forehead, not bothering to try to conceal the action, or the discomfort which had caused it.

The gray-stubbled peasant, sitting easily on a camp stool with fingers interlaced across his ample paunch, remarked that he, Amintor, had never been a slave of the Mindsword.

"True. While you, of course . . ."

"I have been subject to such enthrallment, but for the past few hours I have been free. The weapon called Skulltwister has been smashed—doubtless it could not have held me much longer in any case."

The Baron moistened his lips and tried to appear comfortable. "He has, of course, instructed you to say that you are now free. To try my loyalty."

"No. You know the Mindsword's spells must fade with time. And I can prove what I say." The peasant-demon, settling itself in as if for a leisured talk, went on to inform the man of how he, the Baron, had just allowed Sightblinder in young Prince Stephen's hands to make a fool of him. "But I have not mentioned your failure to the great fool, who thinks I am still bound to him by a broken Sword."

The Baron, staring at the lifeless gray eyes of his informant, felt a chill as the conviction grew in him that for once a demon was telling him the truth: He had indeed been fooled by the Sword of Stealth in the hands of the Tasavaltan princeling.

The demon, as if it could read his mind, nodded slightly. "Your partnership with the Dark King—such as it was—is already ruined. Therefore, Baron, you had better seek to make some other arrangement for your own survival as soon as possible."

Arridu, originally somewhat contemptuous of the Swords, had been forced to concede that they must be respected. To cope with the Sword of Force he needed a human ally, or tool—someone with the nerve and knowledge necessary to wrestle Shieldbreaker away from Vilkata. Ideally, this human helper would be a non-magician, who could be dealt with more reasonably thereafter.

The Baron seemed an eminently suitable choice. The man possessed both nerve and knowledge, and would therefore be worth some effort at persuasion. Amintor was somewhat physically decrepit compared to the magician, the much greater age of the latter having been more than compensated for by magic. But in this wrestling bodily strength was not a requirement.

Amintor, listening to the demon's proposal without yet committing himself, appreciated the skill and daring with which the plan had been made. At the same time, he felt extremely reluctant to agree to anything of the kind without what he considered some enforceable guarantee of his role in the new partnership to follow. Second place in any partnership was generally good enough for him; he was not a man who really wanted to be supreme dictator.

And—wasn't there some relevant old proverb? If not, there ought to be. Only a lunatic, the Baron thought to himself, would ever willingly become a demon's partner.

The question was whether he, Amintor, really had any choice.

"Then I am with you," he said at last, trying to make the agreement sound hearty and whole-hearted.

The tent restored itself to normal interior dimensions as the peasant got to his feet, his small eyes twinkling. "Of course you are," the demon said reassuringly.

"When do we strike?"

"That has yet to be decided. Probably the next time you and the Dark King are together. But let the coming-together be his suggestion and not yours."

Arridu agreed with the Baron that Amintor at this point had best go on trying to rejoin his army.

When the thing was gone, Amintor once more stretched out, shakily this time, to try to get some rest. He wondered whether Vilkata's wide-awake spell was going to keep him from sleeping altogether.

Dozing, or trying to doze, the Baron also considered privately whether it was yet utterly hopeless for him to make a deal with Prince Mark and his royal wife, or with Stephen if and when he encountered the lad again. Amintor was quite ready to ally himself with Tasavalta, for the time being at least, if other choices seemed unsatisfactory. And the Tasavaltans, their capital in enemy hands, were in no condition to be too choosy about their allies.

Darkness was falling outside his tent. His minor demons and his hapless converts went about routine activities. If only he could sleep.

FOURTEEN

THE compact realm of Tasavalta lay for the most part green and beautiful, in sunny early afternoon, some twelve hours after Vilkata's surprise attack on the capital, Sarykam—and approximately two hours after Stephen had confronted Baron Amintor and relieved him of the Sword of Chance.

Ben of Purkinje—massive, heavily muscled, scarred, graying and ugly Ben, who was a couple of years older than the Prince and looked a little older still—and Prince Mark, companions since their early youth, had ridden together out of the village of Voronina before dawn, feeling the urgent need of a scouting expedition in the direction of the city.

Mark was wearing Woundhealer at his right side, and at his left, just in case of untoward encounters, a mundane sword of comparable size and weight, an efficient killing tool.

Captain Miyagi and his small company of soldiers had remained in the village with Princess Kristin, as had the beastmaster and his trained animals, with the exception of one day-flying bird-messenger that went with Mark. In expectation that Vilkata's invading forces would soon renew and extend their assault, the understanding was that the Princess would, at some time during the day, move her field headquarters to a different village. If all went well, her husband, having completed his reconnaissance for the time being, would soon join her there.

Mark and Ben, long familiar with each other's thoughts, had little to say as they cantered toward Sarykam. The morning was well advanced by the time they came in sight of the city's familiar walls.

At this point the pair encountered a handful of people, good Tasavaltan citizens, but now with the look of refugees about them, carrying homemade bundles and wearing expressions of bewilderment. One couple pushed a laden cart built to be hauled by animals. All of these people recognized the Prince on sight, and most of them knew Ben as well. All told at length of the devastation in the capital, and several were eye-witnesses of Vilkata's demons taking hostages by the hundred.

One man had heard a rumor that the Mindsword had been destroyed, but that all the weapons in the armory were captured by the foe. Another rumor was that Vilkata had been slain; and there were less happy rumors concerning things that might have happened to Prince Stephen. The father of the young Prince, well aware of the unreliability of tales in wartime, managed to hear these last without giving any overt sign of great dismay.

Leaving the refugees to settle their concerns of food and shelter for the coming night, Ben and Mark moved on a little way. They were considering whether to approach the city more closely, when in a suburban street one of the death squads dispatched by Vilkata against Mark, half a dozen Tasavaltan converts sent out as assassins, recognized the pair and attacked, shrieking their glorious Master's name.

Some of these men were literally frothing at the mouth with the violence of their hatred, with their joy at the prospect of killing and dying for the Dark King.

Ben had only a moment's warning, but that was all he needed. He met his attackers with considerable skill and overwhelming strength. Knowing that Woundhealer was available, in his partner's hand, made it possible also to fight with an unusual recklessness.

Mark, standing back-to-back with his huge ally, engaged in peculiar Swordplay—every time he thrust home with Woundhealer, or even nicked one of his attackers, the bright steel of his Sword brought swift healing, recovery, to the Mindsword's victims.

First one attacker then another, bloodlessly slashed or neatly skewered, staggered back, dropping weapons, moments later crying out in horror at their own behavior.

The first men so efficiently de-converted were in moments hurling themselves upon their former comrades, grabbing at sword-arms, trying desperately to stop those still under Skull-twister's spell from pressing the attack. The odds in the fight had soon shifted dramatically.

Those injured soon received Woundhealer's swift, sharp blessing, some of them two or three times before the fighting stopped.

In a minute the skirmish was over. After a last round of healing, wiping away whatever wounds Mark and Ben and their opponents had incurred in the deadly business, the Prince, breathing heavily, sat down on a curb to rest. Ben, gasping even more loudly, had slumped beside him.

"I am going," Mark said presently, "back to rejoin the Princess. There will be decisions to be made, and I must learn what reports have come in from around the country. Will you come with me, or scout some more? I leave it up to you."

Ben thought it over for a few more gasps. "I will stay here, or move closer in, toward the palace, and learn what more I can learn. Send me a messenger-bird or two when you can."

Mark nodded. The Prince took Woundhealer with him when he departed to rejoin Kristin. But he left with Ben a freshly acquired squad of de-converted Tasavaltan soldiers to aid him in scouting out the city and trying to establish an organized resistance.

Ben ordered his de-converted squad back into the city, where, without his easily identifiable presence, they could pretend to be still carrying out Vilkata's orders. A tentative plan was made for rendezvous.

Ben himself waited alone for a few hours, indoors in an abandoned suburban house, till darkness fell—then he cautiously advanced, passing inside the city walls without trouble, through an abandoned gate. He was increasingly consumed with the urgent need to find out what had happened to his home, and to his wife and daughter.

It was no secret that Ben had been on poor terms for years with his wife, Barbara, and in fact months had passed since his last visit to his home—or house—in Sarykam. But since the horrible news last midnight, he'd discovered that this degree of estrangement gave no immunity from fear and grief. For years he'd not seen much of his and Barbara's only child, their grown-up daughter Beth, but now he knew beyond any doubt that Beth's fate was still of great importance to him.

It had also crossed his mind that young Prince Stephen, supposing he had somehow escaped the palace, might have come to Ben's house looking for help.

From a block away, Ben saw the ruin of his own dwelling— the upper floor completely gone—without surprise. He knew, without particularly worrying about the fact, that it was extremely dangerous for him to be here in the city, especially in the vicinity of his old house. He did not doubt that the destruction which had claimed this building and much of its immediate surroundings had been meant for him primarily.

Meanwhile, the afternoon had worn on for Kristin, in another little village much like Voronina, but with a different name, and closer than sixty kilometers to the capital, lying outwardly tranquil under a complacent sun.

In this new village Kristin had relocated herself and, thus, the royal headquarters. By midafternoon she was waiting anxiously for, among other things, her husband to rejoin her.

Kristin had not been brought up in a farmer's house—far

from it. But she had learned long ago to put up with much worse, when necessary. Today, like most of the village women, she was wearing trousers and loose shirt of homespun.

The owl which had brought the royal couple their first word of the disaster in Sarykam had come with her to this village and was even now sleeping the remainder of the day away in one of the barns, a bulky alien presence making the pigeons nervous. The Master of Beasts, considering that he had done everything useful that he could do for the moment, was catching a nap there too.

The central village square, enclosed on four sides by rows of little houses, was quiet except for the usual domestic noises of fowl and other farmyard animals, including a barking dog or two.

Surrounding the small settlement, which consisted of no more than a score of houses, were fields now lush with summer crops, demarcated by hedgerows. A range of coastal mountains loomed blue in the distance. The people, like most of their compatriots more or less accustomed to the occasional presence of Prince and Princess, were today for the most part going about their usual affairs, though with uneasy faces and many pauses to search the sky.

Mark, about an hour after leaving Ben, came riding into the village, returning about on schedule from his reconnaissance.

His wife made no great demonstration at Mark's appearance, but to anyone watching her closely, her sudden relief was intense and obvious.

Mark agreed with his wife's suggestion that he get some rest now, while he had the chance. He'd been up since the alarm was sounded, since very early that morning.

For the last few nights, back in Voronina, he had shared with his Princess the tiny spare room—perhaps the only such chamber in Voronina—of a prosperous yeoman's house. This new village was even smaller, and Mark guessed there would be no spare rooms available.

When the Prince had seen to it that his mount was stabled, and heard such reports as had come in during his absence— they seemed of little importance—he lay down in the shade of a tree. The Prince felt comfortingly at home among these country smells and sounds and people. He had grown up in a small village not that much different from this one, and at no enormous distance either, though the home of his birth had not been Tasavaltan.

An hour later, after a sleep troubled by strange dreams, Mark was up again, standing near the middle of the small village plaza, anxiously scanning the afternoon skies, hoping for another winged messenger. Even more bad news—provided it was not too bad—would be, in a way, some relief.

For both husband and wife this waiting, with no knowledge of what the limits of the ordeal were going to be, gave promise of becoming a supreme test of patience. The hours since the first word of the attack had seemed endless, a desert of time to be got through in which it seemed impossible to do anything useful, or anything at all but wait.

As the afternoon wore on, with shadows lengthening, it became impossible for Mark, and Kristin too, to sit without doing anything. While continuing a desultory conversation, the royal couple were soon at weapons' practice, sharing a single battle-hatchet for the purpose. The sound of the thick blade's impact on the trunk of a dead tree echoed repeatedly from the flat house-fronts of mud brick and wood. Soon some of the simpler villagers came to stand gawking in the background. Soon Captain Miyagi came to join the onlookers.

Those who had stopped to silently judge the skill of Prince and Princess, some of them with expert eyes, were favorably impressed. The arm drawn back— swiftly, not giving an enemy a chance to dodge—and then snapped forward. *Thunk!*

First Mark's long powerful legs (next turn, Kristin's, somewhat shorter) strode restlessly toward the target and back again, his (or her) right arm swinging the recovered weapon in a practiced hand.

This time it was Prince Mark who spun around and threw. Again the sharp blade thudded home. Small chips flew from where previous cuts were intersected. Mark's aim was good, mechanically good. Another day or two of waiting, he thought, and the target tree was going to be chewed away to nothing. But no, they would have to relocate once more to another village before that much time had passed.

And every few moments he raised his head, as did his Princess, to scan the skies, on watch for an attack by demons or flying reptiles, but particularly for more news.

One of the problems reviewed by the royal couple while practicing with physical weapons was that of how to obtain the best possible magical help, and as soon as possible. If only Adrian were finished with his studies and were here . . . but in fact Adrian was not ready, and not here, and it was not possible that he could be of help just now. Thank Ardneh, the older son at least had not been taken by surprise, as the younger must have been, in Sarykam.

Karel, too, was ominously out of communication, like everyone else the royal couple had left behind them in the supposed safety of their capital.

At least General Rostov, traveling in another province at the time of Vilkata's attack, had now checked in, sending a messenger with some reassuring word about mobilization there.

Kristin and Mark by now had convincing evidence that Vilkata was the author of this latest disaster. The plenitude of demons in the assault had suggested as much. Refugees' information, such as Mark had now heard first hand, provided more solid evidence. It was true, then: The Dark King had returned to the attack, bringing with him the Mindsword which had been in his possession two years ago when he was hurled away. The Prince could remember all too well the horrible events of two years past, on the night of Vilkata's previous attack, which had resulted in the Dark King's banishment and also Kristin's injury.

In the hours since the first news of the disaster had reached the Prince and Princess, the couple had endeavored to keep up each other's hopes regarding their younger son, still unaccounted for in Sarykam. Their best grounds for optimism lay in the facts that Stephen was more often than not level-headed and responsible for his age—and that he had been granted access to the Swords.

The mother and father of Prince Stephen, once more scanning the skies together waiting, hoping, for the next messenger-bird to appear in the sunset skies, repeatedly assured each other how good it was that they had given their young son that much of a chance.

Holding frequent, almost continuous consultation with his Princess, Mark, since the news had arrived, had been making plans—most of them, so far, necessarily only tentative. Which way would Vilkata move now? Was a fresh assault to be expected upon some other part of the realm?

He was also trying to lay the groundwork for effective countermeasures, as more reports about Vilkata's assault, each in itself fragmentary, reached him. But there was as yet almost nothing he could do, beyond sending warning to everyone with whom he was able to communicate by messenger, that the Mindsword was in the city and the place must therefore be avoided.

Mark most especially wondered what had happened to the Swords in his armory.

It began to be possible for Mark to believe the rumor he had heard concerning the Mindsword. Though Skulltwister had undoubtedly been present last night in the capital, Vilkata was no longer pressing his attack with the enthusiasm that might have been expected had the Blade of Glory been still available. Of course, the Prince dared not disregard the possibility that the horror could be reimposed at any moment.

And Mark's and Kristin's worries continued unabated regarding Stephen, as well as Mark's parents, Jord and Mala, who had been the only other members of his immediate family in Sarykam at the time of the latest attack.

FIFTEEN

M OMENTS after Stephen had shouted his last order at them, Amintor and his search party had departed from the walled garden in the middle of the ravaged city, leaving the young Prince alone with the still-befuddled wizard, Karel.

Stephen, still enduring the renewed burden of a Sword in each hand, stood staring with perplexity at his Great-Uncle, who gazed back at him—rather, at a spot just over Stephen's head—with all the solemnity of confident worship. The young Prince was about to appeal to Coinspinner for help in dealing with this problem when the Sword of Chance suddenly twitched of its own accord. Then it tugged again, the direction unmistakable. It was guiding Stephen to one of the side gates in the garden wall.

Both hands still filled with black-hilted magic, Stephen stepped unsteadily along the indicated course and leaned on the gate to open it. Looking out into an alley, he saw two people half a dozen meters away, both of them frozen in watchful attitudes. Their faces, turned toward him, were studies in controlled fear. Immediately Stephen recognized his cousin Zoltan, a sturdy, brown-haired young man of twenty-four, and the Lady Yambu, a gray but relatively youthful fifty-three. Both were armed and on foot, wearing common pilgrim gray.

Over the past several years Yambu and Zoltan had developed a relationship resembling that of mother and son. They had been out of Tasavalta a great deal, often traveling together on one pilgrimage or another. Meanwhile they had remained on close and friendly terms with Prince Mark and the rest of Mark's family, and it was not surprising that both of them had been in the vicinity of Sarykam when Vilkata's latest attack fell upon the city.

Karel, now doubly deluded, trying to be watchful and protective of his great Master, had followed Stephen to the gate, and was frowning out over his shoulder.

The four people held their tableau for a long, silent moment in which Sightblinder helped assure Stephen that neither his cousin nor the lady were Mindsword-converts. But the lad quickly realized that they might well be seeing him as Vilkata and trying to play the role of faithful slaves.

Actually Yambu's first look at Stephen had shown her the image of the Emperor; but then that form shifted, back and forth, in swift alternation with Vilkata's. At the same time, Sightblinder's magic held her enthralled, prevented her from realizing the scope of its deception. Understanding little more than the fact that something magical and out of the ordinary was taking place, she glared back proudly at the latest image of the Emperor, and stubbornly refused to speak.

Zoltan was seeing the Dark King too, but interspersed with fleeting glimpses of a certain mermaid, a creature of importance in his past. Stephen's cousin, quietly stunned, like Lady Yambu remained silent for the moment.

Stephen, naturally enough, was first to recover from his surprise. Fiercely he ordered Karel to go and stand guard at the other end of the garden, the far side of the grounds surrounding Ben's ruined house—then the young Prince put aside Sightblinder long enough to joyfully disillusion his newly-arrived friends.

Before the three could do more than begin to exchange greetings, the elder wizard was coming back from the other end of the garden. Karel, obviously reluctant to leave his Master in what he perceived as a situation of potential danger, came near disobeying orders, and returned so swiftly that Stephen barely had time to grab up Sightblinder again.

As he rejoined the small group, Karel looked suspiciously and anxiously at Stephen's companions, and to his Master openly expressed his doubts that these people were really true faithful converts like himself.

The young Prince hesitated. He did not dare reveal his true identity to Karel lest the old man try to kill him, as the armorer had done—and Karel was vastly more formidable.

After some argument he persuaded the old man to move away again, long enough for a hasty, whispered conversation to take place concerning him. It was obvious that much craft and energy would have to go into the job of managing the old wizard until he recovered from the Mindsword's lingering influence. There was no known way, as far as any of his three friends knew, to hasten the recovery.

It was Yambu who came up with what seemed a good suggestion. Stephen, speaking in Vilkata's name, ordered Karel to mix himself a strong sleeping potion and drink it. "Something that will make you sleep for twenty-four hours."

Karel, though frowning, was unable to resist obeying a direct and forceful command from his Great Lord. Stephen's Great-Uncle mixed the potion as commanded, dutifully conjuring up the necessary materials, along with a crystal cup, apparently out of nothing.

Having quaffed the draught, the elder, his eyelids already sagging, was put to sleep in a sheltered place under one of the broken walls of Ben's house, in what his friends hoped would be safety, until he should waken, they hoped, in his right mind.

"Will he be all right there?" Stephen asked, leaning against a half-ruined wall. He was feeling an immense relief at having someone he could talk to.

Yambu shrugged. "We can only hope so. What else could we do with him?"

* * *

Half a minute later, Stephen, with a profound sigh of relief, gave his two Swords temporarily into the care of his two friends, and sat down to rest his psyche and his body alike.

There was no question in his mind about one thing: He had been simply unable to deal any longer with the pressure of carrying two Swords. If he hadn't lost Shieldbreaker, he might have been forced to abandon it—to hide it on the slim chance he, or someone, could retrieve it before the Dark King's magic succeeded in discovering the now-ownerless Sword.

Dusk was deepening, and the three were busy comparing notes on recent events, when there came another movement at the garden gate, a cautious opening. The young Prince grabbed up Sightblinder again, then relaxed when the massive figure of Ben of Purkinje came into view. Stephen realized that Coinspinner was still at work for him, bringing him further reinforcement.

Ben, cautiously entering the garden of his own ruined house and coming in sight of the occupants, stopped in his tracks as if he had sustained some heavy blow. He saw Stephen's image transformed into that of a red-haired young woman, tall and strong, and for a soul-shaking moment it was possible for the huge man to believe that his long-lost Ariane was not dead after all.

It was not the first time that the Sword of Stealth had played him such a cruel trick, and in another moment or two he was able to greet his friends in a normal voice.

Karel had obeyed to the letter the command of his Master (as he thought) to put himself to sleep for a full day; but his need to protect and serve that Master actively soon brought the old man to his feet, sleepwalking. Unnoticed by his three friends, now deep in conversation at a little distance, the elder wizard, obviously in the grip of some purpose which transcended sleep, walked out of the garden by another exit, and away.

* * *

Meanwhile, the young Prince was congratulating himself and entertaining his new gathering of friends with the story of how he had swindled Baron Amintor out of the Sword Coinspinner, and had effectively gotten rid of Amintor and his search party—at least for the time being.

Coinspinner had not failed to provide the little band with food. A root cellar under Ben's house, and a small icehouse in his garden, had both been spared demonic vandalism.

But hours were passing and there was only limited time for self-congratulation. Stephen and his friends, finding themselves fortuitously armed with two Swords, now had to determine the best way to put Coinspinner and Sightblinder to work.

Zoltan opened the serious conference by suggesting that they carry the pair of god-forged weapons to Stephen's royal parents as quickly and by as direct a route as possible—Ben ought to know where Mark and Kristin were most likely to be found.

But Ben was already shaking his head. He had ominous and urgent news to relate, eyewitness reports of Vilkata's hostage-taking.

This seemed important enough to compel a change of plan.

Stephen and his friends, still benefitting from Coinspinner's untiring influence, had not got much further with their talk when a messenger reached them from the Prince and Princess—a night-flying scout, a great owl dispatched from village headquarters, discovered their whereabouts in the city.

While the bird rested and ate, Ben took the opportunity to indite a short message laden with good news, written in code and addressed to Stephen's parents. The note informed Kristin and Mark that their son had been located, that Sightblinder and Coinspinner were available, and that the destruction of the Mindsword had now been definitely confirmed.

Soon the messenger, somewhat rested, was urged on its way. Still, there could be no thought of merely waiting now for orders from Mark and Kristin. The need was urgent to do something about the hostage situation, and orders sent from headquarters might never get through.

But everyone in the garden needed a rest before undertaking any substantial tasks. Stephen in particular was grimy and bleary-eyed from digging in the ruins of his grandparents' house and had suffered burned fingers on both hands in the effort to save their lives; his legs and ankles were scratched from climbing through the rubble, his right shoulder had been wrenched by last night's Swordplay, and then Coinspinner, before coming into Stephen's possession, had twisted his ankle, enough to keep him from walking easily or far.

The lad had put in rather more than a full day's hard work in the armory even before the attack fell on the palace, and had enjoyed only brief periods of real rest since then.

Now and then pangs of guilt still assailed Stephen over the fact that he had lost one of the Swords, perhaps the most important, to the enemy. But each time he forced himself to try to think the matter through clearly and logically, telling himself that he had done the best he could manage at the time.

In the hours before dawn—the messenger had been perilously delayed en route—Prince Mark and Princess Kristin received the happy news of Stephen's safety and confirmation of the Mindsword's destruction.

Prince and Princess happened to be awake when the good news arrived because people from an outlying farm had come to the village shouting, pleading, seeking Woundhealer's blessing on a scalded child. This victim was no casualty of Vilkata's attack, but only of domestic accident, a broken table-leg, a falling pot. Even in the midst of war, the other terrors of life went on.

While Mark and the cavalry remained suspiciously on guard against some trickery, Kristin drew the Sword of Love. As always with Woundhealer, the healing was swiftly and easily accomplished.

The child, relieved of pain, shock, and disfigurement, contentedly fell asleep. The grateful parents could not be as easily sent away. In fervent voices the man, named Bodker, and his wife Alta, praised and blessed the Prince and Princess, and the Sword the royal couple had brought among their people.

Kristin, more at ease than her husband in such situations, walked with the parents outside the cottage. Left alone again for the moment, Mark stared with a bitter smile at the Sword of Healing in his hand—one Sword which was never going to do the least harm to any of his enemies. Still, he had come to know the Sword of Love too well not to appreciate the ways in which it could be useful to the fighting man.

With enemy reptiles and demons tending to dominate the sky, flying messengers could now afford the Prince only an intermittent and indirect contact with his son. Messages could be exchanged, some co-ordinated plan of action could be at least outlined. A messenger approaching Stephen and his friends could be as confused by Sightblinder as any human or demonic enemy—but, of course, Coinspinner could help to straighten matters out.

Mark had to assume that Vilkata, with a thousand fanatically helpful converts to call upon, would soon learn to what village his archenemies, the Prince and Princess of Tasavalta, had gone, and when and why. Then—if the Mindsword still existed—the Dark King would soon be marching after them, doing his best to create an avalanche of new converts on the way.

But no such attack seemed to have been launched. Another indication, if any were still needed, that Skulltwister had actually been smashed.

Still, Mark and Kristin warily decided to continue moving their headquarters repeatedly, perhaps several times a day, keeping in touch with their key people by means of galloping couriers and a small band of flying messengers. Even now, in the village currently occupied by the royal couple, someone was getting the riding-beasts ready for the next relocation.

Meanwhile, with hard information gained, more orders could be dispatched to all the outlying districts of Tasavalta and to any reliable allies in the region. Mark's new confidence that the Mindsword had been destroyed rendered a general assault with an army on Vilkata's forces feasible again. Mark and his Princess were both busy, full time, sending reassurance to their people and marshalling troops.

SIXTEEN

WITH dawn, squadrons of flying reptiles, precursors of Amintor's advancing army, patrolled the sky over and around the city, making further Tasavaltan communication by flying messengers, at least temporarily, almost impossible. More couriers, and fighting birds to escort them, were being summoned from the more distant provinces.

Dawn found Karel still walking in his sleep, a man moving with the dazed sense of some unknown, urgent task to be accomplished—the elder wizard was wandering on an erratic course that had already taken him out of Sarykam. Twice minor demons tried to interfere with him, and twice he blasted them magically out of his path, even without becoming fully aware of his surroundings.

With the passing hours, the hold upon him of the vanished Mindsword was decaying, and the old man struggled internally to regain control over his own soul.

At first light, Yambu made her way across the grounds of Ben's ruined house, looked at the place where Karel had been put to sleep, and discovered that he was missing.

There were no signs of violence, nor did it appear that the wizard had taken anything with him, even food or water.

The lady reported her discovery to her friends, but there was nothing any of them could do about Karel now. Rather, it was necessary for the four remaining, having restored themselves with food and rest, to take action quickly to help the many hostages Vilkata had now crammed into the courtyards and cellars of the palace. Ominous sounds from the city streets, drifting in over the garden wall to Coinspinner's charmed

redoubt, confirmed that more victims were being added hourly
to the total.

There could be little doubt that the Dark King's prisoners
were in urgent peril of being slaughtered within the next few
hours. Such an atrocity was only to be expected, given Vilkata's nature and the situation in which he now found himself.

Stephen and his three friends all agreed that the most effective action would be direct, getting in among the hostages with
Sightblinder and Coinspinner. It was entirely possible, even
likely, that the rescuers, in following such a course, would find
themselves facing Shieldbreaker—but the risk had to be accepted.

Naturally the organization of the rescue operation would
have been much easier could it have been postponed for even
one more day. Now it would be more difficult because of the
necessity to save some all-too-willing victims; but in another
day the great majority of Vilkata's converts would be emerging naturally from the mental fog generated by the Mindsword. Hour by hour, even minute by minute, they would
experience first doubts, then confusion, then a full readiness to
rebel against the man who had so briefly made himself their
Master.

But of course it was not possible to wait that long. The Dark
King, anticipating just such a mass reversion, would be planning already to slaughter those he had confined—or to have
them massacre each other, or be devoured by demons—before
they could regain their senses.

Before pushing open the garden gate and launching their
attack upon the palace, Stephen and his companions had to
decide, of course in consultation with Coinspinner, which of
them was going to carry each Sword in among the hostages.

"Who shall carry this?" The Silver Queen, addressing one
Sword, raised high the other.

The tip of the Sword of Chance twitched, tugged decisively.

The task of wielding Sightblinder in combat had fallen to
Zoltan. The young man gripped thoughtfully the black hilt
marked with the symbol of an eye, and in the perception of his
comrades he vanished, was transformed into a series of images
compounded of their own hate and fear and love.

"And this?" Yambu, like a priestess, held aloft the very
Sword that was being questioned.

Coinspinner's magic weighed straight down upon her; and
thus remained in Yambu's hands.

There were a few tactical questions to be settled. Ben, mundanely armed, undertook the job of bodyguard to the now-
Swordless Stephen. The young Prince's chief responsibility
would, of course, be the exercise of his unique power; when the
fighting started, he would banish as many demons as he could,
to as great a distance as possible.

A minute later, Ben yanked open the door leading to the
street. Stephen and his friends, doubly Sword-armed, marched
out of the walled garden and toward the palace. They antici-
pated that on their arrival their work would be for the most
part indoors and in enclosed courtyards; therefore they made
no attempt to equip themselves with riding-beasts, which
under the circumstances seemed more of a complication than
an advantage.

Still the unconverted population of Sarykam had not totally
evacuated the city, though by now a high proportion had fled.
Many old people remained, and a scattering of others, some
simply unwilling to be driven from their homes, had been
hiding from the hostage-taking demons. Zoltan, advancing
with Sightblinder, had not walked two blocks before he began
to attract a following crowd of Vilkata-converts, some no
doubt genuine, some playing the role, all deceived into believing they were following their all-important Master. Among
them a few confused individuals, who beheld in Zoltan an
image of some dearly beloved child or spouse or parent riding

toward them, hastened to give thanks for that person's survival.

In a loud voice Zoltan introduced his three original companions as his faithful servants; then all four began to tell the swelling crowd that an impostor, a false Master, now sat in the palace.

More than once while walking the modest distance to the palace—and later, coming at him in the jammed interior courtyards—total strangers, deceived by the Sword of Stealth into the conviction that Zoltan was someone they loved, still accosted the young man with maudlin apologies, self-accusations regarding old and unknown mistreatment. Again and again his ears rang with tearful pleas that he—or she—come home with them at last.

Less visible, or audible, were an equal number of people who fled from his path in total terror.

Coinspinner, in the hands of the Silver Queen, unobtrusively set the raiders' course. The marching crowd, urged on by Zoltan's shouts, soon swelled into an angry horde. A figure appearing to be, in the eyes of hundreds of onlookers, the Dark King himself, accompanied by a rapidly growing entourage whose purpose was uncertain, pushed through the outer gates and entered the palace grounds.

That company went in unopposed, unchallenged by human or demonic guard, through one of the main doorways of the palace itself.

Complicated, conflicting reactions by the hostages themselves surrounded Zoltan and his close escort when he carried Sightblinder in among them. A roar went up from a thousand human voices, and what had been a passive crowd of captives was transformed in a moment into an utterly chaotic mob.

Eagerly the four invaders began their inside work, shouting into the cellars and improvised dungeons, freeing hostages with sharp commands in Vilkata's name. Even as Stephen and his band began their rescue operation in the palace, the most recently rounded-up contingent of genuine hostages, a scant few, were still being penned up with the others in the inner courtyards. Those interior rooms of the huge building which were most suitable for the purpose had already been filled far beyond their normal capacity. Up till the hour of the raid, in an effort to forestall, or weaken, the inevitable Tasavaltan counterattack, the Dark King had continued to cram more hostages into the courtyards and cellars of the palace, an indiscriminate gathering of whatever men, women, and children could be rounded up by his remaining human converts and his demons.

Aside from elderly folk, or those who had been injured or crippled after Woundhealer ceased to be available, practically everyone who was not a hostage or a direct combatant on one side or the other had by now fled the capital.

Doors and gates were opened in blind obedience, convert guards were trampled, demons hurled away by Stephen, who stood chanting steadily, pointing at one inhuman form after another. Lady Yambu continuously consulted Coinspinner, trying her best to interpret the results and convey them to her comrades amid the din.

In moments, a mass escape was under way.

On the theory that the prisoners most remote from freedom should be released first, or, in any case, must not be forgotten, Zoltan, almost as familiar as Stephen with the palace, urged his comrades to the lower depths, where they found some doors still locked. With shouted commands the raiding party dug people out of cells and an improvised torture-room, then moved above-ground again to visit one courtyard after another.

It was plain from their behavior that demons and converts saw Zoltan as their god, the Dark King, the ultimate object of both love and fear, whereas the non-converts among the prisoners beheld Vilkata as an object of stark terror. Many feared some kind of sadistic trap when he told them they were free, but few dared to let the opportunity slip by.

At the hour when the emptying of the palace began, Baron Amintor was still riding away from the city, heading generally northwest at a steady pace—reversing the route of his entry little more than a day earlier. He was taking his handful of convert troops to attempt a linkup with his own advancing army.

The Baron—still agitated and energetic as a result of the no-sleep spell—was furiously regretting the loss of Coinspinner and making his own private plans to regain control of the situation, when the great demon Arridu came dropping down out of the sky to visit him for a second time.

The little group of riders halted. Arridu, taking the form of a mounted warrior in black, at once informed Amintor that a strong effort to free the hostages in Sarykam was even now in progress by a small band of Vilkata's enemies armed with Sightblinder and Coinspinner.

The demon added: "I would, of course, have rushed to help our glorious Master—but, alas, one of the attackers would see to it that I was swiftly banished, were I there."

The Baron drew a little aside with his illustrious visitor to talk while his mounted escort waited uncomfortably at a little distance, out of earshot.

Eager to hear details of the attack on the palace, Amintor demanded: "And Vilkata? Does he come to meet these raiders with the Sword of Force?"

A smile showed under the black warrior's helmet-visor. "We must expect that will soon happen."

So far, Coinspinner's luck appeared to be sustaining the rescue party in excellent fashion. The Dark King himself, and the great Trump-Sword he carried, still had not taken the field against them.

Until now, Zoltan and his small band of companions had ravaged and emptied the familiar cellars and the prison-court-yards with impunity. Everywhere their orders for a general release of prisoners, shouted in the Master's name, were being accepted as genuine and obeyed.

When some hundreds of people who were still under the Mindsword's spell, guards and prisoners both, came swarming round Zoltan in bewilderment, he ordered them firmly, in the Dark King's name, to return to their homes and their old loyalties, and honor the Prince and Princess of Tasavalta.

The confusion precipitated by the attack among the demons and converts guarding the palace had quickly escalated into total chaos—perhaps it was only chance that some of the Dark King's loyal creatures, discovering him in a high tower, stammered out the story of what they had just seen. They were positive that he, the Dark King himself, had given and was still giving puzzling and contradictory orders for a general release of hostages.

Vilkata, recalled by this alarm from a certain magical enterprise which had distracted him, recognized that some enemy armed with Sightblinder must be attacking—but he had been more than half expecting some such move for hours, and thought himself ready to meet it.

The Dark King looked forward, with the gleeful anticipation of impending triumph, to holding Shieldbreaker in one hand and Soulcutter in the other—and then walking among these Tasavaltans and enjoying watching what became of them.

But the Sword of Despair was not available just yet, and the joy of wielding Soulcutter against his enemies was going to have to be postponed for just a little while.

Scrambling up a ladder to the tower's roof, the Dark King brought into action his secret weapon, a griffin he had recently obtained, and leapt into the saddle already secured to the magical hybrid's back. The great lion's head turned on its long neck, looking back for orders; the vast wings spread, the gigantic eagle-talons scratched at stone in an eagerness to taste soft human flesh.

In moments Vilkata was airborne, hovering over the most central courtyard—the point of riding a griffin rather than a demon was, of course, to render himself immune to being swirled away to the Moon again by Mark or his misbegotten offspring.

The Dark King was holding Shieldbreaker drawn and ready, and in his demonic vision Sightblinder below was no more than a silvery twinkle in the hands of one he recognized as a scorned enemy. And Coinspinner was there too, in the hands of another he had long hated! Today there were prospects for good hunting with the Sword of Force!

In the blink of an eye, Vilkata and his magic mount were hurtling down upon the raiders, ready to put a stop to their daring raid and to their lives as well.

Mass confusion was compounded, with rival Masters issuing contradictory orders. Even when Vilkata was present with the Sword of Force, Zoltan with Sightblinder could still deceive everyone else. To that extent another Sword could indirectly be effective against a leader armed with Shieldbreaker.

The difficulty on the Tasavaltan side was that Stephen and his friends were at times uncertain as to which figure was Zoltan and which Vilkata.

Zoltan was bellowing commands for all that he was worth. *"He* is the impostor, I tell you! But be careful, he carries the Sword of Force. You men, disarm yourselves and seize him."

But there was no use trying to disarm a man flying overhead and out of reach.

Vilkata, gripping his own Sword firmly, swept low over the field astride his griffin, seeing very clearly the doomed impostor issuing orders in his name. With a howl of glee, the Dark

King smashed Sightblinder from Zoltan's hands. The magic Sword of Stealth was transformed into a shower of dead and deadly splinters, and Zoltan fell.

Once more the palace echoed with the violent explosion of a ruined Sword—but in the next instant the Dark King came near falling from his saddle.

His griffin-mount, understanding that something had gone wrong, landed abruptly. Vilkata clutched at the sockets where his eyes had been.

He was freshly blinded, his grip on triumph shaken.

Young Prince Stephen had just hurled into distant exile the latest demon to appear before him—it was Pitmedden, who had been providing Vilkata with his only vision of the surrounding world.

SEVENTEEN

A T the moment Sightblinder was destroyed the great majority of the thousands of hostages were already free, and the remnants of the captive horde were streaming swiftly out of the palace through its many exits, spreading away across the grounds, escaping the Dark King's malevolence in dribbles and gouts of flight and panic.

Among those last to leave the palace were a number of people who fled unwillingly, converts still stubbornly clinging to their conversion; they were now in headlong flight only because they had heard their god, Vilkata himself, order them to do so.

Converted and unconverted alike departed unmolested. Stephen had for the time being banished all of their demonic gaolers, and the human converts Vilkata had assigned as guards were chaotically bewildered and demoralized. Thrown into a panic by their Master's misfortune, those near Vilkata were desperately intent on shielding him from further harm. They were frenzied by his blindness, a deprivation of external help against which the Sword of Force had done nothing to protect him.

Adding to the confusion in the courtyard, the Dark King's griffin-mount, prowling near him on the ground, slashed with lion-claws at the faithful who would still have helped their Master, and bared fangs large as human hands, keeping friends and foes alike at bay.

Vilkata in the courtyard had for a little while remained astride his plunging griffin, though unwilling to trust it airborne when he could not see; soon he had slid from the creature's back. Now, on foot, with Shieldbreaker still firmly in his hand, and guarded from unarmed attack by the griffin and a circle of fanatical human converts, he was prohibitively dangerous for either friend or foe to approach.

Cursing and raging, the Dark King had no demons to bring him quick reports; and still he dared not attempt to fly, to pursue his enemies and their remaining Sword, until one of the creatures should return to provide him with sight. He called out repeatedly to his human bodyguard, urging them to protect him.

Coinspinner was still in the hands of the Silver Queen, but the Sword of Chance would of course be ineffective in any direct action against the man who still brandished Shieldbreaker.

When Yambu, with Ben looking on, questioned the Sword as to how best to defeat their enemy, Coinspinner unmistakably urged her toward the nearest exit from the courtyard.

Meanwhile, Stephen had been separated from his friends and lacked any magical guidance. But he saw that there was no way to attack Vilkata at present, and he too moved quickly to get himself out of the courtyard and away from the palace before the Dark King could recover his sight. More reptiles, and perhaps more griffins, were coming to sweep the place clear of potential enemies.

In the rush to get away, the young Prince left the palace by a different exit from Yambu and Ben. Neither party paid much attention to this fact at the time.

Vilkata was enraged by the awareness that some of his enemies must be getting away—but he was savagely pleased at having achieved the destruction of Sightblinder. That meant there was now one less Sword-prize in the world for which his many rivals and enemies might contend; and his own ultimate goal of dominating the world with a single Sword was further advanced by the same amount.

The Dark King's pleasure was increased on hearing confirmation from his converts that Zoltan, cousin to the accursed Tasavaltan royalty, was undoubtedly dead.

Yambu and Ben, trotting away from the palace at a good pace for folk no longer young, heeding Coinspinner's urging though they scarcely needed it, looked about them as they ran in an effort to locate Stephen, but without success.

And naturally no messenger-birds were available just now; the report to Kristin and Mark would have to wait.

The Silver Queen and her massive escort paused to catch their breath after a few blocks. Ben seized the opportunity to borrow Coinspinner from Lady Yambu. The Sword of Chance assured him that he should remain with her to reach whatever was his most important goal.

Stephen, running in a different direction, had escaped from the palace with his life and little else. He found himself once again moving through almost-deserted streets, still separated from his friends.

This separation was not necessarily any worse than inconvenient. Before launching their raid on the palace, the methodical veterans had designated a point of rendezvous for survivors, if their attempt to free the hostages should somehow miscarry.

Stephen went to the appointed spot—an intersection otherwise of no particular significance—and waited, under cover, for a quarter of an hour. When none of his comrades showed up, he comforted himself with the hope that they had probably survived anyway; and he decided that he had better move along, keeping a wary eye out for flying reptiles.

Mourning the death of Zoltan, but believing that his cousin had not died in vain, the young Prince started to make his way out into the countryside, where he hoped to be able to locate his parents.

* * *

It was late in the day before Prince Mark and Princess Kristin learned, from a winged scout fortunate enough to survive the leather-winged predators, of the attack on the palace by their people armed with two Swords, and the general success of that endeavor, despite the death of Zoltan.

The bird could give its master and its mistress no news of Stephen—or of Yambu or Ben—and Kristin and Mark were once more uncertain of their son's fate, and of the current whereabouts of the Sword of Chance.

The day wore on, and their knowledge of the situation improved minimally as more bits of information came in.

Mark, even before the attack on Sarykam, had heard some rumors concerning the independent army of mercenaries being organized in a neighboring territory by his old foe Baron Amintor.

To Kristin he muttered: "Wouldn't have expected him to have a great deal of success, at this stage of the game; but he appears to have been successful."

Amintor had been too distant from the palace to be caught up in the struggle to free the hostages, or in its aftermath. But his new partner, Arridu, was prompt at bringing him news, including that of Sightblinder's destruction. The Baron smiled grimly to hear of such a serious setback for the Dark King.

Shortly after the Baron had received word and Arridu had once more taken himself away, Amintor succeeded in making contact with the most advanced scouting unit of his own mercenary army, a fast-moving cavalry patrol. One of this party's scouting reptiles spotted him and guided him to the meeting.

To the Baron's considerable relief, his second-in-command rode out to meet him. Amalthea was perhaps twenty years his junior, tall, dark, and slender, an attractive woman and a

skilled magician as well as an effective warrior—a rare combi-
nation and one that suited Amintor perfectly. He understood
very well that only the power of Coinspinner had made it
possible for a man of his own age and condition to recruit a
junior partner who was so eminently satisfactory in so many
important ways.

Amintor felt a fierce joy when he beheld Amalthea cantering
toward him, followed immediately by a pang of regret as he
realized how likely it was, given his loss of the Sword of
Chance, that she would not be with him much longer.

Still, for the time being, their relationship remained secure,
as far as he could tell. Amalthea welcomed her leader in a
warm though not greatly demonstrative fashion. She favored
him with a simple kiss, while the picked mercenaries of the
cavalry patrol looked on impassively.

Then Amalthea drew back a little. "Is there something
wrong with you?" she asked sharply.

No doubt, he thought, her magician's sense detected Vilkata's stay-awake treatment. "A spell—one more spell, more
or less . . ." The Baron shrugged. He was still breathing heavily
from the excitement, the exertion, brought on by Vilkata's
magic.

"What kind of spell? And where is Coinspinner?"

"As for the spell, I tell you it is nothing of importance. Only
a few words from our glorious leader, with the object of helping me keep awake. And Coinspinner has taken itself away."
That last explanation was near enough to the truth, the Baron
thought, to serve the purpose. "You've brought what I asked
for?"

"Of course." Amalthea nodded. But had the woman hesitated fractionally before replying?

Leading Amintor to a little distance, just out of sight of
their troops, Amalthea opened a large bundle of magical
equipment and brought out a certain package—she had taken
care that the soldiers not know that she was carrying it—and

showed Amintor the Sword she had been taking care of for him.

It was another of Coinspinner's gifts, of course.

Her eyes studied her elderly leader with concern as he un-wrapped the weapon and looked it over.

The concentric rings of a target made up the stark white symbol on this particular black hilt. Farslayer. He nodded silently, knowing that he was going to need all the help that he could get.

Having inspected the Sword of Vengeance, the Baron sheathed it again and handed it back to Amalthea.

"And what am I to do with this?" she asked him sharply.

"You are going to have to use it." He smiled at her in the way—if he could remember—that a young man would.

The woman only stared at him in silence, trying to fathom his plan, and perhaps his worth. Then she paused to do a little magic, seeing to it as best she could that they were not being spied upon.

Amintor added: "Use it when I am not with you. But at a time and in a way that I command."

"Of course," Amalthea responded, calm and business-like. "When and where?"

The Baron explained. The Sword of Vengeance was a mar-velous threat, but its actual use was not without strong disad-vantages. Chief among these was the tendency of the victim to be among friends when he was so helplessly skewered, and the concomitant tendency of the bereaved friends to retaliate in kind, when they found themselves so providentially provided with the means as well as motive.

Amintor, considering the matter coolly, as was his wont, thought it would certainly be satisfying to at last rid himself permanently of Mark, who had caused him so much trouble in the past, and continued to do so now. But Amintor was at the same time very reluctant to give Mark's friends a return shot at himself.

Anyway, Amintor did not consider Mark his most immediately pressing danger.

He had barely finished his explanations, given explicit orders, and made sure that Farslayer was again securely hidden, when Vilkata's demonic messenger—not Arridu this time—arrived to bid him hold himself ready for a conference. The Dark King, griffin-mounted, was on his way.

Some of the demons so recently banished by Stephen from inside the palace had been able to return relatively quickly to the Dark King's service. Within an hour of his blinding, Vilkata had regained the ability to see and had jumped back into the saddle on his griffin's back.

Before implementing the next step of his overall plan, which would involve going to the Moon, Vilkata wanted to settle matters between himself and Amintor.

When the two men met, in a small patch of summer forest, Amalthea retreated with her cavalry patrol, leaving Vilkata and Amintor alone except for certain members of the former's escort.

The Dark King sarcastically demanded of the Baron what assurances the latter needed to be convinced that he now faced the genuine Dark King.

Amintor tried to sound conciliatory.

The senior partner, in a black humor, waved Shieldbreaker, and shouted that Sightblinder had now been blasted into fragments, damn it!

Then the Eyeless One, still brandishing the Sword of Force, angrily demanded of his junior partner: "What is the matter with you?" Under the circumstances, this could be only interpreted as rhetorical abuse. It was quite obvious that there were serious difficulties between them.

"Oh, Great King," Amintor murmured, as if in an excess of self-reproach and fear, "pardon me!" And he moved clumsily as if to fall to his knees before his Master—a maneuver that brought him physically closer to his senior partner, by the two steps the Baron judged were essential.

From that position, crouching as if about to kneel, the Baron hurled his aging body forward, in a desperate effort to wrestle Shieldbreaker from its possessor. For once he would stake everything upon one move—because at this exact moment, if Amalthea were faithful, Farslayer should be coming to strike down his foe. If Vilkata dropped Shieldbreaker, he would die, and if he held the Sword, Amintor would wrest it from him.

There came a whistle and a ringing in the air, a flash of silver. The Dark King, Shieldbreaker still held high in his right hand, his countenance betraying no surprise, had withdrawn from his unarmed assailant by a single step.

At Vilkata's feet the Baron lay dead, instantaneously transfixed by a bright Blade. Amintor's body still twitched, fingers closing spasmodically as if to grasp some prize, but his eyes stared lifelessly. He had been slain by Farslayer, flying at him from some unseen hand.

Only a moment passed before Amalthea appeared, emerging from summer greenery some meters behind the Dark King, walking slowly forward among the trees. Her manner was demure and subservient to Vilkata, who was not at all surprised to see her. Obviously they had met before. A look of understanding passed between them. The enchantress had decided she would be better off serving the Dark King directly.

An instant later Arridu appeared too, materializing out of thin air, smoothly assuring his Great Master that had the Sword of Vengeance not killed the traitor, he would have done so.

"It appears you both were right," the Dark King complimented his two assistants. "The fool was planning treachery all along."

In the next moment, brushing aside the congratulations of

his aides upon his cleverness, the Dark King, laughing triumphantly over Amintor's skewered corpse, planted a boot on the Baron's chest, and plucked forth the Sword of Vengeance from the Baron's heart.

For a long moment Vilkata found himself brandishing two Swords, Farslayer and Shieldbreaker, at the same time, a rare experience even for him. His demonic vision suddenly began to play tricks on him. . . .

Or rather, he thought in a flash of insight, he was forcibly reminded of something he should always have kept in mind, but tended to forget—that his self-chosen mode of perception had always been playing tricks.

Whatever its exact provenance, this particular vision was unsettling.

From somewhere there came into his view unbidden an odd glimpse of a small room, stone-walled and cramped, containing a torture-rack and little else, the rack complete with anonymous, screaming victim. And this made the Dark King suddenly feel better—he could get used to this business of the two Swords.

Vilkata was not afraid of casting the Sword of Vengeance in among Mark's vengeful friends—not as long as he, Vilkata, had Shieldbreaker in hand to fend off the likely riposte.

Holding the black hilt of Farslayer at arm's length in both hands, spinning his body gracefully, the Dark King chanted the old rhyme: "For thy heart, for thy heart, who hast wronged me—"

In a blur and a flash, Farslayer was gone, howling away into the distance, from the moment of its launching become invisible with its own speed.

As soon as he had thrown the Sword, Vilkata felt confident (though, as always, there remained a shade of nagging, suspicious doubt) that he'd killed Mark. Only Shieldbreaker could have protected the Prince, and the Sword of Force was still here at his own side.

Hastily he drew his protection, held it ready, smiling as he awaited the counterblow from Prince Mark's grieving friends.

The Prince of Tasavalta was on his riding-beast, leading a growing force of mounted troops and infantry toward Sarykam to reclaim his capital, when the Sword of Vengeance came for him.

Mark was granted no more than a moment of warning.

Only the Prince himself, and a few people who were closest to him, saw or heard Farslayer flying toward him.

It was Kristin, as so often watchfully protective at the Prince's side, who in a flash drew Woundhealer from where it was kept ready, belted at her own waist.

Vilkata's gift came bursting through whatever magical defenses Mark had in place—Karel, recovered now from Mindsword-magic but still at a distance, had seen to it that those barriers had become considerable, though intended only against weaker attacks than this. Neither the Prince nor his chief magician would have wasted time and energy trying to build defenses against this weapon.

The shock of Farslayer's impact knocked Mark clean out of his saddle, impaling him bloodily. No voluntary cry broke from his lips, only the mechanical grunt of air out-driven by the impact of Farslayer's hilt against his chest.

Kristin was no more than an eyeblink later with Woundhealer, which she plunged right into her husband's heart, then did her best to catch his falling body before it struck the ground.

Then, for a few terrible moments, Mark endured having the Sword of Vengeance stuck right in through his breastbone, next to the Sword of Love, the two Blades crossing, clashing, somewhere near the center of his body. His eyes were open, his face working, as if he were struggling to endure, to understand.

The Princess, shifting her grip to the other hilt, pulled Far-slayer from Mark's body and cast it blindly aside.

A swarm of supporters, crying out their shock and rage, at once gathered round the fallen Prince. Meanwhile, the peasant Bodker, grateful and fanatically devoted to the man who had healed his child, and neither knowing nor caring whether Vilkata possessed Shieldbreaker—perhaps possessing little knowledge of any Swords—grabbed up Farslayer and hurled it angrily, muttering his clumsy prayer that it should slay whoever had just tried to kill the Prince. . . .

The Dark King was still waiting alertly, Shieldbreaker pounding and drumming in his hand, when Bodker's gift ar-rived; after a startled moment of noise and glare and flying fragments, Vilkata of course remained unscratched.

Again there had been the Sword-shattering blast—again the lethal spray of fragments of ensorcelled metal.

Nearby demons screamed in pain; their lives, being else-where, of course, were safe.

Meanwhile the Dark King endured a split second in which he feared that his defense had failed him—but after that split second he laughed wholeheartedly at this evidence of what he saw as his own continuing invincibility.

EIGHTEEN

THE two veterans, Ben of Purkinje and the Silver Queen, were making their way in near-silence south along the coast, the east wind from the sea whipping their graying hair. Yambu rode with an almost unconscious queenly dignity, most of the time holding the reins in her left hand, carrying Coinspinner unsheathed in her right. Her wiry arm drooped with the Sword's weight, but her grip on the black hilt held steady, sensitive to its least vibration. The lady's eyes continually scanned the road ahead. Her giant escort, grim-faced and for the moment no more than mundanely armed, kept his large and powerful mount close behind hers.

Since leaving the city behind them, the Silver Queen's companion had twice asked for and been loaned the Sword from her. Twice he had tested Coinspinner's powers with questions containing obscure allusions, phrases that would have been hard to understand even had the wind not whirled the words away so quickly.

Twice the result had evidently been affirmative, for Ben each time gave back the Sword and followed the lady on in silence. It was evident that the Sword of Chance had recommended these two people to each other.

The Dark King now had adopted Amalthea as his chief human aide—or at least had promised her that status—and meant to leave her in control of his army, formerly Amintor's.

Meanwhile he, Vilkata, had other things to do. He told his new assistant no details of his own immediate plans, only that he was going away for a day or two and that she should save what she could of the army which had been Amintor's. Doubtless that would require a temporary—only temporary—retreat from Tasavalta. But the army would be useful when the

Dark King came back to renew his attack with overwhelming force, and it was important that as much of it as possible be preserved.

One of Vilkata's first acts on arriving back on Earth from his two-year exile had been to order his demons to conceal his spacecraft in a seashore cave only a few hours' hike south of Sarykam. The Dark King had considered it prudent to keep this equipment standing by in case some sudden need for it arose. Riding on his griffin now, he was able to reach the site in minutes.

Vilkata, on his way to the cave in which the spacecraft lay hidden, consoled himself, in conversation with Pitmedden, that in the freeing of his hostages he had suffered only a temporary setback. He had driven his enemies from the field in their most recent skirmish, and with his own hand had cut down a nephew of Prince Mark.

But of course those achievements fell far short of total victory. The complete conquest of the realm of Tasavalta, let alone that of the entire world, seemed as remote as ever.

Given Soulcutter and Shieldbreaker both in hand, of course, he would possess the means to rout his enemies for good and all. Arridu whispered, and the great prize beckoned. Thinking he now had a priceless opportunity to obtain the Sword of Despair, the Dark King with his demonic vision eagerly scanned the darkness ahead for the seashore cave.

Ben and Lady Yambu were being guided by the Sword of Chance in the same direction that Vilkata had chosen for his flight. As they rode, they saw him go soaring, streaking overhead, traversing the daylight sky at a much swifter pace.

Coinspinner had provided the Silver Queen and her partner with excellent riding-beasts for this journey—a circumstance which suggested either that speed was important in their journey or that their destination lay at no great distance. Before leaving the city, the pair had come upon a pair of animals, untended, providentially abandoned in the middle of an otherwise deserted street, saddled, well-rested, and fed. Then the Sword, buzzing and twitching in the lady's hand from time to time, led them on a brisk ride out of Sarykam.

After Ben's latest trial with the Sword, the lady confronted him. "Are you asking for something else, big man, apart from some immediate tactical success?"

"And if I am?"

"No harm in it—I was only curious. As we left the square back there, I put a personal question to the Sword myself." After a moment the lady added: "Since we are in retreat already—what I really want, apart from seeing these damned demons and their human lovers crushed, is once more to confront my husband."

Ben was frowning. "Your husband, lady? I thought—"

"Call him my former husband, then. You know who I mean, however you prefer to name him. The so-elusive and mysterious Emperor. The older I grow, the more I am convinced that that confrontation is what I want—nay, what I need—above all else. There are answers I must have, and nowhere else to turn for them."

Before another hour had passed, while, under the Sword's guidance, still heading south along the coast, they had passed several encampments of refugees from the city, and were a dozen kilometers from the capital.

Soon afterward all signs of settlement dropped out of sight. The coastline here was rocky and inhospitable, with few harbors or real beaches. The stony earth held little soil for farming or even grazing, nor were these shallow, tide-riven coastal waters hospitable to fishing boats. Nevertheless, the only indication of the presence of human life was two or three of these craft several hundred meters off shore.

Atop a deserted-looking stretch of cliff, no different in its general appearance from the regions immediately to north or south, they discovered an entrance to a large cave, a gaping hole in the ground at least as big as a small house—no particular surprise in this area, though neither traveler had ever seen this particular cave before.

When Ben and the Silver Queen concentrated their attention on the opening, certain strange sounds and dim lights were faintly perceptible from the darkness deep within the cave.

But Coinspinner was silently tugging its clients in a different direction. Away from the discovered entrance, and down the cliffside, guiding their riding-beasts along an unmarked path which led them to another opening in the rock, right at sea level, quite likely a second entrance to the same cave. Whereas the upper opening was fairly plain on the top surface of a low cliff, the lower was inconspicuous, almost invisible until you were right on it.

Ben dismounted and advanced a few paces, to stand squinting in sunlight, peering into dimness. This lower entrance was awash, at least at the current stage of the tide. Waves continually splashed and roared into the space that had been carved from solid rock by their ancestors over a myriad of years.

The Sword of Chance bade the seekers wade into the cave; the low entrance made it necessary for them to leave their riding-beasts outside.

Some strange inhuman sound, a heavy shifting of great weight upon clawed feet, came out of the darkness ahead, raising visions of deadly monsters in Ben's mind. "Dragon!" he whispered sharply, backing into a retreat.

Yambu's hand was on his arm. "No, a griffin, I can see its wings." Her eyes were evidently better than Ben's in darkness. A leonine growl confirmed her identification. "It must be the creature Vilkata rode—remember, we saw him pass us in the sky."

Ben relaxed a trifle. "What now? The Sword has led us to this thing—are we supposed to climb upon its . . ."

Ben's voice trailed off. A premonitory wave of nausea, a seeming tilting of the watery shingle beneath his feet, warned him at last that the griffin was not the only guardian of this entryway.

Yambu was experiencing the same sensations, and her hand gripped hard at Ben's arm. But the demon had scarcely appeared, a luminous form in warrior's shape drifting in the cave entrance, when the Sword of Chance went into action in defense of its human bearer.

Ben's heartfelt prayer was answered almost before it could take shape in his mind: Coinspinner could as easily visit catastrophe upon a demon as on a human or a beast. The thing had no more than confronted them when its image froze. Ben understood in a moment that some horrible accident had just happened to that demon's life-object, however remote in space that object might be from the manifestation he confronted.

. . . *the thing's eyes stared into some terrible distance, where its hidden life was being menaced . . . no time for it to reach the spot, to try to defend itself . . .*

The blank expression in the doomed demon's countenance turned into one of tremendous shock. In the next moment the image had crumpled, then evaporated, and the watching humans knew it must be dead.

The griffin, indifferent to their presence, mumbled a sleepy lion-roar and seemed to be crouching, turning round, doglike, as if preparing to go to sleep.

The Dark King, observing these events from a place of concealment within the cave, understood perfectly well what had just happened. Vilkata, gnashing his teeth at being so inconveniently deprived of one more demon, was fully alerted to the fact that his enemies were on his trail—and that they must have the Sword of Chance still with them.

Vilkata found the situation quite to his satisfaction. Now, with Pitmedden as usual providing him his sight, in this case letting him see around a corner, he waited in ambush, clutching his Sword, behind one of the gnarled rock formations in the inner darkness of the cave.

In this part the cave was deep and dark enough to keep out most of the sunlight. Some Old World lighting glowing indirectly out of the parked space vehicle provided a partial illumination.

Though Ben and Yambu had so far been given no direct evidence that Vilkata was here, the presence of the griffin and at least one demon certainly made his presence likely. They had to operate on the assumption that the Dark King was still armed with the Sword of Force, and that he might well have more demons with him, as well as a bodyguard of human converts.

Ben, now advancing into the cave, climbing wet rock past the somnolent griffin, warily got ready to throw down at a moment's notice any mundane weapon he was holding. Perhaps he did thus far disarm himself.

He and the Silver Queen were both experienced in Swordmatters, and with a minimum of words and gestures made their arrangements for mutual defense. It was decided between them that Ben would hold their Sword and lead the way.

But Vilkata jumped out of ambush and struck, before Ben, being led by Coinspinner and still trusting in the guidance of that Sword, could throw it down.

When the Dark King, a lunging shape not instantly identifiable, came jumping out from behind a rock, Ben raised the Sword of Chance instinctively, just as Vilkata had raised his weapon in the armory under the palace.

Shieldbreaker emitted a barrage of drumming sounds. In the next instant, with a violent crash whose visual component lit the cave, Coinspinner had been destroyed.

* * *

Flying fragments of the broken Sword stabbed into Ben's head, sent him slipping, sliding, finally tumbling, down a little slope. But the huge man was not immediately disabled, and for the moment could disregard the fact that he was hurt. An instant after the blast, Ben, bleeding from his face and scalp but again on his feet and now unarmed, charged uphill at Vilkata, who was still holding Shieldbreaker.

The Silver Queen, considerably more distant from the blast, had also been injured by stray bits of Sword, but not severely, though momentarily stunned by the concussion.

Seeing the energy with which Ben was coming after him, the Dark King muttered blasphemies, angered that his latest victim should retain such strength—and was coming unarmed.

Vilkata considered hastily whether to retreat, or stay and fight. He was unsure of just what powers or what people were here arrayed against him, and he had no intention of throwing down his own invaluable Sword—that would mean assuming some risk, however small, of not getting it back. Having come to depend upon the matchless, Sword-smashing power of Shieldbreaker in his own hand, the Dark King had no intention of giving it up.

Briefly Vilkata considered trying to deal with the still-advancing Ben by means of some lesser magic, or by hurling rocks. But common magic worked poorly when, as now, fighting blades were drawn. And the Dark King was determined not to be delayed in his trip to the Moon. Rather than deal personally with Ben and Lady Yambu, Vilkata snapped a few terse words to another of his lesser demons and turned away. The thing shrilled an obedient acknowledgment of its Master's command.

The Dark King, with Pitmedden and one other minor demon still clinging to him like tendrils of evil smog, darted to the open hatch of the waiting Old World spacecraft and jumped in. The hatch closed with a soft thud behind him and the spacecraft almost immediately whirled aloft, to go rushing in near silence out of the cave through its upper aperture.

Ben and Lady Yambu, recoiling from this demonstration of the powers of Old World machinery, found themselves still free to move about. Though certain ominous and unfamiliar sensations in his head were now giving the man to understand that he had sustained some serious injury in the latest Sword-explosion.

Warrior-fashion, he did his best to shake off the difficulty.

Yambu and Ben were now closer to the cave's upper entrance than the lower aperture, and moved out of it to stand on the rocks atop the cliff.

Once in the open air again, Ben stood swaying, his head back, mouth gaping upward—he had come out of the cave just in time to get a last glimpse of the Old World shuttle bearing the Dark King before it disappeared at a tremendous distance overhead.

The Silver Queen had followed Ben out of the cave and stood beside him.

Only briefly were the two humans allowed to hope that Vilkata, in his haste to leave, might have decided to ignore them. Scarcely had they time to draw a deep breath before the demon who had been appointed their executioner was with them, making its presence known in the form of a vague, half-human shape.

But before the demon could begin to toy with its all-but-helpless victims, the whispering sound of the spacecraft's passage through the lower air, which had faded only moments earlier, returned. Ben, looking up, saw that the near-spherical shape had reappeared in the sky and was descending rapidly.

Silently and swiftly, emitting no great glare of light, this vehicle approached the upper entrance to the cave, where the two people and the demon who confronted it were standing.

The spacecraft, hard metal scrunching solidly on rock, touched down very near them.

The onlooking demon gaped, as surprised as Ben and Yambu, and perhaps almost as frightened. The clear, glassy surfaces of the Old World vehicle had been turned opaque, and no one could see into it from outside.

The lights inside it dimmed or went out, and a hatch opened.

The head emerging was certainly not Vilkata's. Nor was it even human—or demonic.

The three onlookers watched with utter astonishment as the rest of the emerging form came into view—a figure, despite its size, speedily, gracefully unfolding through the open hatchway, then elongating to its full height of some six meters. A body standing on two almost man-like legs, all clad in glowing fur, a face and body neither quite human or quite animal in aspect, though obviously male.

"Hail, Lord Draffut!" Ben breathed fervently. The utterance sounded like a prayer.

Yambu and the demon were equally quick to recognize Draffut, the famous Beastlord, a being everywhere believed by common folk to belong to the pantheon of gods. What stunned Ben even more than the fact of Draffut's arrival was that of his god-like size and evident power. Ben had heard the appearance of the Lord of Beasts, in recent years, very differently described.

Draffut had no sooner unlimbered his gigantic form from the spacecraft than he growled out a challenge to the stunned demon watching.

Whatever followed between the two beings on the level of magic, in the way of an exchange of threats, even of direct blows, Ben failed to perceive the interaction at all. All he could be sure of was that a moment after the Lord of Beasts confronted the demon, Vilkata's creature had fled, or had been driven from the field.

Now that an oasis of safety had been established, at least temporarily, Draffut greeted Yambu and Ben as old acquaintances, even as friends.

Ben was just starting to reply, when, to his surprise, the throbbing which had been put inside his head by Coinspinner's dying blast rose up and wiped away the world.

When the huge man recovered his wits, he found himself being held, supported like a baby in Draffut's gigantic hands, while Lady Yambu stared at him with concern. Brusquely Ben asserted a warrior's contempt for his own wounds, announced that he was fine, and climbed out of the Beastlord's grip to stand, somewhat shakily, on his own two feet. Blood from his scalp injury was still coming down his face in an occasional thin trickle, and he brushed at it impatiently.

"A long time since we've met, Master Draffut." Ben was too knowledgeable to speak to this creature before him as to a god.

"Many years, Ben of Purkinje." Draffut was half-kneeling now, a position which brought his huge head closer to a level with those of his companions. The great voice was as soft as it was deep.

Ben, his head suddenly once more awhirl, spoke again before he'd taken careful measure of his words. "I remember that we were in a battle together, you and I and a thousand others, and you . . ."

The vast eyes, of shifting colors, stared at him. He thought the inner radiance of the white fur dimmed momentarily. Draffut said: "I killed a man that day. The act was unintentional, but yes, I killed."

That hadn't been Ben's key memory of Draffut's part in the battle, but he couldn't deny that it had happened. Ben did his best to reassure the luminous giant. "Killing is a part of any war."

Draffut only shook his head.

"I had heard . . ." The huge man began, then hesitated.

The Beastlord nodded. "That I had changed. Had been diminished, as a result of what happened to me on that day of war."

"Yes."

"And what you heard was true, for I was changed indeed. Once more, as in my early youth, I ran about the world on four legs, and was content to be again a dog, the form in which I was created. But I have a friend who was not content that I should remain so."

It was Yambu who brought the discussion back to a practical level: "We owe you our lives, Master Draffut. Where have you come from in that Old World device, and why are you here now?"

"I have been sent here, from the Moon, with instructions to bring two people back."

Yambu had never been timid, and now, at her time of life and with her experience, there were very few things that really frightened her. Still she felt a qualm at the thought of embarking upon the shuttle-voyage Draffut was proposing.

Coinspinner was no longer available to provide guidance, but her doubts were thrust aside when Draffut promised the Silver Queen that he could bring her face to face with the Emperor at last.

"You hesitate, great lady. But you are wanted there." And Draffut looked up into the sky—to human eyes the Moon, today risen in early daylight, was now, near midday, quite invisible.

She could not doubt that this gigantic being was telling her the truth. "He himself has said this to you? He mentioned me?"

"Indeed, great lady, the chief reason I am here is that the Emperor has asked me to bring you to him."

* * *

Young Prince Stephen, halfway through a journey to the village where he thought his parents most likely to be found, had taken shelter in a small shady grove, trying to keep out of sight of patrolling reptiles in the sky.

Stephen, who had closed his eyes in weariness, was almost entirely sure that he was dreaming when he opened them at a small sound, to behold his famous grandfather, now sitting quite near him on a fallen tree, and nodding to him in familiar greeting. Stephen recognized the Emperor at once, despite the fact that the Emperor now looked a little younger than his son Prince Mark.

Today Stephen's grandfather, a surprisingly ordinary-looking man clad all in gray, had not chosen to put on one of his famous masks, or play the clown. Instead he appeared in the boy's dream—if dream it was—as armed with many Swords. The familiar figure was carrying them all glittering and gleaming, the bright Blades clashing together harmlessly, in a kind of crude gardener's bag. He opened that container to let the young lad look inside.

But soon the Emperor covered up the Swords again and put aside the bag.

Then he said, as if this were his point in making the display: "They're not really all *that* important, you know."

"What's more important than Swords, Grandfather?"

"A number of things—for example, that you and I have a talk every now and then."

"Really?"

"Yes. Oh, yes. And now seemed like a good time."

Stephen sat up, shifting his position. He now had the feeling that he was wide awake. "I'm trying to find my parents."

His companion nodded. "I know you are. I expect you'll manage to locate them all right. Tell your father that he and I must have a talk again sometime."

"I'll tell him." Stephen blinked. "And I know he wants to talk to you. He spends a lot of time trying to find you."

"Your father worries a great deal, unnecessarily. You might tell him I said that."

They chatted for a few minutes more—about nothing out of the ordinary, as Stephen remembered later—before the Emperor got to his feet and slung his bag—had it really contained Swords?—over his shoulder.

Taking these actions as signals of departure, Stephen said politely: "Good luck, Grandfather, safe journeying—Ardneh be with you."

"Thank you." The man's reply was solemn. "And with you as well."

"I'll see you again, won't I?"

"Oh yes. It might be a while, but we'll meet again. Never worry about that."

Ben and the Lady Yambu, standing with Draffut just outside the seaside cave, looked at each other. Both of the humans at the moment were feeling sharply the lack of the Sword of Chance. But Coinspinner was gone, and that was that.

Following the guidance of the revitalized Draffut, the two humans boarded the Old World spacecraft without argument or serious hesitation, despite the utter strangeness of the device.

Draffut communicated in some way with the machinery. Moments later, the craft and its three occupants were being borne upward at a speed achievable only by Old World technology.

For the first hour or so of the flight, Ben lay on one of the strange beds and briefly slept. When he awoke, the bleeding from his head wound had entirely stopped, but he still felt pain and occasional disorientation. As their hours in space lengthened into a full day, the two human passengers occupied themselves alternately resting and moving about inside the glass-and-metal vehicle, watching the Earth recede and the Moon grow ever larger. It was indeed a mind-bending experience.

Not counting small latrine-bathrooms and a galley, there were three habitable chambers inside the shuttle, which was easily the size of a small house—the largest cabin was capacious enough to house without undue hardship the six-meter length of Draffut as well as the two humans. Particularly as Draffut soon manifested the ability to double his body into a relatively small space with no apparent lack of comfort. The humans now discovered that the movable interior partitions of the craft could be repositioned to provide one long, narrow chamber in which the Beastlord was able to accommodate himself at full length.

The passengers experienced no fierce acceleration even though the Earth seemed to be falling away at breathtaking speed; and the human passengers speculated as to whether the speed and ease of the journey were due to magic or *technology*. "Up" and "down" remained, respectively, the directions of the shuttle's overhead and of its deck; but the sky outside, and the Earth visibly embedded in it, assumed alarming and upsetting positions.

Ben's wounds, though bandaged by the Silver Queen with Old World medical materials on board, still bothered him, and her own minor injuries still pained. Draffut several times administered such healing as he was able to perform by the laying on of his huge hands, and Yambu was greatly helped. Each treatment made Ben feel a little better, though the benefit was only temporary. The Beastlord grumbled that his healing power was not what it once had been, and solemnly promised a more efficacious therapy once they reached the Moon.

Ben dozed repeatedly and dreamed. The cumulative weariness of a hard life seemed to have caught up with him, and he welcomed the chance afforded by these comfortable quarters to catch up on sleep, and also on food, which proved to be plentifully available in several acceptable forms. Draffut showed both human passengers how to control the Old World equipment concerned with health, safety, and comfort.

There was talk of Swords, and of the prospects in the war now raging, among the three now traveling so swiftly together to the Moon.

For their own satisfaction—Ben's in particular—they brought up to date the inventory of Swords as well as they were able.

Yambu had for some years been making an effort to keep track of the Twelve Swords—Draffut announced that he had been doing so too, and now gave his companions his current reckoning in the matter.

After Coinspinner's recent ruining, only Farslayer, Soulcutter, Shieldbreaker, and Woundhealer still survived—and Draffut was not at all sure about the first of those. One by one, over the past forty years or so, all the rest of the output of Vulcan's forge had been reduced to bits of black wood and dull metal, the nothingness of dissipated magic.

The Sword of Despair, said Draffut, was really the one to worry about. The Emperor had told him that.

It was Yambu who theorized that a few of the Swords, including Soulcutter, had shared an interesting property—the Tyrant's Blade never discriminated among individuals. In effect, Soulcutter didn't care who anyone was.

Neither did Woundhealer.

Nor had the Mindsword, before it was destroyed, ever distinguished one person from another apart from singling out its current owner as the supreme object of devotion.

Back on Earth, Stephen had not traveled far from the grove in which he met the Emperor when, to his great joy, he encountered a recovered Karel, whose own magical search had led him to the young Prince. From that point on, under the great wizard's protection, Stephen had nothing to fear from flying reptiles, nor could his reunion with his parents be delayed much longer.

Woundhealer had restored Mark to full health almost instantly upon its application, and now only a nearly-invisible white scar marked the place where Farslayer had come ravening into his flesh.

Prince and Princess together had continued their advance upon Sarykam, recruiting more armed troops readily from the villages, where a number of trained militia were available. Scouts reported that what had been Baron Amintor's army, now commanded by a woman named Amalthea, was trying to reverse course and withdraw from Tasavalta.

And with the loss of Coinspinner's luck, the army gave signs that, lacking some triumphant stroke by the Dark King personally, it would soon break up in internal conflicts.

Coming out from the capital to join Prince Mark were a number of de-converted soldiers, along with the bulk of the general population. With every passing hour, more converts now recovered spontaneously from the Mindsword's hideous spell.

With these and other forces rapidly becoming available, the country moving toward full mobilization, the Prince acted swiftly to harry and punish the force of mercenaries as it strove to withdraw from Tasavalta. General Rostov, and the local leaders elsewhere, had not waited for Mark's direct leadership before organizing and taking action.

The mercenary force was in retreat, threatened with disintegration, united now only for self-defense.

Less than two days after departing the coast of Tasavalta, the three passengers in the space shuttle were preparing for a landing on the Moon.

The lifeless-looking desert globe first became frighteningly large, then ceased to be an object in the sky at all, and was transformed into a world reassuringly below their feet. Draffut, the experienced traveler, meanwhile pointed out certain sights of interest—including the place from which Vilkata had rescued the demons—as they approached, and indicated at least roughly what territory lay definitely within the Emperor's domain.

Yambu gritted her teeth, doing what she could to get ready for a confrontation with that impossible man, who had once been her husband.

The Beastlord also explained, to a pair of human beings too awed and bewildered to understand him very well, how he himself had come to be restored to power and majesty by immersion in what he called the Lake of Life—that had been the Emperor's doing, of course. Draffut told his questioners that he expected they would have the chance to see the Lake of Life for themselves.

Yambu and Ben had both heard of the ancient, legendary Lake of Life, which supposedly had existed at some unknown location on the Earth.

Draffut assured his human listeners that the lunar Lake was a duplicate of the legendary one.

Below the travelers, a smooth area of the Moon's surface that looked like pavement grew and grew.

Ben, long past astonishment, observed some kind of giant hatch or window in that surface yawn open to receive their vehicle.

And then, fairly abruptly and without fanfare, the voyage ended in an intact base or spaceport built securely under the lunar surface.

Back on Earth, at about the same time that their friends' spacecraft reached the Moon, Prince Mark and Princess Kris-

tin were joyfully reunited with their son and the old wizard
who was Kristin's uncle.

Moments later, while Stephen enjoyed the benefits of
Woundhealer, he passed on to Kristin and Mark the most
recent intelligence regarding the conditions in Sarykam, and
what had happened to him in the course of his journey since
leaving the city. Naturally the youth included his most recent
information about Ben and Yambu—and Zoltan.

As a kind of afterthought, Stephen told his parents about
his encounter with the Emperor—adding his continued uncer-
tainty as to whether that meeting might have happened only
in a dream.

Mark acknowledged his son's information about that talk
with a nod, but made almost no comment on the matter.
Everyone, it seemed, got to talk to the Emperor sooner or
later—everyone but him, the Emperor's son. And what good
did it all do, anyway, all these vague signs of encouragement
and advice from the imperial Great Clown?

No one at the royal headquarters as yet had any certain
knowledge of Coinspinner's destruction, or Farslayer's.
Through Karel's art the Prince was soon given warning that
the Dark King was coming back with Soulcutter and more
demons from the Moon.

NINETEEN

W HEN Ben's mind grew clear again, he found himself standing, leaning against the wall, in a long hallway with several distant branches and many doors. The passage was three or four meters broad and considerably higher, smoothly carved from rock, and lighted by peculiar Old World lamps—a strange place, a very strange place indeed.

He was unarmed and still wearing the clothes in which he'd come from Earth.

Most unsettling at the moment was the fact that he could not remember just how he'd been separated from his two companions. He knew his parting from Draffut and Lady Yambu must have taken place—somehow—soon after their arrival on the Moon; but he could no longer recall the circumstances.

The big man distinctly remembered the blasting of Coinspinner into little pieces against the edge of Shieldbreaker back in the seaside cave—and then the menacing demon, and Draffut's timely arrival. But the details of his journey to the Moon were hazy. He realized that his head injury must be producing some serious effects.

However he had come to be here, here he was, standing more than half weightless in this strange lunar corridor, with his companions nowhere in sight, listening to a droning, unearthly background murmur, as of Old World machinery . . . .

He thought that perhaps, buried deep in the sound, he could hear someone calling. Calling his name.

Ben found that he could walk—a little unsteadily, but he could certainly walk. Getting about here was quite easy because of the lack of weight. On he went, sampling the doorways in the long hall, discovering more rooms and tunnels, trying to find some clue as to how he might rejoin Draffut and the Silver Queen—and trying also to accustom himself to the strange lunar environment. Yes, he was on the Moon. That was hard to believe, but in his time he'd seen a few other things that were almost impossible, and he had managed to deal with them.

Vilkata, on returning to the Moon, at a landing place far from Draffut's, had quickly noticed that the mysterious subsurface being, or entity, which he and his demons had previously observed, was now detectably more active than it had been a few days ago.

That was interesting; but just now the Dark King had little time to spare for odd phenomena. He had come here with the fixed purpose of obtaining Soulcutter, and he immediately bent all his efforts toward that goal.

When his attention was caught by the unexpected presence of more demons, fresh exiles from the Earth now gibbering and squealing in the airless lunar distance, he did the best he could, in passing, to gather these hapless creatures under his control. They would be useful, though not essential, when he made his last return to Earth, there to stake everything on one climactic effort to win the ultimate game of power.

Ben still continued his wandering in corridors of stone and Old World glass, trying to read the symbols of unknown languages carved into the stone walls.

Entering a room containing certain objects that struck him as hearteningly familiar, Ben decided he had found what must be a branch of the White Temple. The man-sized carved images of Ardneh, cubistic and vaguely mechanical, and of Draffut, were both eminently recognizable. Ben had never been one for much Temple-going, whether White, Red, or Blue. But under his current circumstances the familiarity of this room's contents seemed benign and reassuring.

At the next door, Ben came upon what looked like a peculiar kind of library. At least part of the extensive chamber was devoted to that purpose, for, besides the incomprehensible Old World machines, there were real books and papers, maps and drawings, spread across many shelves and over tables. The visitor leafed through a few of the papers and bound volumes, discovering several different languages, but none that he could understand.

One book, occupying a place of prominence upon an incongruous hand-carved reading stand, drew Ben's particular attention. The thick volume was printed in the common language that he understood, and the pages lay open at the place where in the ancient scripture the words said: *Ardneh, who rides the elephant, who wields the lightning, who rends fortifications as the rushing passage of time consumes cheap cloth . . .*

Ben looked up at a slight sound, to discover that he was no longer alone. The Emperor had come in and was standing near the doorway through which Ben had entered.

"Hello," said Ben simply, feeling no fear, but a certain awkwardness. He'd met this man before and, though that meeting had been years ago, had no trouble recognizing him at first glance.

"Hello," replied the Emperor, in his unassertive voice. "I thought you'd probably soon find the library."

Ben nodded gravely and looked around. He could feel the latest trickle of blood from his head wound drying on his face, but for the moment he was experiencing no pain or dizziness. "I've also discovered one of the few books in it that I can read."

The other looked sympathetic, and Ben thought he might be about to offer medical assistance. But instead the Emperor asked: "Is there anything in particular you'd like translated?"

"I don't suppose so. I . . . yes." Ben nodded decisively. "Not

these books, though. There were some words on the wall, out
in the corridor—"

The Emperor was nodding. Then, in the manner of one
preparing to convey information, he turned away, with a jerk
of his head to indicate that Ben should come with him.

Two minutes later, the two men were standing in the branch
of corridor where characters in Old World script were carved
or painted on the wall:

> *AUTOMATIC RESTORATION DIRECTOR 2*
> *NATIONAL EXECUTIVE HEADQUARTERS*
> *REDUNDANT SYSTEM*

A word-for-word translation of this legend left Ben little
better informed than he had been; and the Emperor offered
further explanation.

"The first letters of the words in the first two lines form an
acronym—ARDNEH. You see, Ardneh, the Earthly entity
destroyed so long ago, was a machine. A thinking machine of
sorts, what the Old World folk called a computer.

"Doing the job for which it had been constructed, Ardneh
cast a Change upon that world, and saved the world when war
threatened to destroy it. A Change that cancelled the effec-
tiveness of much of the Old World's *technology,* and, at the
same time, brought back magic. What had been nuclear explosions became demons. . . ."

Ben said: "The truth behind the story that the Scriptures
tell."

The Emperor nodded.

Ben felt light on his feet, light in his head. But not bad. It
was perfectly easy to stand here. "But Ardneh, whatever he
really was, existed on Earth. And was destroyed there, two
thousand years ago, along with the demon Orcus."

The Emperor's hand—how human, how ordinary it appeared—reached up on the wall to tap a finger on the last two

words of the inscription. He repeated their translation. " 'Re-dundant system.' Meaning another Ardneh. One might say *Ardneh Two.*" He spoke two words in the old language. "The reason why the Change endures, and magic works, long after Ardneh on the Earth was done to death."

"Ardneh-tu?" Ben repeated unfamiliar syllables.

"Yes. Would you like to meet him?"

Minutes later, at the entrance to yet another chamber carved from deep and ancient lunar rock, the Emperor stepped back, allowing Ben to go in alone.

He noted with little surprise that Yambu was already there, and looked up at Ben's entrance. But before Ben could speak to her, a box of metal, large as a man but built into a wall, greeted him with words of welcome.

Ben stared back at the box, and was reminded of the White Temple's carven image. He asked it: "You are Ardneh-tu?"

"I am." The voice from the box was bland, human and yet unfeeling.

The two humans and the machine were confronting each other in a strangely-lighted room, densely occupied by metal boxes, cabinets, and consoles of unknown materials. There were chests of tools, long cables like multiheaded snakes, interlocking nests of metal and glass.

It was Yambu's turn to ask a question; evidently she and the machine had begun a dialogue before Ben's arrival. Now the Silver Queen, in the manner of one continuing some earlier discussion, asked Ardneh-tu: "Then the Emperor is your creation?"

"No. It would be closer to the truth to say that I am his work. And so are you. All humanity."

Yambu questioned Ardneh-tu sharply: "But you told me that people of the Old World made you."

"That is true."

The lady looked helplessly to Ben, but he could only gesture vaguely with his huge hands, signalling his own hopeless lack of comprehension.

Yambu turned back to the box that spoke. "Then I do not understand."

"Humans are not fully equipped to understand. It is not required of them."

The Dark King, totally ignoring all presence on the Moon save for his own and those of his demonic escort, had been making his way, overcoming one magical barrier after another, to the crevice in deep rock where, according to Arridu's story, Soulcutter had been hidden by the Emperor some twenty years ago.

For once, it appeared, Arridu, even without compulsion, had told the truth.

The Sword of Despair was encapsulated even as the great demon had described it, almost as the demons themselves had earlier been sealed in, embedded in a block of some solid crystalline material, and that, in turn, sunk deep in black volcanic rock.

Around the intruding wizard the rock for half a kilometer in every direction was shaking, breaking, shattering—the demons who were aiding him groaned and labored and cried out in their travail.

Extremely powerful magic was necessary to retrieve the Sword of Despair—a great price, of course, had to be paid to undo the Emperor's sealing. But to a man who had willingly steeled himself to sacrifice his own eyes, no price was too great that still left him able to hate, to strike his enemies.

The job of extracting Soulcutter from the Emperor's sealing required many hours, extreme exertion, and no little pain, even for a sorcerer of the Dark King's power. But eventually, by dint of determined and ruthless effort, the magical procedures were completed and Vilkata was able to draw forth the sheathed Sword—and at that moment he collapsed, overtaken by some disaster against which Shieldbreaker had been able to afford him no protection.

The collapse was not physical, and it was accompanied by no dramatic show, but it was certain, and effectively complete. But the Dark King still stood tall, even as he allowed Arridu to strip him of both his Swords.

The demon standing in warrior form held the gods' sheathed weapons negligently, both hilts clasped in one huge hand, as if he were as far beyond the power of their double magic as they were beyond mere ordinary steel.

Vilkata meanwhile continued to hold up his two empty hands, their fingers still half-clenched as if around black hilts. He gave no sign of understanding that the gods' weapons had been taken from him. He turned his eyeless gaze from one hand to the other, seeing only what he wanted to see there—because Pitmedden had been driven insane too.

"Arridu!" The Dark King's command still crackled with authority.

"Yes, great Master?" The demon's voice this time was thick with mockery.

But Vilkata did not notice. "I want to get back to Earth as quickly as possible. Do you think the spacecraft or on a demon-ride . . . ?"

"Which would be swifter? Why, the great Master must decide that for himself—but is not the Master forgetting something?"

A light frown creased the eyeless face. "Forgetting—what?"

"Why, Unsurpassable Lord, that Your Lordship's greatest enemy is even now your prisoner. And that the torture chamber awaits your pleasure."

"I—yes, of course." And Vilkata, turning in the indicated direction, saw to his delight that all was indeed as the demon had said. There, in the small, cramped room was the rack in readiness, the thumbscrews waiting, the small brazier where a fire of magical intensity heated sharp slivers of poisoned

metal—a whole array of delights for the connoisseur of torment.

Only the victim was missing; and that lack, of course, could
soon be remedied.

The great demon watched with amusement as the blind man
approached the rack. Vilkata set aside, for the moment, his
imaginary Swords, and began the task of fastening himself
upon it. The ankles were easy, the left wrist a trifle more
difficult. The right hand of course would have been impossible—but then it was necessary for the torturer to keep at least
one hand free to work with.

Looking on, listening critically to Vilkata's first scream of
mingled agony and triumph, the great demon toyed with the
hilt of Shieldbreaker and murmured: "Even the Sword of
Force could not save you. Because it was no weapon which
brought thee to this sorry state—only thine own will. Thy
pledge so freely given was accepted, the bargain kept. Still art
thou able to hate, to strike at thy enemies—that thy blows
should actually hurt them was not guaranteed."

The Dark King, slowly, sadistically rending his own flesh,
was now muttering disjointed phrases, cries of triumph min-
gling, alternating, with groans of pain.

Arridu, savoring this suffering, bent a little close to hear
better.

In the intervals when Vilkata was capable of speech, he
spoke of future plans. When Earth was conquered he would
command his demons to carry him off into space, there to
complete his glorious conquest of the Sun. . . .

A few hours later Arridu, contemptuous of any human
resistance which might face him when he arrived, completed
his own swift return to Earth.

He brought with him two Swords, Shieldbreaker and Soulcutter. And he was well aware that on Earth, in the hands of

his enemies, only one Sword, Woundhealer, still remained intact.

Arridu knew the bearer of the Sword of Love and sought him out at once.

The last duel took place in full daylight, upon a grassy summer hill not far from Sarykam, and it was fought between Arridu, carrying both Soulcutter and Shieldbreaker drawn, and Prince Mark of Tasavalta, armed only with the Sword of Love. Other loyal humans stood by ready to help Mark—until the arrival of Soulcutter cast all who were within arrowshot into a deep and paralyzing despair.

Mark, holding Woundhealer embedded in his own heart, was unaffected by the Sword of Despair. And the Prince had no thought, in this climactic confrontation, of simply banishing his tremendous foe.

"Should I do so, he will only come back, sooner or later, to attack me. Or worse, to ravage the rest of the world. Let the matter between us be fought out here and now."

Prince Mark, when the subject of the Sword of Despair had lately been raised in discussion, or when it had come up in his own thoughts, would recall a brief meeting he had about five years ago with his true father. At that time the Emperor had denied possessing Soulcutter, even though Mark had earlier seen him pick up that Sword from a field of battle. And whenever Mark's father made a flat statement like that, Mark had never known it to be wrong.

And now Mark faced a nice, practical, tactical question: How should an unarmed opponent—like himself, for one armed only with Woundhealer was effectively unarmed—how should such a one attempt to fight an enemy who held Shieldbreaker *and* the Sword of Despair?

And Mark thought he knew; his recent experience with Farslayer had helped him acquire the knowledge.

It could be assumed, or gambled, though no one could claim solid proof, that Woundhealer would save the mind as well as the body from ongoing damage—or repair the damage as fast as it was inflicted.

Mark, his left hand still clamping the hilt of Woundhealer hard against his own ribs, feeling the transcendent giddiness of the Sword of Love buried in his own heart, leapt in to wrestle with only his right hand.

Arridu immediately dropped Shieldbreaker—and was at once seized, staggered as he had dared to hope he would not be, by the mortal power of unsheathed Soulcutter still in his other hand. The impact of Despair was strong enough to stun the demon momentarily, send him reeling back. Soulcutter slipped from his weakened grip.

Mark, still holding himself transfixed with the Sword of Love, grabbed up the discarded Sword of Force and struck at the nearest vital target, smashing Soulcutter to bits as the Sword of Despair lay on the ground.

Its poisoned fragments stung him harmlessly. *At least, at last, if all our struggles achieve nothing else, that damned thing is gone. . . .*

Now the great demon, stunned and terrified by the loss of two Swords, turned to flee. And Mark, determined that Arridu should not escape, hurled Shieldbreaker after him . . . he saw to his horror the demon's figure twisting in mid-air, saw the gigantic warrior's hand reach out to seize the spinning hilt of the Sword of Force. Screaming with new triumph, howling like a whirlwind, the enormous demon fell upon him.

Mark started to draw from his own breast the only Sword he had, meaning to meet the last attack full on.

His effort came too late. Shieldbreaker and Woundhealer were smashed together, inside a human heart.

TWENTY

B EN of Purkinje and Lady Yambu walked out of Ardneh-tu's lunar dwelling place together, having been told
by that ancient intelligence that they would each find what
they were seeking on the shores of the Lake of Life.

The path on which Ardneh-tu had directed them lay
through the little spaceport. As the Silver Queen and Ben
traversed that chamber with slow, almost bounding lunar
strides, both humans glanced once more in passing at the Old
World spacecraft which had brought them to the Moon.

"All right with me," said Ben, "if I never have to ride in one
of those things again."

Actually the huge man had little thought or feeling one way
or the other about getting back to Earth. He was rather surprised that the question seemed so abstract, did not seem to
concern him. But so it was.

Nor, he decided, was this attitude entirely the result of his
head wound, because the Silver Queen, whose injuries had
been much lighter than his, muttered some vague agreement
with Ben's remark—her thoughts continued to be concentrated upon her promised opportunity to see her husband
again, a chance to demand some answers from him.

Yambu and Ben, still following their respective directions
given by Ardneh-tu, soon came to another temporary parting
of the ways. Neither was concerned; all sense of danger had
imperceptibly receded; and Ardneh-tu had assured them that
they would be safe if they went where he had directed them.

Ben could smell the fecund moisture of the Lake of Life for
some time before actually entering the great cave in which it
lay. The impression on entering was far from cave-like—a
crystal ceiling, startlingly distant, was lighted by refracted
sunlight. Ben remembered Draffut's mentioning that the slow

lunar sunrise would soon take place in this region of the lunar surface.

On hearing his goal described as a lake, Ben had envisioned some kind of underground pool; but the reality surprised him, even though the Lake itself was not yet in sight. He was standing on one edge of a vast columned space whose glowing overhead suggested an Earthly sky and whose floor sloped down toward a mass of bright vegetation, concealing whatever might lie beyond—presumably including the Lake of Life itself.

He had not advanced much farther when he stopped suddenly in his tracks. All he could think was: *Sightblinder cannot be here. The Sword of Stealth has been destroyed. What I see now must be an image cast by some other magic.*

Or else—

Perhaps fifty meters from where he stood, on the far side of the visible space, in the garden area where the light was brightest, Ben saw Ariane, the red-haired love of his long-vanished youth.

Birds rose in alarm from among the nearer trees as he went bounding and stumbling forward, all else forgotten.

The young woman—to all appearances still unchanged from when Ben had last seen her more than twenty years ago—was dressed in simple but attractive clothing. When he first saw her, she was busy about some routine task—some kind of gardening, troweling rich black and very Earthy-looking soil.

At the sound of Ben's voice, Ariane looked up. His last doubt vanished—it was she. Joy came to her face, but no enormous surprise. In a moment she was running to greet Ben happily, as if she had been expecting him.

For a long, cold moment, the thought of Sightblinder's illusions returned to torment Ben's mind. But he knew, if he knew anything, that that Sword had been destroyed.

Then the moment of renewed doubt was past. Ben clutched the young woman's large, strong body to him, swept her off her feet. This was no illusion. No. His knees had felt weak as she came running toward him, but now his whole body felt strong again.

A minute later, he and Ariane were seated side by side, on the fallen bole of some odd tree or giant fern, quite near the spot where she had been gardening. The whole garden, smelling of damp earth and life, seemed a fascinating mixture of the controlled and the natural.

And peaceful. In a dazed way Ben became aware that this lunar environment, so strange and changeable, sometimes so antagonistic, had in the last few minutes, even apart from the miraculous presence of Ariane, grown astonishingly friendly.

Even the gravity now seemed more like that of his home-world—he wondered if that meant that he was weakening. But at the moment illness and injury were the farthest things from Ben's thoughts.

It required recurrent mental effort to reassure himself that he was really still on the Moon, and not somewhere beside one of the warm seas of his own world. There were green things, some plain, some exotic, spiked with a profusion of multicolored flowers, growing on three sides of where he sat. And in the middle distance beyond the thickest greenery, where the distant crystal cave-walls were no longer visible, a bright mist suggested almost irresistibly that gray sky, and not a cave-roof, lay beyond.

Here and there among the nearby shrubbery, several fountains played—Ben had not noticed them before. The statuary in at least one of them was slowly shifting shape, as if on the verge of bursting into life—and it was into this rippling, unquiet basin that Ariane dipped a crystal cup, then brought it to Ben, saying: "Here, drink this."

Until that moment Ben had not been conscious of thirst, but

having brought the cup to his lips he drank deep. It was, he thought, the best drink he'd ever had.

Feeling refreshed, seeing and hearing everything more clearly, he cocked his head a little on one side. "You know, I hear something that sounds like surf, big waves. Or I think I do."

Ariane glanced back over her shoulder. "Yes, there are waves. It's the Lake of Life just over there. The people of the Old World made it. They made a smaller one on Earth, too—or so Draffut tells me. But that was destroyed two thousand years ago."

"I thought that Lake was only legend."

The waves of red hair bobbed. "Legend, yes. But also as real as Draffut is. He says it was immersion in the Lake on Earth that first made him something more than a dog."

"I think I could use some of it myself." Though at the moment he really felt quite well.

Ariane's green eyes twinkled. "You don't really need it any more—anyway, you've just had some."

Ben nodded slowly, as if on some level he was beginning to understand. What little he could see of this lake through the screen of vegetation, no more than a small glimpse here and there, suggested that it might stretch on for kilometers—or was that only an effect of mist and light? Certainly the forest of growth on this shore was diverse and fertile beyond anything Ben had ever experienced or even imagined.

Ariane had put a hand on his shoulder and was looking him in the face—as if she were looking at a young man, in a way that stirred his blood. Then she smiled and asked him: "Tell me how you came here?"

In a few moments, after a false start or two, Ben was relating the tale of how Coinspinner had been blasted out of his hand in the coastal cave near Sarykam. He added the comment that there must now be very few Swords left on Earth or anywhere else, though he had no up-to-date certainty about numbers.

Ben also expressed his worries about Shieldbreaker and Soulcutter, and how Prince Mark and the rest of Tasavalta were going to deal with them.

But Ariane did not seem at all perturbed. She assured the man she loved that he had done all he could do. He didn't have to worry about such matters anymore.

He protested. "If Mark—"

"You've done all that you can do for Mark."

"I suppose you're right." Ben put his face down in his hands and rubbed his eyes. Then he looked up again. Ariane was still sitting right beside him.

"Are you really here?" he whispered hoarsely. "Am I?"

"I'm really here. And so are you." And the young woman, garbed simply but richly in garments whose shapes showed her strong body to advantage, whose colors harmonized with her red hair, continued to sit close beside the huge man, looking at him lovingly. It was a restful attitude. There was no hurry about anything.

"Ben?" As if she were wondering—not worried, only curious—why he remained silent.

"Ariane? It's really you?"

"Yes, foolish man, are you still worried? Of course it's me." Strong pale fingers pinched his arm.

He rubbed the pinched spot absently. "But how did you get here? On the Moon? And when?"

"You're here, aren't you?" She made it sound like an eminently practical answer. "Well, I've been here, with my father, almost since I last saw you."

Absently he rubbed at his forehead, where his fingers could no longer discover any sweat, or blood. Or wound. He asked: "You mean with the Emperor? Since when?"

"I've just told you. Yes, the man you call the Emperor's my father—but you knew that. Actually, to me it doesn't seem very long since you and I were parted. We were trying to steal some treasure, as I recall. All in a worthy cause, of course." She smiled as at some memory of childhood pranks. She stroked Ben's head, the back of his neck. If there was a little soreness still, pain had receded so far as to be faintly enjoyable, little more than a memory, as happened when a wound or a sprain was almost healed.

He asked: "Just you and your father live here?"

Ariane's laughter tinkled; a delicate sound to come from a body so big and strong. *"No,* Foolish One. There are others. A great many other people. You'll meet them. Some you already know."

"Really?"

He wanted to ask who else was here that he might know, but instead closed his eyes. Whether magic was involved in what Ariane—and her father—were doing for him, or *technology,* or some sweet drug in the drink she'd given him, or what, Ben was being slowly overwhelmed by a sense of blissful tiredness and relaxation. In a little while, he felt sure, he was going to fall asleep. Now there would be time and security in which to sleep.

Ben felt a momentary regression toward childhood. How strange. But he was certain there was no danger, now, in such abandonment. Opening his eyes again, Ben told his love: "I wish I had a father like yours."

She nodded soberly, as at some reasonable request. "He'll be glad to be your father if you want."

Ben thought about it. The last time he had seen the Emperor, the Emperor had looked younger than Ben. Ben started a chuckle but it quickly faded.

Then something occurred to him, to his renascent adult self. An item of information that should be passed along. "Your mother's here," he told Ariane. "Lady Yambu came with me in the shuttle, from—from the Earth."

The green eyes of his beloved opened wide with eagerness;

a delicious little personal trait that Ben realized he had forgotten until this moment. She said: "I want to see my mother—but there's no hurry. Right now I just want to be with you."

Ariane, Ariane. Yes, it had to be twenty years, Ben thought—really a little more than twenty—since he had seen this young woman or touched her hand. But he remembered perfectly how her hand felt, solid and warm and somewhat roughened by active use. It felt just like this.

So many seasons, so many events and people had come and gone that he was finding it difficult to be accurate about the reckoning.

"As I remember the way things were so long ago—you loved me then. You really did."

"I really did. I really do." And at this point the red-haired young woman kissed this man who loved her. Then she got up from her seat and her fingers became busy, rubbing her fingers over the now-painless spot on Ben's head where he'd been wounded, then splashing him gently with more water from the fountain.

It was all delightful. Perfect. But Ben's lingering sense of mundane reality, though fading by the moment, was still strong enough to be offended by this situation. "I was a young man then, when last we met. I'm getting to be an old man now. My wife and my daughter may both be dead, for all I know. They were taken hostage, I think. . . ."

"I know." But here, now, no one's death seemed to be of any great concern. Everyone had some difficulties along that line, but they were temporary. And Ben's beloved, as young and beautiful as memory would have her, put a hand on his arm. Her touch was very real. She only smiled, faintly, as if there was something, some delightful secret, that she was going to explain to him, sooner or later, when she got around to it. But there was no hurry. Ben understood, without having it spelled out for him, that there was going to be plenty of time for explanations. All the time that anyone could want.

* * *

A little later, Ben became aware of other people, moving, strolling, at some distance along the shore of the Lake of Life. He could hear other voices from time to time, though their words were indistinguishable. "Who's that—?"

And at the same time, in a secluded cove not very distant along the shore of this Lake of Life, the Silver Queen, Ariane's mother, was being reunited with her husband.

There was a black-brown curve of sandy beach, lapped by occasional waves, and out beyond the gentle surf the surface of the water in the Lake vanished into a shimmering, indeterminate distance. When the Lady Yambu came upon the Emperor in this spot he was also gardening, driving with his right foot to thrust his shovel firmly and unhurriedly into the black rich soil, getting ready to plant something new in the superfertile soil beside the Lake.

Gladly he paused in his work, wiped a trace of sweat from his forehead, leaned with muscular forearms crossed upon the handle of his shovel, and welcomed his caller with the calm of a loving husband who has perhaps been separated from his wife for a few hours.

In fact he moved at once to kiss Yambu, but she was still wary, and put him off.

The Emperor shrugged, stepped back and did not press the matter. He had all the time there was, and he could wait.

Husband and wife soon found several things that both of them were eager to talk about. One of the first such topics was their daughter.

Another was the fact that the Emperor really wanted the help of the Silver Queen in cultivating the new garden he was planning on this section of the Lake's shore.

"Are you telling me that you've brought me here simply to help you tend a garden?"

This led the discussion to another item: some explanation for the fact that the two of them, despite an obvious mutual attraction, had frequently argued and quarreled.

And Yambu (she was now sitting on a beach-side boulder, the rock's surface mottled with some ever-moving design of life, while her husband still leaned on his spade; and now she noticed, with a feeling of merely confirming what was right and proper, that her long hair when the breeze stirred it before her eyes was no longer gray but jetty black) said to her husband: "It seems to me, looking back on it, that we never got along at all when we were married. And yet, I doubt that I would ever consider marrying anyone else."

He almost frowned. "If I have anything to say about it you'd better not consider that."

"You're jealous." She said it unbelievingly.

"I am."

Her anger rose up. "But of course it's quite all right for you to be promiscuous, because you are . . ." Yambu stopped uncertainly.

"A man? You know me better than to think I would make that excuse."

"You father children everywhere."

"I give them life. It is not behavior I can recommend to every man."

"But, of course, for *you*—"

"Yes. For me."

Yambu shook her head as if to clear it. She meant to come back to argue that point later. "Speaking of your children, do you know your son Prince Mark for years has spent a great deal of time and worry trying to locate you? Even to the neglect of his own family?"

"I know."

"Well?" Impatience flared. "The poor man wants to know who you are, beyond a name, an image. And so do I."

Her companion raised an eyebrow. "You have been my wife

for all these years, you've borne my child—and you don't know?"

"If I had lived with you for all these years, perhaps I could comprehend the situation. As matters stand, I want you to tell me."

The Emperor was no longer leaning on his shovel; his shovel had somehow disappeared. His face seemed plainer, more distinct, than any man's face should be. He said, in a voice not grown louder, but much changed: "Some long ago have called me the Sabbath, or the Covenant—some have called me Wisdom. Some lately have said that I am the Program of Creation."

A long moment passed before the Silver Queen persisted: "And you—? I want you to tell me what you are."

He—plainly her husband once again—stretched out his hand to her. "Come live with me. And argue with me again, and learn. I am the Truth."

Under a balmy Earthly sky a Tasavaltan celebration was just getting under way. And people were considering the result of the last Sword-combat. Arridu was dead, obliterated in the explosion of Shieldbreaker's deadly fragments—and only Woundhealer, of all the Twelve Swords, still survived.

It was Stephen's older brother Adrian, come home from his distant studies as quickly as he could, but just too late to join the fight, who at length deduced and announced an explanation—how Shieldbreaker, once in Mark's heart, had become the Prince's and not the demon's weapon—and how the blast of its destruction, edge to edge against the one Sword it could not break, had slain the demon at close range.

The victorious Prince Mark, his family, and all who stood by them were aware that Ben of Purkinje and Lady Yambu had somehow left them, but they were not unduly worried about either missing person.

Mark had his wife and his children safe, and for the time being he was content.

And it was Stephen, marveling, who discovered, at some distance from the field of combat, the charred, cracked, useless hilt of what had once been the Sword of Force. In the boy's hand the black wood was now suddenly sprouting a green shoot.

Stephen went running to show the marvel to his father.

THE END

FANTASY ADVENTURE
FROM FRED SABERHAGEN

☐ 55343-8 THE FIRST BOOK OF SWORDS $3.95
Canada $4.95

☐ 51934-5 THE SECOND BOOK OF SWORDS $4.50
Canada $5.50

☐ 55345-4 THE THIRD BOOK OF SWORDS $3.95
Canada $4.95

☐ 52058-0 THE FIRST BOOK OF LOST SWORDS: $4.50
Woundhealer's Story Canada $5.50

☐ 55296-2 THE SECOND BOOK OF LOST SWORDS: $3.95
Sightblinder's Story Canada $4.95

☐ 55288-1 THE THIRD BOOK OF LOST SWORDS: $4.50
Stonecutter's Story Canada $5.50

☐ 55284-9 THE FOURTH BOOK OF LOST SWORDS: $4.50
Farslayer's Story Canada $5.50

☐ 55286-5 THE FIFTH BOOK OF LOST SWORDS: $4.50
Coinspinner's Story Canada $5.50

☐ 51118-2 THE SIXTH BOOK OF LOST SWORDS: $4.50
Mindsword's Story Canada $5.50

Buy them at your local bookstore or use this handy coupon:
Clip and mail this page with your order.

Publishers Book and Audio Mailing Service
P.O. Box 120159, Staten Island, NY 10312-0004

Please send me the book(s) I have checked above. I am enclosing $ _____
(Please add $1.50 for the first book, and $.50 for each additional book to cover postage and
handling. Send check or money order only—no CODs.)

Name _____

Address _____

City _____ State / Zip _____

Please allow six weeks for delivery. Prices subject to change without notice.